The Resolute Woman

M.L. Lexi

Titles by M.L. Lexi

The Blind Woman
The Deceitful Woman
The Forgiving Woman
The Grieving Woman
The Guilty Woman
The Loyal Woman
The Noble Woman
The Resolute Woman
The Unfaithful Woman

The Farfalla Family Saga

The Determined Woman
The Persevering Woman
The Invincible Woman

The Fearless Woman Series

The Fearless Woman
The Naïve Woman

Copyright

To family, near, far, and in spirit.

Sometimes there's too much judgement in this world enough understanding.

—M.L. Lexi

Chapter 1

IT WAS SIX thirty in the morning, and the world was silent outside. The spring day was flush with an eastern sun that shone brightly through the sliding door glass and bounced off the shiny, cream-coloured tiles. The kitchen, with smooth oak cupboards, quartz countertops, and stainless steel appliances, smelled of baking muffins.

Eighty-year-old Edith Morgan nicknamed Buzzy for her sharp wit on the comedy stage, had already spent an hour baking. Now, with a jazzy tune flowing from the radio sitting on the countertop, Buzzy flitted about washing bowls and putting away the ingredients she had used to make this morning's blueberry muffins.

Buzzy wore her trademark brown Capri pants and a loose teal shirt. She wore gold at her neck, ears, and wrist and a wedding ring on her finger.

At eighty years old, Edith Morgan was relatively unlined and youthful-looking. She was tall and slim with a commanding presence. She had a cascade of short silver hair. Her gray eyes, undimmed by the years, sparkled with the vibrancy and sharp wit that had been her hallmark. The few wrinkles etched around her eyes and mouth were not signs of age but were the delicate brush strokes of the rich and exciting life she led.

On her bed by the sliding door, Carol Burnett, the two-year-old white and tan Pomeranian, lay still. Carol Burnett's head was on her front paws, and she avidly watched the two squirrels scurry across the fence. Carol

Burnett wore a stylish, floral silk Armani scarf around her neck today.

Buzzy's tenant, Maxine Bassett, leaning on the edge of exhaustion, stumbled into the kitchen and sat at the table. Maxine wore pyjama pants, a pink cotton T-shirt, and black ankle socks. Her dark hair had a roll-out-of-bed dishevelled look with strands sticking out in different directions. Maxine's shoulders slumped, and her once vibrant blue eyes carried the weight of countless sleepless nights.

"That goddamn dog kept me awake for most of the night. They let him out to the backyard, or his outhouse, at eleven thirty p.m., at one seventeen, and three thirty-one in the fucking morning. And as if that was not enough, they let him out at six-goddamn a.m." Maxine's voice was raw with fatigue. "Are you listening to me, Buzzy? Buzzy," Maxine screamed loud enough to get Buzzy's attention.

Buzzy removed her noise-cancelling headphones. "Sorry, dear. Did you say something?"

Maxine reiterated everything she had said with added profanity and summed it up with a frustrated breath.

"Are you sure it's wise to swear as much as you are? One day, you will forget you're not talking to me and let that salty, immoral city language loose on your pious mother and cause her an aneurysm." Buzzy set two cups of coffee, creamed and sugared, on the table with a thump when she noticed Maxine dozing off.

"Christ, Buzzy." Maxine raised her head, resting on the folded hands on the table with a jolt. "Was that necessary?"

Buzzy sat. "That's rather specific timing you tossed out."

The memory of their conversation swam back slowly to Maxine's clouded mind. "Were you not listening? The goddamn dog wakes me up every time he barks, and I have trouble getting back to sleep, so I've decided to keep a log. How do you manage to get a good night's sleep?"

"I wear them to bed. You should get a set. They're not as uncomfortable as they look and filter out most of the noise."

"One, they're expensive. I don't have Buzzy money. I'm a kindergarten teacher. Remember?" Maxine took a swig of the coffee in her hand for the much-needed caffeine shot. "Two, why should I be forced to wear headphones to maintain my peace of mind at home."

Buzzy nodded in understanding and thought better than to interrupt Maxine's agitated rant when she rose to pace the room.

"You're the landlord. You should speak to our entitled, selfish, inconsiderate neighbours about it and tell them to get the dog to shut the fuck up before I commit a deadly crime. I don't mind the moron dog barking during the day, within reason, but Christ, on a fucking tricycle, they can't think that the dog barking at all hours of the night and early morning is reasonable." Maxine's frayed nerves from months of putting up with the dog's incessant barking were unmistakable in her furious tone.

Maxine's booming voice had Carol Burnett's ears piqued with interest. Quick disinterest had Carol Burnett turning her attention back to the fr "licking squirrels.

"I have spoken to them," Buzzy said. "You have also, and in very colourful language if I recall, to no avail. If Becca and Miles, whom you were very friendly with when they moved in, didn't listen to your animated, very loud, profanity-laced rant, what would you have me do?"

Buzzy rose, walked to the stove when it dinged and shut the oven off.

"You're the homeowner. You carry more weight than I, a lowly basement renter. They will listen to you." Maxine watched Buzzy transfer the muffin tin from the oven onto the cooling racks. "That goddamn dog is not a seven-pound yapper like Carol Burnett. He weighs seventy pounds, and his bark goes through brick and my skull. I can't take it anymore, Buzzy. If you don't do anything, I'll have to hand in my notice to terminate my tenancy."

Buzzy stared at Maxine for a moment before her mouth twitched with amusement. "You and I know you're not doing that."

Maxine sucked in air and hissed it out. "No. No, I'm not, but only because you're too generous with my rent, and I couldn't afford to live elsewhere. "

Buzzy's comfortable wealth could afford her a sprawling estate, but she chose to live in the red brick bungalow on Strathmore Avenue. The tiny house was Buzzy's and her husband's, Mortimer, bought when they were first married and struggled to make ends meet.

Buzzy had renovated the one-hundred-year-old house in the neighbourhood with tall trees, green lawns, and a colourful array of floral gardens with a modern open look. There were windows all around to let the sunshine in. Sleek dark wood floors replaced the fading linoleum. Abstract art hung from tan painted walls. The furniture was soft Italian leather, and the tables were polished maple.

Sheer happenstance or perhaps providence led Maxine to Edith Morgan's advertisement for the apartment she had for rent. To Maxine's delight, the apartment was a cozy haven, offering all the comforts a single girl needed: a bathroom, small bedroom, kitchenette, and sitting area. There was a washer and dryer in the room that doubled as a closet. The smell of cut wood and paint still hung in the air. The tile floor shone, and the countertops gleamed. Beyond its newness, the apartment was furnished and reasonably priced, a plus for Maxine, who did not have a dime to her name.

Maxine found her home in Buzzy's basement apartment and a substitute mother and friend in Buzzy.

"What would you have me do?" Buzzy plated two blueberry muffins and brought them to the table.

Standing at the sliding door beside where Carol Burnett lay, Maxine looked up to the sky. She was happy to see dark clouds heavy with water on the horizon. She hated driving to work in the rain, but the dog was not let out to the backyard on rainy days. She would get a day's respite and hopefully some sleep tonight.

"Call Animal Control and submit a complaint. Talk to Miles and Becca's parents when they visit." Maxine sat at the chair she had vacated when Buzzy signalled her to sit.

"Oh, honey, you're such an idealist. Where do you think they learned their entitled behaviour? I'll call Animal Control later today, but everyone knows they're the least effective governmental department. Their specialty is scraping dead raccoons and skunks off the road. Anything beyond that requires applying thought and logic, which is short in supply where Animal Control is concerned. They'll tell me the dog has every right to bark as long as it's not incessantly and often."

"But it is incessant and often," Maxine snarled.

"You need to calm down, dear. Being young does not guarantee that you won't experience a coronary event." Buzzy sat. "Animal control will always put the animal's well-being above that of humans. Eat the muffin. It's warm. As you like it."

"I can't get a good night's rest. I'm exhausted. I can't concentrate. I'm always irritated, stressed, and anxious. It's not fair to my kids. Christ! It's not fair to my sanity." Frustration edged into Maxine's voice. "I'm cratering here, Buzzy."

"I'll speak to Becca and Miles again." Buzzy tossed a few pieces of muffin to Carol Burnett when she strolled over. "But you know what they're going to say."

"Yeah. 'The idiot dog is a dog,'" Maxine pronounced it dwog as Becca did. "'And dogs bark and have to go potty when they must, regardless of the time of day or night. I miss Rose and Henry. They were great neighbours, quiet and uneventful. I wish they never sold the house to Becca and Miles. I wish I had the money to buy the house when they put it up for sale." Maxine refreshed her cup of coffee, and Buzzy's when she held up her cup. "Their parents must be so proud of the self-centred and inconsiderate people they've raised."

"They are. They've raised them to their image. And isn't that what you said to them during your last outburst?" Buzzy tossed Carol Burnett another piece of muffin and waved her back to her staring spot.

Maxine nodded. "They both stared at me with the same dumb fuck look their idiot dog does."

"The dog's name is Bobo, and let's not blame him for his parents' stupidity."

Maxine rolled her eyes dramatically. "I know that. He's still an idiot."

"You really hate that dog," Buzzy said.

"I don't hate the dog. Maxine rested her head on her updrawn knees. "The dog is collateral damage to the detestable, thoughtless owners who believe the world revolves around them and to hell with their neighbours."

Maxine's lips curved into a pleased smile when the clouds opened, and the rain fell thickly. Bobo would not go out to roam on wet soil in the backyard. Fingers crossed, the rain would persist all day as the weather network predicted, and Maxine would get a good night's sleep tonight.

A run to burn the calories of the second celebratory blueberry muffin Maxine planned to have was in store.

Part I

The Beginning

One simple act can lead to a marked change in your entire existence.

—M.L. Lexi

Chapter 2

MAXINE SWAPPED HER pyjama pants for gray leggings, a pink tank top, and a hooded jacket and set off on her run under the wall of rain that came down from dark skies. The harder the fall of rain, the better, Maxine thought, hoping to wind her anxiety and anger down before heading off to work.

"The girl is wound too tightly." Buzzy stood at the window with Carol Burnett cradled in her arms and watched Maxine push through the rain. "Imagine the best option she has to relieve her tension is exercise. What the girl needs is a good man and a good lay."

Carol Burnett yapped her agreement.

Maxine Basset was too responsible, and that made for an average life.

Maxine Basset was a twenty-six-year-old kindergarten teacher who never missed a workday. Buzzy boasted that Maxine was the ideal tenant: quiet, pleasant, headache-free, and she paid her rent on time.

Maxine did not come home drunk. She did not bring home strays, which women her age tend to pick up at bars for one-night stands. Maxine was more concerned with her personal growth than sexual gratification. Fit and flexible Maxine, at her sexual peak, had gone years without sharing a bed with a man.

"Maxine is a lovely girl, but she is as persnickety with her love life as her daily goings-on. She renews her driver's license months before its due date to give herself what she calls system failure time. But then, which one of us doesn't have our quirks? Hmmm?" Buzzy raised her brows to stress the point to Carol Burnett, who she had set on the sofa cushion beside her. "Beyond that, in the four years she's been my tenant, we haven't seen a man in her apartment. She's one frustrated young lady."

Carol Burnett lapped her muzzle once and yawned.

"It's not as if she can't attract a man. She's a good-looking girl." Buzzy ran a hand over Carol Burnett's fur as the rain pattered on the windows

Maxine was medium-height, with striking blue eyes concealed behind the thick lenses of her black-rimmed glasses. Her mouth was wide and generous, her cheekbones high on an oval face darkly tanned under the spring sun, and her nose had aristocratic markings. She was lean and athletic due to the five-mile runs she did three times weekly.

"Maxine could leave an impression on a man if she saw herself as anything other than ordinary and made an effort, but she doesn't bother to do so."

Carol Burnett let out a bark.

"Yes, I know she won't listen to us, Carol Burnett." Buzzy reached for the television converter and tuned it to the news.

Rain, murder, and mayhem were the news of the day.

"She wears those reserved outfits: buttoned-up shirts, knee-length skirts, conservative dresses, and loafers. Grant it they're befitting a teacher of young, impressionable students. Still, she doesn't have to dress like that after hours. She also doesn't have to wear muted makeup. Imagine how great she would look if she upgraded from the simple touch of rouge on her cheeks, pink gloss on the lips, and a dusting of bronze eye shadow bought at the local Dollar Store. God, if I had her stunning looks, I would milk it until dry."

Saving money above her appearance was high on Maxine's list, and Buzzy could not change her mind.

Buzzy could not talk Maxine into having her long, wavy, charcoal-dark hair cut and styled by a professional rather than those butchers at the local hair-hacking shop. Maxine would instead tie her hair into a ponytail.

Maxine ate the same lunch daily: ham and cheese on white toast with tomato and lettuce. She did not add mayo, as it added too many calories. Maxine had a banana for her morning break and a delicious red apple during her afternoon break. The rare time Maxine treated herself, she substituted a multi-grain bar for the apple.

"Predictability and restraint are Maxine's middle names. She holds out for the perfect man and has been man-less forever, it seems. For Christ's sake, she drinks tap water, not coffee, not because it's healthy but because it's cheaper. One positive, I guess, is that she's accumulated an impressive amount of money in her Buy-a-Home account over the past four years. It won't be long before she has her down payment for her dream home. I know because I've seen her scheduled deposits on the Excel file she keeps on her laptop computer. Really, Maxine, even your password, m-a-x-i-n-e, is predictable," Buzzy said to Carol Burnett, who had slid into sleep.

Maxine drove a second-hand Honda, which had too much mileage and required frequent maintenance, but the insurance was reasonable, and the car got her from point A to point B—most days.

Maxine loved her job and the children who, year after year, fell under her care, but when she got home, reality slapped her in the face. She was average and boring. Her life was average and boring.

"Maxine needs a change to her uninspiring life. It's why she's so tightly wound, and you and I, Carol Burnett, will be instrumental in that change." Carol Burnett's response was a loud snore. "Sure, I'll do the leg work, and I'll get to it now," Buzzy said, picking up the telephone and making the necessary calls.

I's had to be dotted, and T's crossed.

Chapter 3

THE THREE DAYS of rain came and went, as did the smile on Maxine's face and the bounce in her step. The sun shone again, dried the ground, and Bobo roamed the backyard and barked at eleven p.m., midnight, one thirty a.m., and six a.m.

"He's out there again." Maxine's back pressed against the wall and cast a look out the bow window to get a better look at Bobo.

The air in the kitchen was a clash of fried eggs, bacon, coffee, and toasted bread. Buzzy plated the food on two plates: eggs, one bacon strip, and one buttered toast slice onto Maxine's plate. Buzzy plated twice that amount onto her plate.

Maxine pointed to the headphones on Buzzy's head and mouthed, "Take off the headphones, Buzzy."

"Sorry, dear." Buzzy removed the headphones and set them on the kitchen counter. "Did you say something?"

Buzzy wore red Capri pants and an unbuttoned white cotton shirt over a pink tank top. Her face was expertly made up, and her hair was carefully styled. Carol Burnett, spread out by the sliding door, wore a red Fendi scarf with a matching bow on her head.

"Bobo is out there again. He's staring right at me through the fence slats." Maxine pushed her glasses on her nose and aimed a cold, steely glint of those blue eyes at Bobo. She was sure Bobo returned a taunting stare when he barked at her. "It's six thirty in the goddamn morning. These people have no respect or regard for their neighbours. The world revolves around them. How could they think letting their dog out at dawn to bark is acceptable behaviour? They're off-the-chart retarded. Sorry mentally retarded for the politically correct in the room." Maxine made a choking motion with her hands when Bobo let out more barks while staring at her.

It had been days since Maxine got more than six hours of restful sleep. Even with the three-day break, Maxine was so exhausted from lack of sleep that she had no strength to change out of her pyjamas or brush her hair. Maxine's hair was matted and flat on the side she had slept on. Maxine had dark circles under her eyes, and her face looked drawn and unforgiving.

"I think the words are mentally challenged," Buzzy corrected with a slight smile that faded when she saw the scornful look in Maxine's eyes.

"All this aggravation because a fish decided to explore dry land millions of years ago. Because of that curious fucker, I have to put up with asshole neighbours raised by plebeians and, by extension, their fucking dog." Maxine shot back with temper.

Carol Burnett lifted her head and looked up at Maxine with a raised eye.

"She didn't mean you, baby. She's talking about a distant cousin." Buzzy reassured Carol Burnett.

With her head held high, Carol Burnett signalled the sliding door to be opened so she could head outside. Maxine obliged with an apologetic look.

"Might I remind you, you're a kindergarten teacher. One of these days, that salty mouth will get you in a heap of trouble. And God forbid your pious mother heard how the city has corrupted her virginal daughter."

"Do I look like I give a rat's ass," Maxine said in a tone that was harsher than she had intended, and Buzzy's response was an expressive raised eyebrow. "Sorry, I didn't mean it, Buzzy. I'm just worn out."

"You're forgiven. Sit back down and eat your breakfast. We have bacon," Buzzy said loudly enough for Carol Burnett to hear.

From the backyard, Carol Burnett raced into the house and slid toward the table.

"How are people like that allowed to live amongst us? I'm all for Game of Thrones-type vengeance." Maxine ran a finger across her throat in a slicing motion.

The comment caused Buzzy to lift the other brow.

With broth brows raised, Buzzy said, "That's a bit dramatic, even for you, dear." Buzzy tossed Carol Burnett a slice of bacon, which she caught mid-air.

Maxine shook her head. "Becca and Miles made me reconsider my peaceful stance, and I am now in favour of severe and ruthless punishment for anyone who disrupts your good energy."

"Honey, you need to let go of all that anger. You're letting that dog get under your skin. You need to let loose and laugh." Buzzy poured freshly squeezed orange juice into two blue glasses with yellow daisies. "If you feel your life is at an impasse, spice it up."

"Who said anything about me being at an impasse? We're talking about Bobo." Maxine absently bit into a slice of bacon. Her taste buds were shocked into happiness. Why did everything good have to be fattening?

"Honey, you've become obsessed with a Bedlington terrier. You sleep and breathe, Bobo."

"Have you been listening, Buzzy? I haven't had a good night's sleep in weeks. I'm exhausted and…." Maxine set off on the rant Buzzy was too familiar with,

Buzzy motioned Maxine to drink orange juice to silence her. "Honey, as I said, you're at an impasse in your life." Buzzy held a silencing finger when Maxine opened her mouth to speak. "Let me finish. Think about it. Your sole focus, twenty-four-seven, is Bobo. A dog. Not a man, not an accomplishment in your life, and not life." Buzzy tossed another slice of bacon to Carol Burnett, who looked up with the beseeching big, brown eyes she knew could not be denied.

Maxine went thoughtful for a moment as she considered. Buzzy was right. Her life was circling the drain. It had been since Jesse committed the unthinkable and then left her suddenly. It had taken months of therapy to unsee the unexpected sight of Jesse's naked body in bed when she walked into their bedroom.

What Jesse did to Maxine was unjustifiable.

Jesse Fletcher was Maxine's first in every sense of the word. Jesse was her first boyfriend, her first lover, and the first man she loved. As inexperienced as Maxine was, Jesse made her comfortable with the physical, but the emotional whirlwind he caused in her made her feel drenched in love.

Jesse showed Maxine the meaning of unconditional love. Maxine always thought they were halves of a whole and would be together forever. But then Jesse did the unthinkable and broke her.

With that grief-stricken look that hit Maxine when she thought of Jesse, she brought back the words that pulled her out of despair.

"The psychological impact of Jesse leaving you will stay with you, Maxine. It would stay with any woman. You're not unique in that respect," said Dr. Hammersmith. "Accepting what Jesse did was his decision and not in any way your fault will help you move on."

The words stuck in Maxine's throat when they came to her but helped her move on—every time. Now, was no exception.

Those words ingrained in her mind had helped Maxine find the strength to remove the engagement ring from her finger. When she did, Maxine was able to pick herself up and out of her depression and pushed on with her life. Without Jesse, Maxine found her way into an empty world. At least, Maxine thought she had.

"How can my life have already hit a hard brick wall at my age? I'm just starting my life. I'm an accomplished woman with a degree, a job I love, and a quasi-pleasant life." Maxine's voice sounded drained.

"You have all that, Maxine, but we all have our demons, which take hold of us," Buzzy said to mollify the despairing look on Maxine's face, which she had seen often but had yet to find out its cause. "You know you can talk to me about anything."

Maxine fell silent, her gaze fixed on the distant point she always focused on when discussing Jesse. Buzzy did not press further. When Maxine was ready to talk, she would tell her what cut so deep it broke her. Everything had a shelf life—even secrets.

"Anyway, your life adds up to boring." Buzzy stretched the word "boring" for emphasis to distract Maxine from her sad thoughts.

"Thanks for that, Buzzy." The sarcasm rang clear in Maxine's voice.

Buzzy smiled, pleased to see the anger slice at the eyes drenched in sadness. The feisty Maxine that Buzzy knew was back. "I'm calling it as I see it, dear."

"It's nothing to smile about."

Buzzy brought two cups of fresh coffee to the table. "Get the sweetener and cream."

"I'm going for a run after breakfast and don't think the best food option is fattening cream and bacon."

Buzzy's intense gaze motivated Maxine to stand up and walk to the refrigerator. Over the years of being Buzzy's tenant, Maxine had learned that saying no was not an option when she gave you the dark and still look she did then.

"Christ, Maxine. One slice of bacon and some cream will not kill you." Buzzy turned to Carol Burnett and threw her the last slice of bacon she made for her. "That's it. There's no more, Missy."

"You won't feed the bacon to Carol Burnett, but you will me."

"She's had three slices. Now, get outside and chase something, Missy. Get some exercise," Buzzy said to Carol Burnett.

Carol Burnett gave an imperial tip of the head before trotting across the tiled floor and past the sliding door when Maxine opened it.

Spring was unfurling, and the garden was alive with colour. Bees and hummingbirds flitted about the red and white tulips, hyacinths, and peonies in bloom that Buzzy had planted in the corner patch of the back garden. The budding maple and lilac trees embraced the shining sunlight.

"And remember, no barking. Otherwise, Auntie Maxine will wish you death," Buzzy called out to Carol Burnett, who immediately got busy chasing the butterfly flying around the yard. "Now, at the risk of sounding like a broken record, what you need is a good man to tingle your senses and drive you to erupt like a volcano as he drives himself into…."

"All right." Maxine cut in, feeling the flush work up her throat to her cheeks. The dignified and poised Edith Morgan turned into a feral sexual creature when she dived into sex talk. All semblance of grace evaporated, and her language became too explicit. "I get it."

"I don't think you do, dear. You're far from home, living in the basement apartment of an old woman's home with a Pomeranian with an attitude." Buzzy laid out the facts.

"You're not old. My mom, decades younger than you, would struggle to keep up with you." Maxine sipped at her coffee, sitting across from Buzzy.

Buzzy's mouth lifted at one corner. "I have always been a powder keg of energy. Still, what I'm saying is you need company. If not that of a man, at least that of people your age. Spending too much time alone in your apartment, watching television and planning your lessons, kills the spirit."

"I spend time with you and Carol Burnett and have friends at St. Boniface." Maxine forked scrambled eggs and chased it with a bite of toast.

"Honey, your school friends are colleagues. You don't entrust colleagues with your secrets, sleep, or do anything remotely intimate with them. It doesn't work out well when you do. Colleagues who come to look closely into their coworkers' lives and don't like what they see will cause a whole lot of hurt. And although Carol Burnett wouldn't admit to it, she's of the canine species. As for me, I'm asleep by nine. It's why I'm baking at six in the morning." Buzzy looked over at the pecan pies resting on the counter. "At nine p.m. is when a girl your age starts her night."

Maxine fell silent for a moment. "I must admit I wouldn't mind some excitement in my life. Passing excitement, not the permanent type. I'm not the impulsive type. I like stability in my life, but right now, what I want is…."

"A friend with generous benefits. If you know what I mean." Buzzy gave Maxine a wink of pure mischief.

"Is sex all you think about?"

"Oh, dear, what else is there? No strings attached is the best way to find your Prince Charming. You can't steer romance your way. It'll come when you meet the right man. I met my Morty when I least expected it, and he hit me like a shovel over the head." Buzzy looked thoughtfully as the flood of memories of her and Mortimer over their fifty years of marriage engulfed her.

"That happy look you get when you mention Morty is the one I want to come over me when thinking of the man in my life." Maxine nibbled on the remaining bacon on her plate, trying to prolong the joyful dance in her mouth.

"Take a hardy bite of that bacon, Maxine. Come on, swallow. You can do it." Buzzy encouraged, and Maxine did. "Was that so difficult to do, dear?"

Maxine's brow lifted sardonically. Still, she ate the remaining bacon pieces on her plate when the flavour explosion hit her senses. "Christ, that's good."

"A little bit of fat, sugar, carbs, and sex is good for the soul." Buzzy grimaced when the flashes of memory assaulted her. "My Morty was a tiger in bed. He would…."

Maxine cut in to stop Buzzy from talking. "I don't think I need that visual, thank you."

"Right. Anyway, your Morty will come along when you least expect it. There's someone out there for each of us."

Maxine, pffht that.

"He will, dear. Just don't rush things." Buzzy watched as Maxine eyed the fattening cream but couldn't bring herself to pour it into her coffee. "Have the cream already, Maxine. Live on the dangerous side." Buzzy reached for the cream carton and added a double pour to Maxine's coffee cup when Maxine could not bring herself to do it. "You need to hazard to become more adventurous, dear. Take risks. Stop overthinking everything so much."

"Cream is high in fat, leading to an undesired thick waistline." Maxine drank cream-laced coffee, letting it roll on her tongue to savour it.

"Tastes good. Doesn't it?"

Shit, yeah! Maxine thought. "It's okay."

Buzzy's mouth bowed up. "That's the taste of excitement, dear. The uncharted to be explored." Buzzy rose and slid the door open when Carol Burnett demanded to be let in. Carol Burnett pranced past Buzzy without looking at her and out of the kitchen. "And what's the worst that can happen by venturing to try something you think is risky but placates the appetite."

Maxine raised her eyebrows at Buzzy. "You're not talking about the bacon anymore, are you? You're talking figuratively."

Buzzy scooped the remaining egg on her plate with a piece of toast and filled her mouth with it.

Maxine threw her head back and stared at the ceiling momentarily before saying, "Unpredictability is not me, but let's say it was. What do you have in mind?"

Something changed in Buzzy's eyes, and she smiled the sweet smile that always made Maxine feel the uneasiness creep up her spine.

Looking straight at Buzzy, Maxine took a long, slow breath. "This conversation was part of your calculus all along. Wasn't it?"

Buzzy's mouth tipped up at the corners.

The woman was the living embodiment of mischievousness transcending age and time, Maxine thought.

Buzzy squared her thumbs and fingers and aimed them at Maxine's face, contemplating the infinite possibilities.

"Shit. What am I getting myself into?" Maxine murmured.

Chapter 4

MAXINE SAW BECCA and Miles walk out of their home with Bobo on his lead. Bobo's tail swished in excitement at the prospect of going for his walk.

Maxine killed the ignition on the driveway and shouldered her tote. Slamming the car door closed, she marched toward Becca and Miles. A woman on a mission. She wore a tan leather jacket over a knit dress.

Bobo let out a bark at Maxine that caused her more irritation than she already felt.

"Thank you for letting Bobo out at one thirty in the morning." Maxine's bark was louder than Bobo's.

Becca's face crunched up while Miles stood beside her, stiff and silent. Both wore jeans and hoodies. Miles was inches taller than his medium-height, slim wife. Becca's hair was bound in a messy ponytail, while Miles's short, dark curls hung loose around his round face.

"Bobo had to go potty," Becca said as a matter of fact, and Bobo let out a piercing bark in agreement.

The evening air was cool. On the horizon, the sun was fading from the sky as it descended for the day. The whooshing sound of Mr. Matlock's sprinkler, two houses over, as it showered the grass, sounded in the quiet neighbourhood. A bouncing ball echoed as the Miller boys played basketball in their backyard.

"And he has to bark in the middle of the night and shock everyone around him out of sleep?" The fury was hot and pulsing behind the lenses of Maxine's glasses.

Miles reached for the lead in Becca's hand, and the dog and man put distance between them and Maxine.

"He's a dog," Becca pronounced it dawg, "Barking is what dogs do."

"He woke me up, and I couldn't get back to sleep for hours." Maxine's agitation was making it difficult for her to breathe. Maxine stopped talking, inhaled deeply, and went on. "I was awake for hours before I managed to get back to sleep."

"I can't help it when he barks." Becca's face neither radiated sympathy nor concern.

"This is why God invented dog trainers and muzzles. You can put one on your dog," Maxine mimicked Becca's dowg lilt, "When nature calls in the middle of the night and early morning." Maxine's voice was loud enough for the neighbours to peek their heads from the windows.

Miles and Bobo put another few feet of distance from Becca and Maxine.

"I can't put a muzzle on Bob. He's family." Becca's eyes were small, dark and still.

Maxine's blue eyes went wide in disbelief. "I know the world revolves around you, but see everyone here," Maxine waved her arms to encompass the entire neighbourhood. "Including my work. We need our rest. Every second home on this block has a dog, but Bobo is the only dog heard barking all day and night." Maxine's voice quivered, rising a few octaves as adrenaline surged through her, causing her to struggle for breath.

Bobo lapped his muzzle once and yawned.

"I work, too. I can't control when Bobo has to go out."

Maxine's wide eyes went to slits after the shock waned. "Your parents must be so proud of their demon spawn."

Becca squished up her face in confusion.

Maxine began to speak again but closed her mouth when Buzzy appeared and took hold of Maxine's arm. "Don't aggravate yourself further, Maxine."

"I'm not done, Buzzy."

"You are, dear. You'll get nowhere with her. It's like talking to a brick wall. Thick and dense," Buzzy said, tugging at Maxine's arm to urge her inside the house.

A red flush brightened Maxine's face, and she aimed a look at Becca, which could have caused her to self-combust before Maxine followed Buzzy into the house.

Chapter 5

A SENSE OF foreboding crept over Maxine. The pleasure in Buzzy's eyes was almost sinister. It was as if Maxine was staring into the eyes of a she-devil, ready to claim her soul.

Maxine's eyes filled with apprehension. "I take it back. I don't want any change in my life or anything to do with what you have in mind."

Buzzy waved a dismissive hand. "I see you as—" There was a long silence while Buzzy gnawed on her cheek. "Maxi Bass. Yes, Maxi Bass is who I see you as."

Maxine frowned. "Maxi Bass? What are you talking about, Buzzy?"

"That will be your stage name."

Dropping her fork with a clank on her dinner plate, Maxine gaped at Buzzy. "Stage name? What are you going on about?"

Buzzy's kitchen was lit bright, and the air was painted with the smell of baked lasagna and toasted garlic bread. Carol Burnett happily munched on her slice of lasagna, her tail wagging in delight with each tasty bite.

"You said you wanted change. Performing my Ba-Dum-Bump Comedy Club will bring the change you need." Buzzy took a healthy bite of garlic bread.

Jolting up in her seat, Maxine caused her glasses to slide down her nose. "Perform on stage at your comedy club? I can't perform on stage. There is no way I can do that. Look at me. Aside from knowing nothing about comedy, having a funny bone in me, or knowing how to deliver a joke or write it, I have no stage presence." Maxine slid her slipping glasses high on her nose.

Buzzy sat back in her chair and locked eyes with Maxine. "You will have all that when I'm done with you. You will have a dominating presence, or at least Maxi Bass will."

"Me, have a dominating presence," Maxine said, sounding surprised. "Have you been drinking this early in the morning?"

"Honey, you forget I've created many comedians in my lifetime who went on to achieve great success." Buzzy brought a forkful of lasagna to her mouth.

"I don't know, Buzzy. I'm not funny, let alone have a commanding presence." Maxine nibbled on garlic bread.

"Not to toot my horn, but you have the best coach in the country. Me. Who better to teach you than the owner of the most famous comedy club in the country? Again, not to boast my very accomplished self...."

"Don't hold back."

"If you insist. I was a kick-ass comedian in my day and creator of many others. I believe I can turn you into a successful performer. I have the contacts and know-how and own the venue. You can't have it better than that."

"I've never performed on stage. What makes you think I can?"

"I know you can." Buzzy placed a placating hand over Maxine's. "It's all about the right coaching, which I will give you."

"What about my appearance?" Maxine raised a hand to her matted hair.

"Honey, that's a simple tweak. The right clothes, makeup, and a suitable hairstyle will fix this." Buzzy held up her palm and circled it over Maxine's hair and body.

Maxine raised her eyebrows and left it at that.

Buzzy looked Maxine up and down. "You can do so much better than this. You have a hot, fit body and nice hair if you bothered to do anything other than bind it into a ponytail. And, honey, real makeup, not the dollar store stuff you buy, can transform this face into a man-magnet."

Maxine rolled her eyes. "You really should hold back sometimes, Buzzy."

Buzzy flashed Maxine a lopsided smirk.

"Okay, so you tweak my appearance. I'm not an entertainer." Maxine crossed to the coffee pot sitting on the hot plate and brought it to the table.

"Honey, I've worked with worse than you and created miracles." Buzzy held out her cup for Maxine to refill.

"Thank God I'm not suicidal," Maxine said under her breath.

"As for the entertaining. You do that already in your classroom every day," Buzzy finished when Maxine squished up her face.

Maxine stopped the coffee pour midway. "You're kidding me. They're children with the attention span of gnat."

Buzzy waved Maxine on to finish her coffee pouring. "Pfft, the same applies to the adults that comprise an audience at the club. They're better because most nights, they're intoxicated or high."

Maxine did not hide her surprise at the comment. "Be that as it may, I'm not a comedy writer. I correct misspelled words such as cat and dog with a red marker."

"I wasn't a comedy writer either. I learned as you will," Buzzy said with confidence.

"I don't know, Buzzy. You have a flair and talent I don't possess." Maxine refreshed her coffee cup, absently poured a healthy dose of cream, and added sweetener to compensate for the calories. "There are certain things you can't learn. Talent is one of them. Talent can't be acquired no matter how much training you get, and an aptitude for comedy is one that you genetically inherit. My father is a pastor, and my mother is a staunch follower of his preaching. Religious people have no sense of humour, are uptight, and rarely laugh. That's my genetic makeup. I have no funny bone in me."

"I will teach you everything you need to know," Buzzy said, noticing the worry deepening in Maxine's eyes.

"Will you teach me how to land a joke? I have no sense of comedic timing. Delivery is the most important tenet of comedy."

"Comedic timing is one of the most difficult acting skills to teach, but I will teach you the ways of comedy." Buzzy watched Maxine haul herself to her feet to pace the room with nervous energy.

"And will you teach me how to write—what do you call it?—the script?"

"I will help you write your material once we determine the type of comedy most suited for you. More importantly, I will teach you how to watch people and read the humour in everyday situations you encounter. That's where the best comedic material is." Buzzy removed the dirty dishes, cups, and cutlery from the table and brought them to the sink. "I will teach you delivery, how to use the non-verbal elements for comedic effect, and everything else you need to know to give a perfect performance."

Maxine picked up the cream and sweetener containers off the table and put them away. "That's a lot of learning and a lot of change."

"And I know how resistant you are to change." Buzzy washed and set the rinsed cups and cutlery on the dishrack.

"I'm not resistant. I'm…."

"Defiant to change," Buzzy interjected. "Not bragging, but I was a kick-ass comedian in my day. Grant it, I made my name on my saltiness, but I got my name out there. Risqué sells, and that's how I see it for you."

"I can't do risqué. I don't know how to do risqué. Not to mention that I risk losing my job if I do this. The management at St. Boniface Elementary will not look well on me moonlighting at a comedy club as a minx."

Buzzy picked up the dishtowel and dried her hands. "One, what you do on your off hours is none of their business. And two, some of my favourite words are unpredictability, risk, and impulsiveness. They light a fire up your ass, which is what you need," Buzzy said in a casual, pleasant tone, but the look in her eyes gave the impression of a panther ready to strike.

Maxine had to admit the idea exhilarated her. It was the first time in a long while Maxine felt simultaneously alive and terrified, invigorated and unnerved. It felt great.

"Okay. Let's do this."

Buzzy smiled. "Good decision. I will make you look fabulous and memorable and *muy caliente*. Maxi Bass, I will all teach you." Buzzy mimicked Yoda's voice.

Chapter 6

MAXINE GRADUATED AT the top of her class and, days later, got herself hired by St. Boniface Elementary to take over the retiring Mrs. Brown's kindergarten class in the fall. Maxine made the bold decision not to return home and remain in the city, leaving behind the small rural town where she grew up her parents, and the security of the familiar.

Alone in a big, crowded city that offered the feeling of loneliness, Maxine set off to pursue her dreams and ambitions.

From her first day of school, Maxine loved her children and teaching. She got on well with her fellow St. Boniface colleagues. Maxine even liked the school's managing staff, whom her colleagues disapproved of and disliked. Coming from a small town where gossip, assumptions, and people having an opinion on how you should live were a way of life, St. Boniface was a breath of fresh air.

On Maxine's first day at St. Boniface, she connected with Beth Caplan, and the two women became best friends. Beth, a grade eight teacher, was ten years older and had as much experience in teaching at the school. Beth happily took Maxine under her wing and helped her navigate the maze of St. Boniface's academia.

St. Boniface Elementary teacher's lounge bustled. The air was ripe with the scents of microwaved pasta, leftover pizza, and brewed coffee, punctuated with conversation and laughter. From the windows, the glittering sunshine spilled over the round tables and the sitting area where the office staff on the sofa and two wing chairs dug into their food. A television in a blonde wood cabinet aired the day's news.

Beth and Maxine sat at their usual table by the window overlooking the park awash in green. It was a bright, sunny day with a clear blue sky.

Dipping her head slightly, Maxine lowered her voice and said, "Buzzy wants to put me on the stage. To do comedy nonetheless."

"That sounds exciting. What brought this about?" Beth spread her lunch on the table: a chicken wrap, potato chips, a chocolate pudding cup, and a banana for the healthy component.

She maintained her five-nine figure slim and fit for the copious amount of food Beth ingested. Her eyes were a striking shade of blue, and her honey-blonde hair cascaded like a sunlit waterfall down her shoulders to her waist. Beneath the straight-cut bangs, her makeup was flawless. In contrast to Maxine's lacklustre wardrobe, Beth's choice of school attire was colourful and stylish. Today, Beth wore a red pantsuit, a hot pink blouse, and matching slingback patent shoes. Gold hung from her long, slim neck, ears, and wrists.

"Buzzy says my boring, predictable life needs spicing up and performing will do it." Maxine reached into her lunch bag for the ham and cheese sandwich, bit into it and chased it with black coffee. Maxine would have preferred apple juice, but the coffee was free.

"She's not wrong there," Beth remarked, with the corners of her mouth curled slightly.

"Thank you." Maxine took a bite of her sandwich and wished it would magically transform into the thick foot-long chicken wrap with gobs of mayonnaise Beth unwrapped.

"Well, is she wrong?" Beth took a mouthful of the chicken wrap. Mayonnaise dotted the corners of her mouth.

Maxine let out a long sigh. "No. She's not."

"Then this is a good thing." Beth wiped the mayonnaise that dotted the corners of her mouth when Maxine pointed it out.

"I don't know." Maxine watched Beth toss a handful of potato chips into her mouth.

Maxine resentfully bit into a carrot stick. "I don't understand how you can eat so much and stay slim."

"It's called good metabolism, which comes from having good sex. Often," Beth said and flashed Maxine a smile.

Every woman she knew was a nympho. Birds of a feather did not flock together, Maxine concluded. It had been a long time since a man had heated her bed and body.

"Anyway, Can you see me speaking or performing before a live audience?" Maxine said.

"You do it daily in your classroom. It can't be that much different than speaking to a room of kids with short attention spans." Beth stuffed her mouth with the remaining chips in the bag, and Maxine reluctantly finished the last of the carrot sticks.

"Buzzy said the same."

Beth moved on to the banana, peeled it, and took a bite. "And she has one hundred-plus years of wisdom behind her."

Maxine snorted a laugh. "She's eighty years old, Beth, not a zombie."

"Whatever. And doesn't Buzzy have experience in the comedy circuit or own a comedy club or something?" Beth finished eating the banana and tossed the peel into the trash can before walking to the coffee station. "I hope you gave Buzzy your blessing to proceed with the transformation," Beth slapped her hand on the table when Maxine started to nod off.

That startled Maxine wide awake. "What? What?"

"You were nodding off. Bobo still keeping you awake?"

Maxine gave her a half nod. "I nodded off in class as well. While standing at the blackboard, drawing a cat. The children's giggles brought me back."

"Do you want me to get rid of the dog? I'll be happy to do so?" Beth stuffed her mouth with more banana.

"Jesus, Beth, I don't want the dog killed."

"How about having the owners tar and feathered? I have connections." Beth watched the thoughtful look cross Maxine's face as she considered the offer. "Hello, Maxine. Joke."

"I know, but I can fantasize," Maxine said quietly.

"I said, Buzzy was in the comedy business, wasn't she?"

"Yes, Buzzy was a well-known comedian in her day. She owns a famous club downtown." Maxine bit into her sandwich and wondered how tastier her ham and cheese sandwich would be without the edges. But cutting it off would be a waste of money she did not have. "But I don't know about the performing. Look at me. I'm not stage-spot-light material."

"Venture into the unknown, Maxine. Buzzy will share the century years of wisdom and mould you into a comedic star." Beth drank coffee with cream and real sugar—none of that sweetener stuff for Beth.

"Buzzy said that too, but I don't know. I don't think she can transform me from an ordinary teacher to a stage presence, let alone a comedian. Look at me." Maxine pointed to her hair loosely tied in a ponytail. Her hand continued downward over her face with muted makeup and down the pink puffy-sleeved shirt buttoned to her neck down the floral skirt that hung to her shins. "I'm as conservative as they come. I'm a small-town girl."

"You're all that, but as you said, you're also a teacher. You know that schooling, training, and coaching are powerful tools for personal development. Education gives you the knowledge and skills to pursue your ambitions."

Maxine raised a dark brow. "Wow! You should become the spokesperson for the school board."

Lifting her coffee cup, Beth said, "You're right. I should. But you know I'm right. You can do this, Maxine. Let Buzzy do her thing."

Maxine moved to eat her apple when she finished her sandwich. "I don't know. It's so much learning and change at my age."

"At your age? Christ, Maxine, you're a spring chicken. You have a semi-empty canvas waiting to be filled with information." Beth pointed a finger to her temple. "As I see it, you have a choice. Remain leading the life of a boring school teacher, man-less, sexless, devoid of any form of excitement, or let Buzzy light you up. Were it me in your shoes, you know what I'd choose." Beth looked up when Norman McDonnell walked up to their table." And speaking of spicing it up. Hey, Norm, how's it hanging?"

"Oh, geez," Maxine said under her breath.

"Heavy and fruitful, Beth, and ready for the handling." Norman grinned, showing blindingly white teeth.

Norman wore a plaid shirt over a red T-shirt, tan chinos, and running shoes. Norman McDonnell taught grade eight and had the quintessential look of a geeky computer nerd. His hair, nut-brown, short and curly, was combed practical and unassumingly. A trimmed beard traced the round face that seemed perpetually on the brink of a thoughtful frown. Norman displayed nerdy confidence, an uncommon trait in the geek fraternity.

"Good to know, Normie." Beth's blue eyes crinkled.

"Hello, Maxine. You look very nice," Norman said, although she looked tired.

Norman could see the thick foundation layer below her eyes, attempting to conceal the dark circles. Norman's shoulders slumped at the thought of another man keeping her awake at night. For months, Norman hoped he would be that man.

Maxine looked at Norman above the rim of her glasses. "Thank you, Norman."

"Did you pass on my message to Maxine, Beth?"

"Shit, no. Sorry, Normie, I forgot. Ask her now." Beth waved a hand at the empty chair beside her.

Norman sat. "We need chaperones for the school dance next week? I thought you might, well, you know, consider volunteering." Norman groped for words.

Maxine pushed her glasses up on her nose. "I'll think about it, Norman."

"Are you going to be there, Normie?" Beth said playfully.

"Of course, I will be. Those peckerheads need a watchful eye to make sure they don't get out of hand and become teenage mommies and daddies." Norman's eyes did not leave Maxine.

"And you're the man for the job." Beth levelled a teasing look at Norman.

"You know it. Thumping music and testosterone is never a good combination. It elevates emotions. I was a teenage boy myself with raging hormones. I know exactly what's going through these boys' minds. I know the tempting pheromones, those seductresses in short hemmed dresses and exposed cleavages purposely discharge on said boys," Norm said with conviction.

Beth stifled a laugh. Given the choice, a geek like Norm would have been more interested in the video game du jour over a teen girl's exposed flesh.

"Why are we having the dance if it triggers so much depravity?" Maxine said.

Norman held Maxine's eyes. "Because it's fun."

"Well, you have help in preventing any fluid sharing from happening at the dance because Maxine and I will be chaperoning with you," Beth said.

That came as much a surprise to Maxine as it did to Norman.

"I'm happy to hear that. I'll make sure to save you a dance, Maxine. And I'm going to shut up now," Norman said when Beth shot him a look that said he should stop talking.

"Maxine and I are happy to do our duty for the little bastards. Aren't we, Maxine?" Beth looked at Maxine with a full-on encouraging grin.

Maxine sighed. "Sure. Yeah."

"I'll pretty us up, Normie, and we'll emit a batch of seasoned, sexier pheromones for you to enjoy," Beth said.

Norman saw the pink blush rising on Maxine's neck to flood her face and found it alluring.

"Looking forward to it," Norman said, touching Maxine's arm lightly before he walked away.

Maxine's glaring eyes stared at Beth. "What did you do that for? Stop encouraging him."

"He likes you."

"I've told you I have no interest in a relationship with Norman or any man."

"Looking as you do, you don't have to worry about attracting anyone."

"Thank you for that."

"I'm your best friend, and say this with love. You look like crap, Maxine." Beth waved at Scotty, sixth-grade teacher extraordinaire, when he walked in.

Scotty was one of the few single men in school. Eyeing Scotty like an eagle at mealtime, Beth let her thoughts wander. Christ, what she would love to do with him. Beth set her sights on leaving with him after the dance to fulfill her aspirations.

"It's the goddamn dog. He woke me up three times last night. The last time I was so anxious and nervous I couldn't get back to sleep. I've been up since four this morning. I don't understand how his idiot parents get any sleep or how they deem his barking outside at all hours of the night appropriate." Maxine's rant went on for another five minutes before Beth flicked her attention away from Scotty to Maxine.

"Have you called Animal Control?"

"Buzzy did, and it went as she predicted. They sent an officer to talk to Becca and Miles and told them the dog has as much rights as anyone to be outside as long as he doesn't bark for long periods. So, Bobo's idiot parents interpreted that to mean they could let him out all day for a few minutes at a time to bark his head off. He's a seventy-pound dog with a loud, piercing bark. The dog is giving me PTSD. I hear him in my head when he's not barking. I haven't had a restful sleep in weeks." Maxine's head dropped limply onto the folded arms on the table.

"My offer to take care of the dog stands."

For a moment, Maxine remained silent as if seriously considering Beth's offer. Desperation had a way of making the irrational appear sane.

The laughter and conversation died to a hum when Sister Fisk, the school's principal, opened the door to the teacher's lounge. When Sister Fisk stepped into the room, she brought a cold front with her.

Sister Fisk was a short four-foot-two, but she made up for her lack of height in vigour. Her round face was in proportion to the rotund body. Her eyes were gray, and her thin lips were firmed in determination. The silver cross at her chest gleamed against the white of her blouse. She wore a serviceable jacket with large pockets and a skirt that rode to her ankles. Her shoes were matronly, with thick, low heels. Her long, gray-blue hair was tightly bound in a bun on her head.

All eyes followed Sister Fisk as she crossed the room toward Maxine's table and watched her tap Maxine on the head with a sausage-thick finger.

Maxine cocked her head. "No, Beth, I don't want Bobo killed. I just—" Maxine stopped when she collected herself.

"Hello, Ms. Bassett. Thank you for joining us, and who is it you don't want murdered?" Sister Fisk said, and all eyes in the room shifted to Maxine.

"I'm sorry, Sister Fisk. I was … dreaming."

"I should hope so. You need to get yourself to bed earlier. A good night's sleep is essential to our performance during the day. It's why I'm in bed by nine and up at six. Eight hours of sleep is beneficial, but I like to get that extra hour in for good measure."

"If you don't have a life," Beth murmured.

Sister Fisk's slanted a look over her shoulder. "Did you say something, Ms. Caplan?"

"I'll try to get more sleep, Sister Fisk." Maxine jumped to Beth's rescue.

"See that you do, Maxine. You're moulding young minds into productive adults, and we need you at your best to do so."

"Yes, Sister Fisk, I will."

"Good. It's one o'clock. Don't you all have classes to attend?" Sister Fisk said, and the room cleared faster than a house on fire.

Chapter 7

MAXINE EYED THE fire-red body-hugging dress Buzzy bought to transform her into Maxi Bass. Maxine considered taking it for a test run at the school dance tonight. The dress was too short and cut too low, with thin straps that exposed her shoulders. It was a bold statement.

Maxine returned the dress to its hanger when Norman's reaction at seeing more leg and cleavage than he should flashed in her head. Then, there were the reactions of her fellow teachers and Sister Fisk, the school principal, to consider. Maxine imagined the authoritarian and staunch supporter of decorum and respectability Sister Fisk's reaction to her kindergarten teacher exposing cleavage full-on. Even the rule-breaking Beth abided by some amount of modesty—most days.

No, the school was not the place to test her new look, Maxine decided. Maxi Bass had to remain concealed from her school life and colleagues, especially Sister Fisk.

Maxine opted for a denim jumper dress over a white quarter-sleeve shirt with a lace neckline. A look her colleagues and Sister Fisk would find acceptable. Maxine applied a light dusting of bronze over her eyes, a touch of blush on her cheeks, and her lips glistened with gloss. Maxine dabbed a touch of the Opium perfume, on loan from Buzzy, on her wrists and neck. Her long, dark hair cascaded in waves around her face tonight.

Maxine approved of the conservative look reflected on the dresser mirror, which was in her comfort zone and a shield against Norman's ideas. For a nerdy geek, Norman's hormones raged often and too much.

Maxine knew Norman's interest in her went deeper than small talk, but she was not ready to enter into a relationship. Her relationship with Jesse had been remarkable. Maxine and Jesse were like-minded and had similar values. Jesse, too, had wanted to become a teacher. Jesse, like Maxine, wanted to make the world a better place.

Jesse was Maxine's soulmate, her perfect match, and he complimented her like chocolate and peanut butter. They had plans to marry, have a family, and make a home. But then Jesse did the unthinkable and left her. There was no warning sign, no indication that Jesse wanted to leave her. When he did, it left Maxine in shock and broken—so very broken.

Maxine hated Jesse for the longest time. She hated him for leaving her, for letting her find him in their bed as she did. For the longest time, Maxine had blamed herself for Jesse's abandonment. She told herself she drove him to it and that it was her fault. She had not given him the attention and love a man needs. She had not satisfied his needs.

Mostly, Maxine was angry with Jesse for not telling her what he needed. She was not a mind reader. How was she to know he was not happy with her?

Although Maxine's anger had abated over the years— anger wanes over time—she could not bring herself to get involved with another man. As much as she missed the emotional connection and a man's physical touch, she was not ready for a relationship.

Walking into St. Boniface's gymnasium, Maxine's eyes went wide in wonderment.

The Social Committee had transformed the space into a whimsical Alice's Wonderland. Painted posters of Alice, the Cheshire cat, the Queen and King of Hearts hung throughout. On the left side of the gymnasium, a long table covered with a white tablecloth overflowed with bowls of fruit punch, lemonade, and orange juice. Finger sandwiches and petite pastries were arranged on tiered stands. Alongside elegant floral teapots, cups, and saucers, there were various potato chip bowls.

Strobe lights cast a kaleidoscope of colours on the walls, while the spinning disco ball on the ceiling, suspended over the makeshift dance floor, scattered dots of light like stars across the dimly lit room. At the front of the room, the disc jockey had set up his equipment and several large speakers on the stage.

Grade seven and eight students, the girls dressed to the nines and boys wearing T-shirts and jeans, trickled into the gymnasium. Bruno Mars's "Grenade" played deafeningly from the speakers.

"Maxine, I didn't think to see you here." Sister Fisk wore a sturdy-looking navy blue jacket over a white shirt buttoned high and a skirt that reached her ankles.

"Yes, well, here I am." Maxine raised her voice above Bruno's.

"And it's good to see you're dressed appropriately." Sister Fisk threw Maxine a quick look. "You know these boys' eyes and minds wander to places they shouldn't. The work of the devil that is."

"Ahh. Yes. " Maxine stammered, grateful she had the good sense not to wear the red dress.

"Don't let these children manipulate you, Maxine. Give them an inch, and they'll take a mile. It's what teenagers are wired to do. As the adults in the room, we mustn't allow it. May I count on you, Maxine?" Sister Fisk stared with the forcible look that always put the fear of God into Maxine.

"You can, Sister Fisk," Maxine replied, more out of fear than commitment.

"Good, Maxine, because you are easily manipulated. If it were up to me, we wouldn't have these dances and open ourselves to the children's scheming. These children bring debauchery, drugs, and alcohol if we allow it," Sister Fisk murmured with quiet ferocity. "So, be vigilant, Maxine. Be very vigilant, indeed. And get some sleep, for goodness sake. The thick makeup to cover those dark circles under your eyes might fool some. Not me. Enjoy your evening, Maxine." Sister Fisk's stern face did not offer a smile.

"Hello, Sister Fisk," Beth said, her white sling-back heels clacking on the wood gymnasium floor.

Sister Fisk looked at Beth's body-hugging violet dress that hugged her shapely curves and gave a dramatic roll of her eyes.

"There you are," Beth said as she walked toward Maxine. "What words of wisdom did Darth Vader have for you tonight?"

"Sister Fisk said nothing of interest." Maxine watched Sister Fisk march toward the disc jockey stand and stab a stiff finger in the air as she set off on a Godly rant. "You look great."

Beth was the rare St. Boniface staff member who could get away with such a risqué dress. Beth's strawberry-blonde hair floated in waves around her perfectly painted face, her bangs a perfectly straight line. She was a beautiful woman who turned heads when she entered a room and Sister Fisk's boil on her butt.

Beth's poise and self-confidence could intimidate any man. It had Dan and made him the type of possessive husband who could suffocate any woman. It was unsurprising that Beth had walked out on Dan after ten years of marriage.

"Thank you. You look—" Beth eyed Maxine up and down. "You couldn't wear something more umph?"

"Umph is not me. I don't carry umph well. You know that," Maxine said, admiring the thick gold necklace at Beth's neck and the hoops at her ears that gave her an umph quality. Both pieces were fashion jewellery, but Beth made everything she wore look luxuriously classy.

"It could be if…."

Maxine cut the conversation off at the knees. This place looks fantastic. I'd never guess this was our gymnasium."

Only Maxine would refer to the gym as a gymnasium, Beth thought. "Yeah, Normie did an amazing job. Normie, geek extraordinaire, transforms into Mr. Roarke. You know? The tall white suit-wearing guy from Fantasy Island. Like Mr. Roarke, Norm clicks his fingers, and voilà. Fantasy Island. A wasted effort for these ingrate kids, but it is what it is."

The news took Maxine aback, and her surprise was evident on her face. "Norman did this?"

"I did." Norman pushed his glasses high on his pointed nose. He wore an open plaid shirt over a white t-shirt, chinos, and loafers. His hair was a messy crown on his round face, but his beard was freshly trimmed. "You like it, Maxine?"

"I do, Norman. You caught the essence of Alice in Wonderland. It's one of my favourite books."

Norman smiled at Maxine. "Mine too. It's why I chose it as this year's spring theme." Norm brushed off Beth's winged brow. "Don't tell anyone. I don't want that information to get around to my geek squad. They'd lose respect for me."

"Too late for that, Normie boy." Beth elbowed him in the ribs, but Norman's eyes were laser-focused on Maxine. "You kids fraternize. I'm going to grab me a spiked glass of punch." Beth sauntered toward Scotty, whom she planned to get to know better tonight.

Norman's brow furrowed. "This room is full of underage children, Beth. It's a virgin punch and better remain that way."

Bruno Mars segued into the techno tempo of Britney Spears's "Toxic," and the dance floor filled with excited kids.

"Not for long." Beth reached into her handbag for the vodka bottle.

A quick jolt of panic came over Norman. "You can't go lacing the bowls with vodka. Sister Fisk will blame me if anything goes afoul."

"Is afoul another word for fun?" Beth winked and went on her way, leaving Norman's eyes burning on her back.

"Beth, you get back here." The alarm was audible in Norman's voice.

"Relax, Norman. She won't spike the bowls of punch. She will spike her drink and the teachers' glasses. I'm sure most of them, too, have a bottle hidden away somewhere," Maxine said to calm Norman.

Norman exhaled a breath. "Yeah, you're probably right. That Beth is a loose cannon. I never know when to take her at her word or not."

"I know, but she's joking in this instance," Maxine replied, hoping her voice sounded more confident than she felt.

Now, Norman stared at Maxine. "You look great tonight, Maxine."

Maxine blushed at the compliment. "This is my first chaperone job. What exactly am I supposed to do?'

"You keep a close eye on this bunch to ensure they don't cling to one another too tightly and end up in the maternity ward in nine months. Also, we need to keep an eye out for contraband: booze, joints, and other types of drugs. Anything that will make them happy and royally piss off Sister Fisk. Although she could use a spliff now and then."

The shock flew into Maxine's eyes. "These are twelve, thirteen, and fourteen-year-old children. They may drink some, but they don't do drugs or have baby-making thoughts."

Naïve Maxine, who thought the best of people. It was one of the qualities Norman liked about her.

"Sure. As the chaperone, you separate them when they get too close. As for the booze and drugs, you confiscate them and bring them to me.

A brow raised in interest. "And what do you do with it, Norman?"

"I dispose of it, of course," Norman replied with a mischievous wink.

Chapter 8

BETH STASHED HER share of the evening's confiscated items: five joints, two bottles of tequila, three bottles of rum, a handful of OxyContin and Ecstasy pills under the spare tire in the trunk.

"I'm off, children." Beth opened the driver's side door and slid behind the wheel. "Don't do anything I wouldn't do. See you at school Monday unless I win the lottery on the weekend, then I bid my farewell now."

"Wait. You wouldn't share your winnings with us? Me?" Norman said. "I've been your partner in crime for…."

Beth brought a finger to her lips. "Shhh. There are ears everywhere. Ciao, babes."

Maxine waved at Beth as she tore out the parking lot when Scotty drove past her Mustang and signalled to follow him. "She'll share her winnings with us."

"You tell yourself that," Norman said.

"How long have you and Beth been partners in crime?"

The late-night breeze carried the scent of rain and rustled the damp green leaves. The nearly empty parking lot glistened under the glow of the lamplights. A mosaic of puddles reflected the darkened sky, where a bright moon peeked out from clouds heavy with water.

"It's not so much partners in crime and more share your loot with me, and I won't turn you in partnership. And it's been long enough." Norman leaned back against his closed car trunk. "You won't say anything about this, will you, Maxine? To anyone. I mean, I can cut you in the loot sharing. Beth won't be too pleased. She enjoys her loot too much."

Maxine shook her head. "I don't want your loot, Norman, but wouldn't I be getting half of your share if I did?"

Norman stared at Maxine blankly and said nothing.

Maxine stifled a smile. Norman the influencer of young minds. "Right. Anyway. Do you always bring in such a big haul at these dances?"

"Tonight was a particularly good one. Spring's in the air." A faint smile touched Norman's eyes.

"How do you know the kids won't turn you and Beth in?" Maxine asked.

"They won't," Norman said with confidence.

"You sound sure of yourself," Maxine said.

"I am. They don't know Beth and I divvy up the haul. They think I destroy it. Two, if Sister Fisk found out what the peckerheads were up to, their fate would be inked on a gravestone in God's righteous graveyard. So you see, the alternative to Beth and I not taking it home would work out worse for them."

"Or you could get rid of it altogether," Maxine suggested.

"Why let it go to waste? They spent good money on it. Someone should enjoy it." Norman's mouth tipped up at the corner. "What's funny is that mostly the A students bring the stuff."

Maxine gave Norman a dubious stare out of blue eyes.

"Hand to God." Norman brought a hand to his heart. "Did you enjoy yourself tonight, Maxine?"

After a moment of reflection on the night, Maxine said, "I did. It was fun."

For the first time since Jesse had left, Maxine allowed herself to be in a social setting with people and enjoyed it. Maxine mingled and joined in conversation. To Maxine's surprise, she let Beth prompt her onto the dance floor, which led to her twice accepting Norman's invitation to dance with him, which led to her joining the conga line.

"Are you hungry, Maxine? Those tiny sandwiches don't quell the appetite of a grown man. I know this nice dive not far from here that serves the best burgers with a side order of oily fries. Don't turn me down, Maxine," he said when he thought she was working on the polite words to wriggle out of the invitation. "Burger and fries, and maybe a milkshake. That's all."

Maxine shrugged. "Okay. Sure."

"I'll drive. No use taking two cars." Norman clicked the passenger door open and waited for Maxine to get in.

Maxine slid into the passenger seat and wondered what else the night had in store for her.

Chapter 9

NORMAN DROVE MAXINE to the Blue Plate Diner, a popular and only restaurant he knew. Norman pulled his SUV into the only parking spot available.

The exterior and interior of the restaurant were a nostalgic walk to the fifties. A vibrant red neon sign flashed the words Blue Plate Diner above a streetcar façade. The restaurant's interior was visible through the numerous windows, featuring a nostalgic ambiance with checkered floors, gleaming chrome accents, and pastel-coloured booths. From the jukebox, Elvis's classic tune "Don't Be Cruel" rocked the house.

It was close to midnight, and the place buzzed with late-night diners. Scanning the room, Maxine noted that many booths were filled with students and teachers who attended St. Boniface's dance that night. Teachers and students waved at Norman and Maxine when they walked in. The students caught sneaking illegal substances gave Norman a menacing stare, and he responded with a grin and a finger-and-thumb gun gesture.

"Doesn't this place scream fun?" Norman said, returning the wave from his students Timmy, Lorna, Stan, and Jeanine, seated at a booth.

"It does. This is great, Norman," Maxine said, taking it all in. "I never imagined our kids enjoying a fifties-themed restaurant or listening to jukebox Elvis. They're even drinking soda fountain-style milkshakes."

"Why wouldn't they be? They're great." Norman steered Maxine toward the host desk. "Hey, Marlow. You think you can round up a table for two?" Norman said to the fifty-something woman with flaming red hair, wearing a vintage pink uniform with a white collar and a lace apron around her waist.

"Hey, Normie. I can do better. I can get you your usual booth," Marlow said between chews of bubble gum. "You and your young lady friend, the only one I've seen him with ever," Marlow winked at Maxine, "follow me."

Maxine's brow winged. "I don't believe that."

"Honey, I'd know. He's here every day for lunch and at least three nights for dinner." Please follow moi." Marlow picked up a couple of plastic-covered menus and led the way to the booth by the window.

Norman sighed. "Don't start, Marlow."

"Don't complain, Normie. I'm giving you and your lady friend our premium seating. Only the best, so you can make a good impression." Marlow turned to give Maxine a wink from her heavily mascaraed lashes.

"I'm not his," Maxine cleared her throat, "lady friend."

"Ignore, Marlow. She suffers from my-mouth-likes-to-run-off syndrome." Norman's dark eyes went baleful. "She's joking about the premium seating. There is no such thing in this dump."

Marlow smiled in return. "Anger is not a good colour on you, Normie. And you love our food."

Elvis's voice went silent, and Jerry Lee Lewis belted "Great Balls of Fire" from the jukebox speaker.

"Fine. I'll admit I like the food in this dump."

"And we like having you, Normie. You class up this dump." Marlow snorted a laugh as she tapped Norman's cheek with the flat of her hand, hard. "You, young lady, sit and enjoy."

"Thank you." Maxine slid into the vinyl upholstered seat.

"You're welcome, honey." Marlow wiped down the table and laid the menus before Norman and Maxine. "I'll send Rosy over to take your order. We have Angus burgers and a great Cabernet Sauvignon or Syrah for the grownups who can afford premium prices served in white coffee cups. We also have imported beer, served to look like ginger ale," Marlow said to Maxine before she turned to walk back to the host desk.

"She seems friendly," Maxine said.

"Yeah, as friendly as a snake," Norman muttered.

"Three days a week for dinner and lunch, too, Norman." Maxine raised a brow quizzically, picking up the menu and scanning it.

The menu was fifties diner food. There were several hamburgers and hot dog options, a BLT, tuna, and egg sandwich, and a blue plate special of bacon, eggs, and toast. All the meals came with a side order of fries. For dessert, there was cherry and apple pie a la mode and lemon meringue pie. Drinks included a selection of milkshakes, a variety of pop bottles, coffee, and tea.

"Bachelor, remember. This place is within walking distance from my house. The food and ambiance are enjoyable even if the cougar woman who owns this place flaps her gum too much," Norman admitted with a wry smile.

"Marlow owns this place?" Maxine said, eyeing the front and back of the menu.

Norman nodded. "She inherited it from her father, who got it from his. It's been around for seventy-five years.

Aside from the Angus beef, wine, and imported beer options, the menu is the original her father set when he opened the place. If I know Marlow, it will remain the same until the end of time. And that's fine with her clientele because it's all great food."

"Hey, Norm." Rosy set down two glasses of water on a round coaster with the diner's name printed in white against red. "It's simple food, but good. We have a top-notch chef in the kitchen," Rosy added.

Rosy wore a uniform similar to Marlow's. Her hair was a short blonde bob that fountained the young face with dark brows over dark eyes and cherry-red-painted lips.

"Didn't expect to see you tonight. I thought you were studying for the bar exam. Rosy is planning to become a criminal lawyer. This is Maxine, a fellow teacher." Norman pushed his menu toward Rosy, who picked it up and slipped it under her left arm.

"Nice to meet you, and I wrote the exam this afternoon. Now the waiting begins." Rosy flipped her notebook open and reached for the pencil nested in her hair.

"I'm sure you did fine. After all, you had the best tutor around." Norman aimed two thumbs at himself.

Maxine gaped at Norman. She was learning a lot about him tonight, which surprised her. "You helped Rosy study for her bar exam?"

"He did, and he was great. Norm helped me study and shared his memory technique that helped me bank things I wouldn't otherwise remember." Rosy pointed an index finger to her temple. "And I think it worked out great, Norm. I remember loads and think I did well."

Norman broke out in a pleased smile. "Good to hear, Rosy."

"I owe you big, Norman. The meals on me."

Norman merely shook his head. "You owe me nothing, Rosy. I want you to succeed in your endeavour and become the next Greenspan."

"Thanks. That's the goal." Rosy grinned and gave Norman a fist bump.

"I may need your services one of these days."

Maxine watched Rosy and Norman interact and saw a side of him she had not seen before. Tonight, Maxine saw many sides of Norman she did not see in school. Maybe Beth was right when she told Maxine she had much to learn about Norman.

"The natives are restless," Rosy said when the occupants of booth five called her over. "Do you know what you're having yet, or do you need more time?"

"Give us a few more minutes for the food order, Rosy, but you can bring us each a vanilla milkshake to start," Norman said.

"Sure thing, Norm." Rosy jotted the milkshake order on her pad and moved on.

"You're good with vanilla, Maxine?"

"Vanilla is my favourite." Maxine continued to peruse the menu.

"I know," Norman said absently.

"How do you know?" Maxine asked swiftly.

"I pay attention and have good memory skills. Remember?"

Beth was right. There was more to Norman than met the eye, and he was getting Maxine's attention.

"How does a hot dog with onions, hot peppers, tomato, and mayo sound? With a side of oily French fries," Norman said, making Maxine's face light up with obvious pleasure.

"I don't know, Norman. That sounds like a lot of food and calories for so late at night."

"Live life on the edge, Maxine. If only for tonight."

From the hot dog selection to the toppings and mayo, Norman's choices were what Maxine liked and thought to order. Norman awakened feelings in Maxine that had been dormant since Jesse's departure, the only person who had known her so well.

"That sounds perfect, Norman. Thank you," Maxine said.

The night was heading in a direction Maxine had not anticipated and liked.

Chapter 10

BOBO BARKED AS Maxine stepped out of the shower—for the fourth time since six that morning. Wrapping herself in the pink terry towel and her hair dripping wet, Maxine climbed the step ladder to look out the basement window levelled with the ground. She saw Bobo roaming and sniffing the feces and urine-infested backyard before his head rose to let out a piercing bark. Maxine raised her middle finger when he looked her way. Bobo barked more loudly.

"Fucking, Bobo," Maxine muttered, the heat of anger rising from her belly to her chest.

Storming toward the laptop on the kitchen island, Maxine flipped it open and opened her email. Maxine searched for the email addressed to Marlene Rowan, Animal Control Supervisor. Edgy and anxious, Maxine vigorously typed her umpteenth email to Marlene.

An update to my email of a couple of days ago.

I want you and your entire incompetent, ineffective department to die a slow and painful death while a pack of dogs circle your bodies as you die and burst your eardrums with their ear-splitting barks.

Maxine read the typed words and would have laughed at their absurdity if she had not been as angry and frustrated as she was. Reluctantly, she deleted the email.

Maxine typed.

I wish you, everyone at Animal Control, and elected officials to be plagued with the kind of shitty, inconsiderate, entitled, ignorant, selfish, moronic neighbours like Becca and Miles Levin. Only then will you be as traumatized as those of us who are at the receiving end of the dog warfare waged on the neighbourhood by dead-brain neighbours. Only then will you do your actual fucking job and take goddamn action against insufferable dog owners like Becca and Miles Levin, who believe the world revolves around them.

Maxine read and deleted. Too much aggravation was taking hold and preventing her from writing a persuasive email.

Maxine huffed out a tired breath and ran her hands over her hair. Only then did she realize it was dripping wet.

Pushing off the stool, Maxine headed for the bathroom and dried her hair. Running a brush through it, she bound it into a ponytail. Looking at her reflection in the cabinet mirror, Maxine touched her face with subdued colours and composed the email to Animal Control in her head as she did.

"Goddamn it, the words animal control is in the title of your fucking department," Maxine said to the reflection in the mirror. "Listen to me. Buzzy is right. I need to take the swearing down a notch or two. I'm swearing like someone with Tourette syndrome and one day will forget who I'm talking to."

By the time Maxine finished applying her makeup, she had the outline of a composed email in her head. Slipping into a floral print dress with a tiered skirt, Maxine slid her feet into black patent flats and made her way to the laptop. She wanted to pen the authored words to the email before she headed to work.

Calmer now, Maxine typed.

Ms. Marlene Rowan
Animal Control Supervisor

Since you spoke to Becca and Miles and informed them that their dog has more rights than I, a law-abiding taxpayer, Bobo has been let outside to serenade the neighbourhood every twenty-five minutes or so with his deafening, piercing bark for fifteen-minute concertos.

As much as we appreciate the free performances, it's seven thirty in the morning now, and Bobo has already been let outside to serenade us with the song of his people.

Each opus has been an awakening performance that stirred emotions I wasn't aware I had.

I want to thank you. If it were not for your advocacy of Bobo's ongoing performances, it would not have been possible for us to enjoy such wondrous recitals all last night through to 1:30 am and at 6:00 am, 6:25, 6:58, and 7:10 am.

Maxine stopped typing for a moment and listened. She picked up where she left off.

Ah, there he goes again. The dog has an incredible doggedness and vocal range. Pavarotti would be envious. Unfortunately, I can't stay for his upcoming performances as I must get to work and attempt to teach my students on three hours of sleep.

Thank you for your good work.

Maxine

Maxine spelled check her text and pressed send. Nothing would come of it, as usual, but the venting was good therapy.

"The sarcasm will go right over her head," Maxine murmured, heading out the door with Bobo's barks following her.

Chapter 11

BEFORE SETTLING INTO retirement life, Buzzy was a skillful comedy writer and coach. She had written monologues, sketches, and scripts. Buzzy wrote for prominent and up-and-coming comedians. Buzzy had coached comedians whose names shone on marquis around the world, went on to sign million-dollar deals with streaming services, and became household names.

Decades later, Buzzy wanted to use her talents to launch the career of her last mentee. But before delving into the transformation of a nondescript teacher into a successful comedian, Buzzy needed to get the essential details out of the way so she and Maxine could focus on the task at hand.

"Was he a good kisser?" Buzzy said.

Behind the reflection of Maxine's glasses, Buzzy saw her tired eyes but made no mention of her observation. Doing so might shut down the conversation, and Buzzy was keen to find out about the first man Maxine trusted enough to bring home—even if it was only as far as the front stoop.

That got Maxine's attention, and she lifted her head off the table. "How?" Behind her glasses, Maxine's weary-looking eyes went wide under the arched brows.

Bobo's barks had made it impossible for Maxine to get the nap before dinner that she had looked forward to all day. Bobo's barks, as usual, shocked Maxine minutes after she fell asleep. As usual, anxious, nervous, and aggravated, Maxine could not fall back asleep, and she lay in bed staring at the ceiling, plotting.

The gloves were off now, and the game was on.

The anonymous letter Maxine sent Becca and Miles, outlining the benefits to their neighbours for using the muzzle she had enclosed and bought with her hard-earned money, went ignored. Becca and Miles showed no interest in using the muzzle.

"I watched you on the security camera last night." Buzzy set pork chops and salad on two plates and walked them to the table, and Carol Burnett followed closely. The smell of sautéed garlic lingered in the spotless, brightly lit kitchen.

Buzzy was up at five a.m., but unlike Maxine, who looked tired, stressed, and anxious, Buzzy looked wide-eyed and well-put together. Buzzy wore yellow Capri pants, a green open shirt over a matching tank top, and Roman sandals. Buzzy's silver hair looked like she had visited Francoise that morning, and her face was airbrushed to perfection.

"But you don't know how to work the security system on the laptop. Or at least that's what you told me." Maxine had traded the dress she wore to work for snug jeans, a flowing lavender blouse and running shoes. Her hair remained in a casual ponytail.

"I don't know how to work it on that contraption that folds close." Buzzy grabbed a warm, freshly baked roll from the breadbasket and carefully placed it on Maxine's plate. "It's still hot. Eat."

"You mean the laptop." Maxine picked up the roll, tore a piece, and tossed it into her mouth.

"Yes, that's it. Too many buttons and mouse clicking for my feeble brain, but you were nice enough to set up one-click access on my telephone. Remember? Butter. We need butter for the rolls and wine," Buzzy said and walked to the refrigerator.

"We don't need butter or wine. What were you doing up at one in the morning? I thought you were in bed by nine." Maxine watched Buzzy set the butter tray on the table and pour wine into their glasses.

"You also set up an alarm on my telephone when the cameras are triggered, and you and Norman emitted enough heat to trigger it. It was one seventeen in the morning, but potato, potahto. I even watched you skulk around the backyard in darkness, spraying that stinking citronella oil. Carol Burnett can't enjoy the backyard until the smell goes away." Buzzy tossed a few pork chop slices to Carol Burnett, who rose on her hind legs to catch each one mid-air.

"And here's a thought, Maxine. If our camera has infrared technology, theirs may too."

Maxine was left pondering this revelation. She quickly put a stop to her mind racing with the implications. She was in her backyard, her property. Why did she need to skulk on her property? Why shouldn't she be able to spray what she wanted and do as she pleased?

Buzzy waved a dismissive hand when Maxine opened her mouth to speak. "So, was he a good kisser? He looked like he enjoyed the task."

Maxine choked out chardonnay. "Jesus, Buzzy. You watched us."

Buzzy shook her head but confessed when Maxine's eyes froze her with her stare. "I did, from beginning to end. Well, don't keep me guessing. Was there tongue or not? I couldn't make that out on the video. The angles weren't right."

The flush rose to Maxine's cheeks. "Christ!" Maxine

"No need to be embarrassed, honey. Lip locking is a natural process between a man and a woman who are attracted to one another. What follows is physical excitement. The man will get an erec…."

"All right, that's enough," Maxine interjected to stop Buzzy from getting into a graphic sex tutorial. The woman had no filter.

"You may as well answer my question, dear. By now, you know me well enough to know I'm not letting up until I get answers."

Carol Burnett lay at Buzzy's feet, patiently waiting for more pork chop bits. Carol Burnett wore a chic Prada red print scarf around her neck that matched the ribbon on her head.

"He was a good kisser," Maxine said and blushed. "He drove me home after…. I had too much to Syrah. Okay? I drank too much alcohol. There, now you know." Maxine paused and waited for Buzzy's comment.

Displaying no reaction, Buzzy dug into her salad.

Starring at Buzzy, Maxine, too, speared lettuce with her fork. "These rolls are tasty."

"Thank you, dear." Buzzy delighted Carol Burnett with more pork chop. "What's the young man's name?"

"Norman McDonnell." Maxine stuffed her mouth with pork chop. "He's a teacher at St. Boniface."

"Norman MacDonnell, like the great comedian, whom I take no credit for." Buzzy looked at Carol Burnett, who lapped her muzzle and looked up with those big brown eyes. "It's her coercive stare, but she can't have more pork chop. She's had far more food than her quota for the day. She'll be pooping nonstop. Ignore her."

"Norman spells his last name with an M-C, not an M-A-C like Norm MacDonnell. Potato, potahto. You need to buy more citronella oil. We're running out. It has kept Bobo from our fence and pushed him towards Mrs. Hathaway's side. If she's claiming Bobo's barking doesn't bother her, I feel no guilt for causing him to keep closer to her house and inches from her bedroom window. Let her suffer for refusing me when I asked her to complain to Animal Control."

"You know that old biddy is half deaf." Buzzy spread butter on the roll, which she had cut in half, and Carol Burnett lapped her muzzle twice. "You're not getting any more food, Carol Burnett. So, be on your merry way," Buzzy said, watching the dog gaze soberly before strolling to her bed by the sliding door and settling in.

"Mrs. Hathaway is only deaf when it's convenient for her, and as for the citronella smell keeping Carol Burnett from enjoying the yard, war is not pretty, and people, or dogs, must make sacrifices."

Buzzy would have laughed at the puerile comment, but Maxine was dead serious. "Did you speak to the surrounding neighbours?"

Maxine nodded. "They denied being able to hear Bobo's barking, and I'm telling you, that's straight-up bullshit. Bobo's bark is volcano-loud. What's happened to sense community?"

"You're right that they hear Bobo. They don't want to get involved." Buzzy watched Maxine eat the last of her pork chop and sponged the plate with a piece of bread.

"Are you telling me our neighbours would rather put up with the sleepless nights than get involved?"

Buzzy saw the shock and disappointment flashing in Maxine's face. "That's what I'm telling you, dear. They've seen how put off and aggravated you are by Bobo and expect you will do what they can't, which is what's best for the neighbourhood. It is where we are, dear. They will not get involved even after all the baking I share with our neighbours. You're on your own."

"Well, then I demand you stop sharing your baking with them and stop being so accommodating. Stop making cakes for their kids' birthdays when they ask. Stop baking brownies and muffins for their school bake sales. Just stop it. It's not even as if you charged them."

Buzzy gave Maxine a pointed look as her brows lifted.

"If they don't want to get involved in the dog controversy, I'll go to war alone." Maxine hissed between clenched teeth.

Buzzy smiled at Maxine wanly. "War? Dog controversy? Really, Maxine, do you see the hold Bobo has on you? You need to occupy yourself with something other than that dog. You need to get busy with your young man. Is he a nice young man?"

"He's not my young man, and don't change the subject." Maxine's stance was angry, and she stared at Buzzy. "I'll pick up the citronella oil, but you're paying for it," Maxine blustered.

"Order what you need and give me the bill," Buzzy said calmly and softly, hoping not to agitate Maxine further.

"He is a nice man," Maxine said after a short silence, regaining her calm. "Norman is a good man, funny and kind. He's not very good at math, but he's respectful. I enjoyed his company," Maxine added, not sure why she had.

"All good qualities."

"Yes, they are." Maxine's face was full of contemplation.

"And you had a good time last night with him?"

Maxine reflected on the events of the previous night. She had enjoyed a good meal over intelligent, witty conversation and shared dreams with a man who listened to her—as Jesse had. As Jesse was, Norman was attentive, caring, and entertaining. Norman was not judgmental when to quell her uneasiness at being with a man for the first time since Jesse drank too much wine. Instead, Norman helped Maxine slide into her comfort zone, resulting in her enjoying their night together more than she imagined.

At the night's end, after her third glass of wine, Norman refused to let Maxine drive herself home. When he walked a somewhat inebriated Maxine to her door, he pecked her on the cheek and stepped away. Maxine pulled Norman back and stood on her toes to lock lips with his. Maxine would not volunteered that bit of information to Buzzy. Not because Buzzy would disapprove. Buzzy would not. Some secrets were hers to keep.

"I had a great time 'with him," Maxine admitted more to herself than Buzzy because she did not imagine happiness would find her again after Jesse.

"Good." Buzzy rested her hand on Maxine's. "I'm happy for you, Maxine. It's been years since Jesse left you, and it's time for happiness to fill your life again. You will see Norman McDonnell, with an M-C, again."

Maxine was silent.

Chapter 12

TO SAY NORMAN was taken aback when Maxine called out of the blue to accept his invitation weeks after asking her to dinner is an understatement. Once the surprise waned, a big smile touched Norman's mouth. Maxine had put Norman off for weeks, claiming she was working on a project with Buzzy. Maxine would not tell Norman what she was working on; she only said that the project required her full attention.

Norman told Maxine his weekend was wide open. The stack of tests to be graded, the year-end graduation dance to plan, grass mowing, oil change on the car, and much more on Norman's to-do list could wait. Norman had a dinner to plan.

It would be their first official date. All sorts of thoughts swelled in Norman's head, and he was hopeful his kitchen aptitude would lead to them. His heartbeat quickened.

Women appreciated a domesticated man, and Norman was out to prove himself to the woman who had a hold of his heart since meeting her. Norman planned to make lasagna, garlic bread, and his famous roseMarlow-roasted chicken. If that did not impress Maxine, the strawberry panna cotta topped with fresh whipped cream Norman planned to make would.

Norman McDonnell aimed to impress the woman who was living in his head.

Norman went about making his house presentable. Maxine was the fastidious sort, and it took Norman most of the day to make his house look exceptional. Once, every critical room in the house sparkled: the kitchen, bedroom, dining room, and bathrooms. Norman went to the supermarket to purchase the necessary ingredients to make dinner. Next, Norman stopped at the liquor store and bought a bottle of Sicilian Nero d'Avola, the perfect pairing for lasagna.

Back at home, Norman got busy in the kitchen while Maxine, in her brightly lit basement apartment, debated whether to give Norman a glimpse of Maxine Bass, as Buzzy suggested she should.

"Honey, you need a hot, sweaty roll between the sheets. Nothing oils the body and mind like good sex," Buzzy told Maxine again and again.

After a short while of intense thought, Maxine decided to slip into the ruby-red dress.

The dress would send the message to Norman that Maxine was not sure she was ready to transmit. Her brain, however, was duelling with the hormones playing tug-of-war since their shared kiss. Norman was the first man since Jesse to stir Maxine's yearning and desire, and self-servicing was not doing the job anymore. Maxine's body needed quelling. It required a man's touch.

After Jesse, Maxine had not met another man she wanted to let into her heart, let alone her bed. As the years passed, Maxine settled into a life of solitude. It was better than letting anyone into her heart and allowing them to tear it into a million pieces as Jesse had. Love, Maxine learned from Jesse, was fleeting, but the pain of heartbreak was permanent.

Norman was caring, gentle, respectful, and dutiful. Geeky guys were, and they weren't high maintenance. Maxine appreciated those qualities, and they filled her with the comfort she had not felt in some time.

In the bathroom, Maxine styled her hair and let the long strands of coiled dark hair fall to her shoulders and around her face. Reaching for the makeup bag, Maxine returned to the bedroom. Sunlight streamed through the windows. Dresses were strewn on the bed, covered in the plum conformer that matched the walls. Shoes lay where she had kicked them off after deeming them non-date material.

Pushing aside the dresses on the bed, Maxine sat at the edge and emptied the contents of her makeup case, which Buzzy recently upgraded to the best brand names. Maxine touched her face and lips with colour and set the gold hoops in her ears—a Buzzy loan.

Maxine looked at the image in the mirror behind her bedroom closet door. Confounded by the woman she saw and barely recognized, she stared at herself for a moment longer.

"Buzzy is right. You do clean up well, Maxine," she said, turning this way and that in front of the mirror. "But I don't know if this is the message I want to send Norman."

"It is indeed the message you want to transmit." Buzzy's unexpected voice startled Maxine when she walked into the bedroom with Carol Burnett meandering behind her.

Buzzy wore floral capris, a flowing silk shirt, and white ballerina shoes. Her striking silver hair was elegantly styled around her face, and her makeup was flawlessly airbrushed. Carol Burnett proudly wore an Armani turquoise scarf around her neck.

"Christ! You startled me. You have to stop letting yourself into my apartment unannounced, Buzzy. I have rights as your tenant," Maxine said but knew they were wasted words. Buzzy was going to do what Buzzy wanted.

"You're a beautiful woman, inside and out, and should flaunt it. If I were as young as you and cleaned up as great as you do when you invest the time to care for yourself, I'd be out there getting laid every night."

"Oh, Christ!" Maxine murmured to herself.

"Take it from me, dear; you must take advantage of your current vigour and the gravitational force working in your favour because both will be snapped when you least expect it. Then, you'll barely have the energy to put on your underwear, let alone remove them when the opportunity presents itself. Not that you'll want to with everything sagging as it begins to do after you hit forty." Buzzy reached for her breast, raised it, and released it to prove her point. "See what I mean. Everything, and I mean everything, hangs southward."

Maxine shuddered at the mental image that popped into her head. "That is way too much of an overshare, Buzzy."

A slight smile settled on Buzzy's face. "I brought you this." Buzzy handed Maxine the delicate gold chain with a heart pendant. The feeling of happiness and love that floated from Buzzy when she lay the chain on Maxine's hand told her it was a cherished memento. "Morty gave it to me on our first anniversary."

When Buzzy set it on Maxine's hand, she looked over the chain and the diamond-encased pendant. As thin as the chain was and as tiny as the diamonds were, it spoke of Mortimer's love for Buzzy.

"It's lovely, Buzzy. But I can't take it."

"You're not, dear. It's on loan. I want it back in the morning." Buzzy unclasped the chain and set it around Maxine's neck.

Frowning slightly, Maxine said, "What makes you think I'm not coming home tonight?"

Buzzy gave Maxine an eye over. "There's too much effort in all this for only dinner."

"Shit, too obvious."

"Not at all. The necklace looks great around your long neck. You look great."

Maxine followed Buzzy to the living room when she left the bedroom. "You don't think it's too much? That I'm sending the wrong message."

Buzzy shook her head. "It's sending the message you want to convey. That you want to roll like thunder under the covers. I'd add more concealer on those dark circles under your eyes if you want the look to get you some tonight."

"Christ, Buzzy. Have you no filter?"

"It is a consequence of being a comedian. Unlike intense you, I see everything through a satirist's eyes and see humour." Buzzy sat on the sofa and crossed one slender leg over another. Carol Burnett leapt next to Buzzy and rested her head on her lap. "To write comedy, you must see the humour in our daily existence."

"Sure. That's the reason you spew whatever comes to mind. And ending up in Norman's bedroom is not what I want to get out of my dinner with him."

Buzzy creased her face into doubtful lines. "Of course it is. Don't talk yourself out of some much-needed fun, dear. You must strike while the iron's hot. And right now, you look *muy caliente*."

"How is it you always know what I need?" Maxine reached for her phone on the coffee table when it rang and, to her detriment, did not look at the caller's identification. "Hi, Mom. How are you?" Maxine's lips curled in a shaky smile.

"I'm fine, Maxine. How are you?" Georgiana said in her typical derisive, stern tone.

Georgiana Basset was the polar opposite of Edith Morgan. Georgiana Basset had no sense of humour and saw everything through the judgmental eyes of her church and the Bible, which she deemed the only suitable book on the planet. But then, Georgiana had to espouse Pastor Barret Basset's—her husband and Maxine's father—code of belief.

Although the Bassets lived in a small, inconsequential town, Georgiana elevated herself to the local First Lady. Georgiana believed the town's residents closely watched and revered her actions and movements. Everything Georgiana did, everything in her life, her thoughts, beliefs, clothes, down to the matronly gum-soled black shoes, was puritanical. Conforming to the sin-free life her husband preached was how Georgiana lived her life and relished it.

Maxine attributed her mother's rigidity to her lack of curiosity and interest in how the rest of the world conducted its life. Living in a bubble closes and limits your mind.

Georgiana and Barret did not own a television, and Maxine was allowed to read only a handful of her mother's pre-approved books. The Bible was one of those books. There was a Bible in every room, and crucifixes hung from the walls of the small red brick home.

Maxine woke up each morning to the carved wooden crucifix with Jesus Christ staring down at her in judgment until the day she left for the city. The scholarship Maxine earned enabled her to attend the teaching school in Toronto, and she was shocked and thrilled when her parents agreed to let her leave home to go to the city. The move saved Maxine from a life of boredom and the religious nonsense her father spewed with fervour and her mother enforced.

Maxine had Jesse to thank for opening her eyes to a life filled with unconditional love, free thinking, and the common sense she did not think possible. Jesse was a political aggressor, protesting the wrongs of the world. Jesse aimed to become a teacher and dedicate his life to teaching the underprivileged in the third world.

Maxine's parents saw Jesse as noble as fulfilling God's work, and they condoned her relationship with Jesse. That is until Georgiana and Barret understood that Jesse was transforming their daughter into a free spirit. Jesse opened Maxine's eyes to a world she only had glimpses of at the school library's computer. It was one of the many reasons Maxine loved Jesse and resented him for leaving her.

"I'm fine, Mom … No, Mom, I'm not living a life of depravity … Yes, I'm still living with Buzzy … Yes, Buzzy keeps me from engaging in the life of corruption the city propagates." Maxine gave Buzzy her back to avoid her laughing eyes.

"Good to hear, Maxine, and I hope she and you devote time every night to read the bible and pray for salvation," Georgiana said.

"Of course we do," Maxine replied, forcing herself to smile at Buzzy as she glanced back over her shoulder.

Carol Burnett had checked out from the moment and fallen asleep on Buzzy's lap. Maxine envied Carol Burnett's carefree, unburdened existence.

"Put her on speaker. I want to hear what she says." The smirk twisted Buzzy's lips.

"Is that Buzzy, I hear? Let me speak to her." Georgiana's remark was more of a demand than a statement.

Maxine thought it prudent to keep Buzzy from speaking to Georgiana, and she said, "It's the television, Mom. Buzzy's not here right now. Umm, Saturdays, Buzzy does the Lord's work by volunteering her time to the food bank at our local church." Maxine covered the telephone's speaker to prevent her mother from hearing Buzzy's burst of laughter.

"Good woman, Buzzy. You let her know the Lord has a special place in heaven for her."

"I have told Buzzy the Lord has special plans for her," Maxine said and muted the telephone when Buzzy sputtered out a laugh.

"And you stay away from that television, nothing but degeneracy and wickedness there for impressionable young girls like you. I've heard they show women in sexual acts. I can't imagine what good that does to anyone," Georgiana exclaimed.

Maxine pictured her mother crossing herself in her religious, all-consuming manner. "Sorry. Yes, I will, Mom. Is there a reason why you called?"

"Yes. I almost forgot. I'm sending you a package. I saw a couple of dresses in the church's collection bin, and I thought they'd be perfect for you. They have a white lace collar, three-quarter sleeves, and are ankle length. One is pink, and the other is sky blue."

Maxine smoothed the front of her dress, wondering what Georgiana would say if she saw her now and knew what she planned for that night. "You don't need to do that, Mom."

"There are also two new Bibles and a hymnal book that your father purchased for the church from the generous donations from our parishioners." The sense of pride flowed from Georgiana's voice.

"Mom, you shouldn't do that. Your parishioners donated the money to the church, not to me."

"Your father asked for their and God's permission to send them to you, and both agreed you and Buzzy should have them. He and I are praying for you, Maxine."

Maxine closed her eyes as the wave of distress that hit her when speaking to her mom washed over her. "I'm sorry, Mom, but I've got to go. I'm meeting a friend for dinner tonight, and I must get ready."

"A female friend, I hope."

The silence at the end of the line persisted.

"Your father and I pray for you every night, Maxine. Living in the city with temptation at every turn, we pray for your virtue and wholesomeness. That boy Jesse corrupted your mind. He wasn't a good man, Maxine. He wasn't good for your soul," Georgiana said sneeringly. "After his … unexpected departure, your father and I rejoiced because you became the girl you once were again. Your father and I wish you to remain as such."

There were times when Maxine wondered if Georgiana listened to her father's preached words of love, acceptance, tolerance, and understanding.

"I have to go, Mom." Maxine ended the call before her mother got another word in and turned to Buzzy. "Don't expect me home tonight." The look of purpose was clear on Maxine's face as she reached for her purse and car keys.

"Atta girl. Nothing ventured, nothing gained, I say. Enjoy your night and do everything I can't." A smile brushed over Buzzy's lips.

"I will. Oh, I so will."

Part II

The Middle

You can change the narrative of your life anytime.

— M.L. Lexi

Chapter 13

NORMAN FROZE AT the door, staring at Maxine. Unable to take his eyes off Maxine, dumbfounded and speechless, Norman's mouth hung open as, for a long moment, he admired the woman before him.

It was the first time in a long while Maxine had considered herself attractive.

The dress whispered over curves Norman did not think Maxine possessed but was happy to see. Gone were the thick-rimmed glasses replaced by contacts. With the dusting of blue-pink eyeshadow, her eyes seemed bigger and bluer. Her full, red, kissable lips looked like those men loved to nibble on. And those long legs looked longer in the tall, red pumps.

Norman liked how his head filled with the sweet scent of her perfume. He liked how the waves of midnight-black hair fell around her face, loose and untamed. Better than that, Norman liked Maxine's display of confidence.

Who was the woman before him? Norman asked himself.

When Norman found his voice, he said, "You look, wow, yeah, incredible," stretching each word for emphasis.

"Thank you, Norman." Maxine's voice was almost a purr that left Norman staring a moment longer. "Are you going to invite me in?"

Maxine waved a hand, signalling Norman to step aside and let her into his home. When she walked past him, he breathed in the subtle hint of her perfume and felt his insides tingle.

Maxine set her clutch bag on the hallway table and let her eyes roam the open space. Sports paraphernalia in dark wood frames hung from the walls painted olive green. Blonde wood floors gleamed. The masculine and modern furniture sat on thick pile carpets. A bookcase built into the wall displayed an impressive and eclectic selection of books that Norman had read. The air was rich with the scent of garlic and lasagna, accompanied by the soft instrumental of "Samba Pa Ti."

"Santana, right?" Maxine said after a short listen.

Norman nodded. "You know your seventies music."

Norman wore tan chinos and a white shirt with the top two buttons undone and the sleeves rolled up to the elbows. He had perfectly styled hair and well-groomed stubble. The scent of Polo cologne enveloped him.

"I'm a big fan of Santana's music—any seventies music, for that matter." Maxine looked around the house for signs of confiscated drugs. She was pleased to see none. "Best songwriting, best lyrics, best rhythm and blues and rock bands, Queen, Led Zeppelin, The Bee Gees, the Eagles. Great music came out of that era no matter the genre."

Norman's face brightened, pleased by Maxine's musical knowledge. "Agreed. I don't believe you were even born in the seventies."

Maxine lifted a single dark eyebrow. "And you were—what?—five?"

Norman smiled back at her. "Touché."

"You don't need to live in the times to appreciate the music, Norman," Maxine said.

"True that. I'm stuck in the seventies, music-wise, that is."

"You have a lovely home, Norman. I have to say, I didn't expect it to be so orderly and clean. I'm impressed," Maxine said, following Norman to the kitchen.

White cabinets, countertops, and stainless steel appliances gleamed under the sun, spilling through the sliding door's double pane glass.

"It was my parents' home, which my brother and I inherited on their passing." Norman indicated Maxine to the stool pushed against the kitchen island.

"I'm sorry about your parents."

Norman pushed his glasses high on his nose. "They died months apart. My mom went first. Ovarian cancer got her. My father, possibly due to loneliness, followed her three months later. They were married forever."

"That's lovely. Not that they passed, but that they were so simpatico with one another." Maxine swiftly corrected.

"I know what you meant, and you're right about them being simpatico. I should be so lucky to meet a woman as compatible as my mom was with Dad. Anyway, I bought my brother's share of the house. He lives in Europe and wasn't planning to live in the house. I wanted to keep our childhood home in the family. It's our home, where we grew up and made memories. Dad worked his ass off to buy us this house. You know?" Norman spoke with such compassion and reverence that Maxine felt her heart fill.

Maxine nodded her understanding.

Over the speaker, Santana segued into Paul McCartney's iconic "Band on the Run."

"I mostly renovated it myself. It took me a long time and energy, but I think it turned out pretty good."

Aside from being moved by his outpouring of emotion, Maxine was impressed by Norman's skill. "It looks like a professional job. And you have a great eye for style and design."

"Thanks." Norman looked over his work with a prideful smile. "I'm sorry. I haven't offered you anything to drink. I picked up a great bottle of wine this afternoon."

"Wine sounds good." Maxine watched Norman set the garlic bread pan into the oven before walking to the refrigerator.

"And I hope you like lasagna, garlic bread, and roasted chicken." Norman uncorked the wine bottle.

"I like all of the above. You cooked all that yourself?"

"Guilty on all counts." Norman poured wine into two crystal glasses.

"I'm impressed."

"I enjoy cooking. It's relaxing. I don't do it as often as I should. I mean, cooking for one is tedious. You cook?"

Maxine gratefully accepted the offered glass of wine and sipped it to taste. "I hate it. Not the wine, the cooking. The wine is wonderful. Cooking stresses me out. The preparation, cutting, and measuring of ingredients drives me to insanity. Buzzy feeds me. Not as well as she feeds Carol Burnett. Her dog," Maxine informed when Norman's brows furrowed.

Norman's eyes lit with laughter. "Does setting the table stress you out?"

Maxine hopped off the stool. "I can do that. Point me to the dishes, cutlery, and whatever else you need to set out."

Norman reached into the cupboard for the dishes and pointed to the cutlery drawer. "We'll need forks, knives, dessert spoons, and coffee spoons. The placemats are in the drawer next to it. The coffee cups and saucers are in the above cupboard."

While Maxine set the table, Norman cut into the steaming lasagna and plated it on white plates with a gold trim. He spooned the chicken and garlic bread onto platters. Norman put the plates on the table and lit the two candles before he helped Maxine to her seat and sat beside her.

"Enjoy," Norman said, and the two touched glasses.

From the speakers, Kansas kicked in with the prophetic words of their seventies hit song "Dust in the Wind."

Throughout the meal, Maxine and Norman shared amusing work experiences. They exchanged stories about their students' shenanigans. Norman told Maxine about his childhood and his parents. Maxine volunteered little about her childhood and life. Norman did not press, reasoning that when Maxine was ready to share, she would.

Maxine spoke fondly of Beth and Buzzy's friendship, and Norman listened intently, absorbing everything she said. "Both offered me the guidance and mentoring a young girl from a small town alone in a big city needs. Buzzy opened her home to me and gave a broke student a comfortable, clean, and safe home. I was fortunate to have met them both when I did."

Norman poured the remaining wine, half in her glass and half in his. "I hope you consider me a friend too, Maxine."

Maxine's head swam in enough wine that her inhibitions faded, and her true feelings prevailed. Stretching her lips into a smile, she leaned into Norman and touched her lips to his. Norman's brain staggered at the warmth of her lips and the sweet taste of wine on them.

"Does that answer your question?" Maxine said with a smile.

Norman's brain shut down, and there was a continuous silence. Then Norman said, "I made panna cotta for dessert. With fresh whipped cream. And coffee."

Maxine rested a hand on Norman's thigh. It felt tighter than she expected. It inflamed her insides. "Let's skip that for now."

"Okay. Sure. It's homemade panna cotta. Are you … sure?" Norman stuttered, trying to process what was happening.

The smile on Maxine's lips bloomed. "I am."

Maxine began to kiss Norman again, and when she found his tongue and tangled hers with his, ecstasy flooded through them like a swelling river.

Maxine stood up and extended her hand.

Norman's heart beat thickly as his hand whipped up to meet hers.

"I don't know your house well enough. You're going to have to lead the way, Norman," Maxine said when Norman remained rooted in place.

Norman nervously pushed his glasses up on his nose. "Yes. Yes, of course," he said, leading her up the stairs.

The orderly bedroom smelled of the vanilla air freshener plugged into the outlet. The bed was king-size, with a walnut wood bed frame. It was topped with a turquoise comforter and two brown pillowcase-covered pillows against the tufted headboard. The dresser, too, was walnut, with a square mirror above it. Lamps with rectangular shades adorned the night tables on either side of the bed. The tall picture window, flanked by brown blackout curtains, bathed the room in moonlight.

"Do you have quixotic seventies music up here?" Maxine said.

"I do." Norman opened the laptop on the nightstand. After a few clicks on the keyboard, the romance of Saturday Night Fever's "More Than a Woman" suffused the silence.

They stared at each other, letting their thoughts wander.

Maxine took his right hand, and her left arm went around his waist. She let him spin her around the room. "Are you all right with this, Norman? With me being here, in your bedroom?" Maxine said.

"I've dreamed of this moment for a long time," he confessed.

"I'm sorry I made you wait for so long."

"I would have waited forever," Norman said, eliciting a warm smile.

"You don't know me well enough, Norman. I come with emotional baggage. Lots of it."

Norman brushed the hair from her face. "The same can be said of a lot of people, Maxine. The difference is I don't mind. I'm happy to help you sort through whatever weighs you down."

"You better mean that, Norman. I don't sleep around. It's not who I am. And I can't handle having my heart broken—again."

Maxine could not allow another man to rip her heart out as Jesse did. She had taken precautions from a repeat incident by remaining unattached. She would have continued her relationship-free life if Norman had not tapped into her loneliness and amplified it to the point of making her yearn for male companionship.

"I know you're not a one-night stand type woman, and I will never hurt you, Maxine. Of that, you can be sure."

Maxine looked into Norman's eyes. The sincerity she saw in them sealed Maxine's decision to be with him as the right one. Norman was the man to help her move forward and into the next chapter of her life. She had waited a long time for the right moment to let go of Jesse and let another man into her life, and Norman was that man.

"I believe you, Norman," Maxine said, taking hold of Norman's hand and walking him toward the bed. "It's been a long time since I've been with a man, and I've only been with one. I may be an anticlimax to your expectations."

"You could never disappoint me, Maxine." Norman reached up to stroke a fingertip over Maxine's cheek.

"I hope not to," she whispered against his cheek as she unbuttoned his shirt and slid it off his shoulders.

What Maxine saw surprised and pleased her. Norman was not athletic, but he was not soft. He looked strong and fit. Norman was not overweight or thin. He was Norman, and Maxine liked what she saw.

Maxine gave him her back, and Norman slid the dress's zipper down until it whispered over her body and dropped to the floor.

The subtle swell of her breast over the simple line of her red lace bra and underwear stole his breath. Her body was shapely with seductive curves. Her legs were long, and those pumps added umph to her sexy look. The musky scent of her perfume drove him to insanity.

Norman took a moment to catch his breath.

"You're stunning," he said, nuzzling her neck. "I've ached for you, wanted to be with you since the first day I saw you. I've wanted to touch and make love to you."

"Then, let's get to it." Maxine slid his glasses off his face.

Norman lifted her in his arms and gently laid her on the bed. He skimmed his hands over her body, awakening nerves that, for too long, were dormant.

Now, on top of her, he kissed her everywhere, kindling needs she had not felt in too long.

Arching her body, she said, "I want to feel your hands and mouth all over my body."

And she did. The feel of Norman's hands and mouth electrifying her skin and places that had not been touched by a man in too long made her shudder. Her body tensed when he cupped her breast and gently bit the hard, erect nipples, first one and then the other. When he explored further and delved deeper into the folds of her body, it drove such thrills to surge through her, and she cried out in pleasure.

Hearing her cries and moans, he felt his hardness growing, throbbing. His need to force himself into her intensified, but he pulled himself back. Pleasing her was what he wanted to do, and he did.

She responded ardently. Calling his name and moaning the passionate cries of an aroused woman at his hand was music to his ear.

The taste of her exploded inside him when the glorious burst of heat thundered through her and drove her to orgasm.

Her arms went around his back, as did her legs, and he drove himself inside her hard and fast. Bound together, she rocked with him and matched his passion. Like rapid-flowing waves cresting over the sea walls, she took him to new heights until his feral cry filled the stillness of the room as he crested on the wave of ecstasy and emptied himself inside her.

Chapter 14

MAXINE'S MUSCLES RELAXING now, she felt weightless, like a feather floating in the air. Threaded between Norman's arms, she pressed her naked body close to his naked body. The scent of man filled her senses. She thought it was a glorious scent and momentarily lost herself.

"You're quiet, Maxine. Are you okay?" Norman played with her hair.

"I'm better than okay. Thank you, Norman," Maxine said, feeling a sense of completeness that had eluded her for a long time.

"I should be thanking you." Norman flashed her a wicked grin. "You were amazing for someone who claims to be out of practice. And you're very agile. You're a regular contortionist."

The flush rose to Maxine's cheeks, and she elbowed him in the ribs. "Don't embarrass me. I'm thanking you for making me feel … whole."

Buzzy was right about Maxine needing to "oil" her body, mind, and soul. Norman had done that. Norman had not whispered the loving words a woman likes to hear before, during, or after lovemaking, but Maxine had not expected it. It was too early for such intimacy. Still, Norman had made her feel desirable, beautiful, and a sexual woman. Norman made her confidence soar— feelings that should fill every woman's life.

"I'd be happy to make you feel that way again if you like. In, say, twenty-five minutes." He skimmed his fingers over her arm.

"For a middle-aged teacher, your stamina is admirable." Maxine flashed him a bright smile.

The strains of Roxy Music declaring love was the drug that hooked him echoed from the speakers.

"Who are you calling middle-aged?"

"You're close to pushing forty, and if my math is right, that's middle age for the average human being. I'm sorry, old man, but them's the facts," Maxine said in a consoling voice.

Norman formed a silent wow with his lips. "Thank you for that insightful comment."

"You're welcome," she said, smiling all the while.

"Would you like something to drink? I have a second bottle of wine I can pop open."

Maxine shook her head. "Just lie here with me."

In Norman's arms, Maxine felt the comfort and safety she had once felt with Jesse. It was nice to have those feelings fill her again. Too lovely to let intrusive thoughts of Jesse rob her of her enjoyment as he had all these years. So Maxine pushed them from her mind.

"I can do that." Norman gently drew her closer to him and held her tight.

In comfortable silence, wrapped in his arms, Maxine and Norman's eyes focused out the window. The sky was dark. A half-moon surrounded by twinkling stars glowed brightly. They listened to nature and the steady nightlife drone filling the night silence.

"I have a confession to make." Maxine pulled away from Norman and turned to him until their eyes met.

The hesitation in her voice did not go unnoticed, and Norman worried that their shared moment had come to a swift end.

"Sounds ominous." He looked into her eyes.

"I came here with the idea of having sex with you to spite my mother," Maxine confessed.

Norman stifled the heavy sigh of relief and merely smiled. "I'm glad to oblige."

Maxine gazed at Norman. Women took a wrong to the grave. Men, however, possessed the singular, extraordinary superpower not to carry a grudge. "I thought you'd be upset that I was using you?"

Norman shook his head. "Not when the outcome was what we shared. Besides, I don't believe you did use me to spite your mother. It may have been the purpose you came with, but it wasn't what went through your mind during our shared intimacy." Norman linked his fingers with hers. "Am I right?"

"You are." Maxine touched her lips to his.

Norman's eyes glinted with satisfaction. "Can I ask you a question?"

Maxine looked into Norman's eyes. "After accepting my confession and what I let you do to me a few minutes ago, you're entitled to ask as many questions as you like. However, it doesn't guarantee I will answer."

"I preface the questions with, not that I'm complaining because I thought you looked amazing, but I'm curious to know why the sudden change in appearance and mannerisms." Norman watched Maxine's eyes cut away from his. "I'm sorry I asked. You don't have to answer."

Did the man have to be so proper and gracious?

Propping herself on her elbow. "Can you keep a secret?"

Norman, too, propped himself on his elbow and met her stare. "As good as the next person."

"No. You have to keep this secret better than that."

Norman brushed back the loose strands of hair that curtained her face. "It'll take everything from me, but okay. I can do it."

"Norman, if you want to know about my transformation, you must swear not to tell a soul. I could get into trouble if my secret got out." Maxine's impatient voice and the urgency in its tone told Norman she was serious.

"I swear I won't tell a soul." Norman crossed his heart.

"Buzzy talked me into doing standup comedy at her comedy club."

"Buzzy owns a comedy club?"

Maxine nodded. "Ba-Dum-Bump."

"I've been there. It's downtown. From time to time, Ba-Dum-Bump features A-list comedians."

"That's the one. So you know it's famous and has been around for decades. Buzzy and her husband started the club to put food on the table, but it soon became the go-to place for aspiring comedians seeking exposure and recognition. Many comedians who found great success after performing at the club expressed their gratitude to Buzzy and Morty by returning to perform and promote it. Notable performers such as Candy, Myers, Chappelle, Colbert, Seinfeld, and Short passed through the club as unknowns and returned as successful aspiring comedians."

Norman blinked, eyes wide in shock. "Seriously?"

"Yep. My first scheduled gig is on Wednesday. I'm nervous as all hell, but Buzzy's been coaching me on comedic timing, cadence, delivery, and so much more. She's taught me the mode of pacing I'm to use to land a joke. It's important to a comedian. It's why I've been so busy these past weeks."

"Hmmm." Norman absently curled the tips of her hair around his finger.

"The outfit I'm wearing tonight, my appearance and mannerisms are what Buzzy sees as my on-stage persona. Maxi Bass is the stage name she concocted." Maxine's beaming face denoted her excitement, and Norman kept his thoughts to himself.

The reality of the situation was not lost on Norman. He was not thrilled about Buzzy's plan to have Maxine look gorgeous while exposing more skin than she should to get the audience's attention. Mostly men's attention. Every hormonal guy in the audience would ogle Maxine. A hormonal man himself, Norman knew the sexual acrobatics their minds would weave with Maxine as the main character.

Maxine appeared too excited for Norman to say anything and spoil her high. Instead, he let it spoil his.

Maxine made a face. "Is that all you have to say, Norman?"

Norman twisted up his lips. "I didn't say anything."

"That's my point." Maxine rolled out of bed, taking with her the bedsheet, which she used to wrap around her naked body. Maxine's hair, so black it almost shone blue, was a sexy, stark contrast against the white bedsheet." I'm pouring my heart out to you."

As good as Norman thought, Maxine looked with her temper on; he felt it best to derail the conversation and calm her down. Turning the conversation about her—a secret taught to Norman by his father, the wisest man he knew—was the way to do it.

"Is it something you want to do?" Norman asked.

"It wasn't initially, but the idea grew on me." Holding the bedsheet tightly against her body, Maxine paced the room as she spoke.

"Sounds like an exciting proposition," Norman added to the conversation, but Maxine overlooked the comment.

"I'm not a fan of the persona Buzzy manufactured. I mean, I look like a cheap slut. I know that."

"I think you look great in that red dress. And those high heels, mm-hmm," Norman said.

"She's written racy Maxi Bass's first monologue. And let me tell you, it's spicy and shocking, and it's why no one can know about my moonlighting as a comedian. If St. Boniface or my students' parents find out their kindergarten teacher is acting … improperly, I could lose my job. I love my job, but I need this, Norman." Maxine excitedly stalked the room as she spoke.

"During my recent rehearsals, my monologue delivery was polished and came easy. I'm not sure it did because I like its spiciness or because it's something I want to do," Maxine told Norman, although he suspected the observation was more to convince herself than enlighten him.

"I imagine you will kick ass. You have a great stage presence. I'll give you that. You caught my eye and sent my glands doing a joyous jig," Norman said, unsure she had heard.

"I hope so, Norman," Maxine said, missing the message Norman meant to transmit. "I'm looking forward to it."

"I'd like to come to watch you in support of Maxi Bass," Norman said.

Maxine's eyes popped wide. "Really. You do? You don't think this is all nonsense and that I'm promoting the Maxi Bass character to rile men's hormones for their attention? Yes, Norman, I've listened to every word you said," Maxine said when she saw the surprised expression on Norman's face. Maxine walked around to his side of the bed and sat on the edge. "You know, this Maxi Bass thing started because I felt lost and beaten as if I were living a stagnant life going nowhere. You know? Like the hamster on a wheel going round and round with no direction."

"I didn't know you felt that way, Maxine. I'm sorry that you do," Norman said.

Norman had not rebuffed Maxi Bass or given her the look of disappointment she expected. Maxine added compassion, understanding, and kindness to the pro column of the list she kept for Norman in her head. Those qualities included being highly skilled in bed, a decent cook, confident but not vain, and looking good naked.

Maxine gave Norman a big smile. "But after tonight. Well, you changed that, Norman. Not completely because, as I said, I have baggage that will take some time to unpack, but it's a start. The point is that you were instrumental in changing my state of mind. Even if this is about two friends having fun, you've put some of the sparkle taken from me back in my life." She lifted her hand to his cheek. "Thank you."

Norman reached for the hand Maxine rested on his cheek and kissed her fingertips, one at a time. "It can be more than two friends having fun. If you want to work toward that."

Without a second thought, Maxine said, "I want."

Norman patted the bed beside him, and Maxine slid in. "You have options. First, my energy level is replenished." Norman gave her a wink.

Maxine's lips stretched out in a smile. "Hmmm, tempting. What's option two?"

"If you're up to it, you can tell me some, or part, or none, up to you, of the baggage weighing you down. I'm a good listener."

Maxine gnawed her bottom lip momentarily as she fell into deep thought. "I'm going to take option one to begin, and depending on how good you are to me, I may just tell you some of the baggage I come with over the panna cotta dessert we still have to get to."

With a slow, curving lip, Norman said, "Challenge accepted. I better get to work. I'm a much better listener after great sex with a complicated, beautiful woman."

Maxine flashed a smile and tossed the bed sheet onto the floor. Norman was a keeper.

Chapter 15

UNDER THE POOLING light of her stoop, Maxine rummaged through her clutch bag for her house keys. Startled by Bobo's bark, Maxine dropped her bag, causing its contents to fall onto the flagstone stoop.

Maxine's chest tightened into that familiar ball of anxiety and anger.

Turning her gaze towards the bark, Maxine caught sight of Bobo peering at her through the narrow gap in the fence slats. So much for the citronella oil, Maxine thought. The dog was invincible.

Maxine shot Bobo a glare that would have set him aflame. Bobo's response was to let out a series of deafening barks.

That triggered Maxine to shout, "Shut up. Shut up. Shut the fuck up, you stupid mongrel. Take control of your goddamn dog," Maxine screamed at Becca when she heard her ordering Bobo into the house.

Bobo gave Maxine one last look before he strolled across the yard and into the house. Maxine was sure she saw laughter in Bobo's eyes.

"There should be a license requirement to breed. How do people raise such ignorant, self-centred children?" Maxine murmured, gathering her handbag contents off the ground and stabbing the key into the apartment door.

Upon entering her basement apartment, fear eclipsed Maxine's anger. Maxine went utterly still. The apartment glowed bright with light. She was sure she had turned the lights off before leaving for Norman's. The smell of brewed coffee permeated the air. Maxine wondered how that was possible when she had unplugged the coffee machine to prevent it from automatically brewing in the morning.

Anger and fear from Bobo's barks and the conceivable intruder in her home, Maxine's mind was unfocused, and she could not remember if she had unlocked the door to let herself in.

Maxine took three deep, calming breaths and took half a step forward into her apartment. "Who's here? I'm calling the police."

"You think you would be more relaxed after your night in Norman's bed." Buzzy's voice startled Maxine, and she jumped.

Maxine lifted her hand to her chest. "Christ, Buzzy. You scared me to death."

Buzzy sat on the sofa with a steaming cup of coffee while Carol Burnett lay beside her. Carol Burnett had been to the spa and looked freshly groomed. She wore a floral bandana around her neck and a pink butterfly ribbon on her head.

"You did spend your night with your young man? Because I know you didn't come home." Buzzy looked at Maxine through the rising steam from her cup.

Buzzy wore floral capris stamped with large, yellow sunflowers and a flowing yellow shirt over a red tank top. Her silver-gray hair, too, was freshly styled, and her face was polished to perfection.

A deep sigh slid out of Maxine. "You shouldn't be here. Haven't we discussed landlord-tenant boundaries?" Maxine kicked off her pumps and dropped her handbag and keys on the coffee table.

Maxine's hair tied back into a ponytail drew attention to the face with the afterglow of great sex. The pep to her step and the persistent smile on her face she could not wipe off if she scrubbed it was additional proof of her sinfully good night.

"You've had several discussions with yourself about the landlord-tenant regulations. I only saw your lips flapping," Buzzy said as Carol Burnett decided to hop off the sofa and raced to greet Maxine.

"Hello, Carol Burnett. You're such a good girl. Nothing like your idiot cousin next door or as intrusive and nosy as your owner." Maxine bent down to delight Carol Burnett with head scratches.

"Spill," Buzzy demanded.

"If you must know…."

"I must," Buzzy cut in. "And I want the truth, not the bull shit story that you're concocting in your head."

Maxine stopped her head scratches, and Carol Burnett returned to the sofa, spread out, and let her head rest on Buzzy's lap. "Fine. I was with Norman all night."

"And?"

"And what?' Maxine fell back into the wing chair beside Buzzy and stretched her legs.

"Details, dear. I must have details."

"I don't kiss and tell, Buzzy." Carol Burnett raised one eye, then the other, and Maxine's eyes narrowed. "Is she judging me?"

"Carol Burnett knows, as I do, your face gives you away every time. I can read the night of debauchery that you spent on your face like a bold headline. You may as well tell me about the man responsible for putting that smile on your face because I ain't leaving without the details." Buzzy pointed to Maxine's smiling lips.

Not realizing the blissful smile was on her face in full display, Maxine pursed her lips. "I'm not smiling. Did you hear Bobo bark at me when I walked to the apartment door? I sprayed every inch of the fence with citronella oil. I even got it on myself, and that stuff is putrid. It took two showers to get the smell off me, and I had to wash my clothes three times. If I detest it so much, why couldn't Bobo? His sense of smell is supposed to be more heightened than mine."

Maxine was deflecting, and Buzzy said, "Don't change the subject, Maxine. You couldn't be more obvious about getting some. Enjoy having had a wonderful time with a man who could put that bounce in your step and smile on your face. I would sing from the rooftops if I were in your shoes. What I would give to share a night with a man doing…."

"All right, that's enough." Maxine stopped Buzzy from putting images into her head that she couldn't unsee.

Settling back on the chair's pillow, Maxine stretched her legs out. "We, that is Norman and I, were engaged for most of the last night, this morning, and afternoon in…." Maxine mulled her choice words for a minute, "Laborious activity."

Buzzy's brows shot up high on the approving gray eyes. "Laborious sounds calorie consuming."

"It was. Very much so," Maxine's lips absently curved.

"Hmmm. Does he look good naked?"

"He looks good naked. Not a romance cover good, but…." Maxine's thoughts leapt to last night, and her smile widened.

"That good. It sounds as if that surprised you?"

Maxine nodded. "You don't expect it. He's kind of geeky-looking. You know? But what surprised me most was his competence. He was very ah, masterful in," Maxine groped for the right words, "his maneuvers. More so than I imagined he would be."

"Because he's geeky looking."

Maxine nodded.

"And?" Buzzy made a rolling hand gesture to speed Maxine along.

"And he's quite creative, you may say innovative—you know?—in there and there." Maxine tilted her chin toward the bedroom and kitchen. "Besides being great in the bedroom, he's a great cook. He made me homemade lasagna and panna cotta. I did not even know what panna cotta was, but Jesus, it was good. We used some of it in—" Maxine stopped as she realized she had said too much.

A wistful sigh escaped Buzzy. "Oh, to be young. I can only imagine how you feel right now. How do you feel, dear? Do share."

Maxine thought about her response for a moment. "I feel desirable, wanted, treasured, and prized. I feel unencumbered. Not completely yet, but more unencumbered than I've felt in a long while," Maxine said, wishing she could speak to her mother as openly and frankly as she did with Buzzy.

But her mother was a desiccated woman, uptight and close-minded. Besides that, one must enjoy sex to be able to speak about it as openly as Buzzy did. But then, Buzzy was an enthusiastic participant, whereas her mother, Maxine imagined, was not. Georgiana was more the type to have terminated any sexual activity once she got pregnant because sex between a man and a woman was for reproductive means only, not pleasure. The Bible said so. It was likely the reason for the rumours circulating in the town since Maxine could remember her father having an affair with Bonnie Kershaw, the church secretary.

Buzzy rose to her feet, ensuring not to disturb Carol Burnett, who snored blissfully. "Well, that certainly is reason for celebration. Let's have a brandy."

"You know I can't afford to stock alcohol."

Buzzy reached far back into the pantry, where she had stashed a bottle of brandy. "Voilà." Reaching into the cupboard for two glasses, Buzzy poured two fingers of the amber liquid into both glasses.

"Because you don't have enough booze upstairs. Now, you must stock my pantry. When I'm not home."

"My sage approved it. Right, baby?" Buzzy said, and Carol Burnett snored her response.

"Namaste," Maxine said, taking the offered brandy glass.

"Is your young man a good listener? He must be, Maxine. Women have a knack for the gift of the gab, and we need someone who will listen, or in the least pretend to."

"He is that. We talked a lot about everything. He was attentive and understanding." Maxine sipped contemplatively. "He wasn't critical or close-minded."

Understanding the double entendre in the words, Buzzy said, "You told him about Maxi Bass."

Maxine nodded.

Buzzy sat next to Carol Burnett, making sure not to wake her. "And was Norman supportive of your quest to fulfill the void, which may not be so anymore?"

Maxine nodded again.

"I need words, dear." Buzzy drained part of her brandy.

"Norman supports the Maxi Bass idea and my upcoming performance this Wednesday. He wants to be there to support me."

Buzzy smiled broadly. "Good, because I have a feeling Maxi Bass will knock them dead."

"Norman believes so, too."

"So, you're ready for the performance."

Maxine lifted her glass in salute and offered a confident smile. "Ready and psyched."

Chapter 16

"SHE'S NOT READY and psyched herself out of the performance tonight," Buzzy said over the telephone while Carol Burnett barked her encouragement at Maxine from the opposite side of the locked bathroom door. "Shush, Carol Burnett. I'm on the telephone with Norman McDonnell, with an M-C. You know? Maxine's fornicator."

Carol Burnett did not go silent, but Norman did.

Sensing Norman's discomfort, Buzzy smiled to herself. "I am sorry to bother you, Norman. I found you on Maxine's telephone. Your texts have been *caliente*."

Norman set down the beard trimmer on the bathroom counter with a thud. "You went through her phone and read her texts?"

"It's an emergency, dear. I'm allowed."

Norman got a sick look on his face. "Why? What's happened? Is Maxine okay?"

"She's as good as Maxine could be."

Norman turned off the bathroom fan when its whirring sound grated on his nerves. "What does that mean, Mrs. Morgan?"

Buzzy twisted up her lips at Norman's politeness. "It's Buzzy, dear. You know how Maxine overthinks everything. Well, she's driven herself to a nervous wreck about tonight."

"It's understandable. Tonight's a big deal. Maxine will be on stage, in unfamiliar surroundings, before an audience who may disapprove of her. It's a lot for anyone to deal with. It's a lot for Maxine. Maxine is simply reacting to the oppressive fear of failure." Norman reached for the bottle of Polo aftershave and dabbed it on his face, winced when it stung him.

Understanding and sympathetic, Buzzy thought. "Thank you for that, Aristotle."

"Plato is more my cup of tea. Did you know that Aristotle was his student?" Norman responded.

"I did. A grade school student who's a scholar. Your talents are wasted." Buzzy attempted to shush Carol Burnett with little success, who could be heard continuously barking in the background. "You appear a lot on Maxine's telephone call log. You have been in communication much since this past weekend. That is understandable since your sexual prowess is legendary, according to Maxine. She hasn't stopped smiling since rolling out of your bed."

A smug, self-congratulatory smile bloomed on Norman's lips.

"You can wipe that smile off your face, dear."

Norman screwed his face into a frown and looked around his bathroom for the cameras. "How?"

"I possess the special power of conjecture. Now, back to what I was saying. Don't get too cocky. Maxine has only had two men in her life. Comparing beige to beiger is hardly the compliment you think it is," Buzzy said in her typical blunt manner.

Norman's instincts told him it was best not to say anything in his defence, and he did not.

Buzzy pressed on. "Anyway, she won't listen to my pleas or Carol Burnett's, and I thought you're the only person who can talk her down before she gets … creative in there."

Fear welled in Norman. Taking Buzzy off the speaker, Norman raised the telephone to his ear. "Talk her down from what? You said she was all right? What do you mean by creative?"

The worry and concern Buzzy heard in Norman's voice pleased her. It was that of a man not solely interested in sex but in love.

"Maxine's fine, dear. As I said, she's locked herself in her bathroom and refuses to come out. She says she won't perform tonight. You're the only other person who knows about her performance, and I need your help."

"She hasn't done anything crazy, has she? Do you think she will?" Norman said, his voice strained.

Buzzy overlooked Norman's anxious tone and questions. "I've tried everything, but she won't come out of the bathroom. Hopefully, she'll listen to you. She's due to go on stage at eleven, in two hours. I require your assistance, Norman. If not, to get her on stage, to ensure she doesn't do anything other than sit on the bathroom floor crying."

"Yes, of course. I'll be right over." Norman dropped the towel around his waist and stumbled into the first pair of jeans he snatched from the closet. "Just ensure she doesn't do anything crazy until I get there."

"She won't, dear, and I appreciate it. Norman, are you there?" Buzzy asked when she heard the thump.

"Sorry, I dropped the phone." Norman's frantic voice came through the line when he picked up the telephone off the floor.

"Honey, calm down. She's not popping pills in there."

Norman stopped buttoning his shirt. "You think she'd do that?" His voice rose to a panic level.

Men are such simple but confident creatures. They would never suspect their loyalty was tested, as Buzzy did then. Maxine was like a daughter to Buzzy, and protecting was what she did.

Satisfied that the boy had fallen hard and showed genuine concern for Maxine, Buzzy smiled and said, "No, dear, I don't think she would do that. That's why I said she's not popping pills in there."

"Good. Good." Norman said in a steadier voice as he finished buttoning up his shirt and raked fingers through his wet hair.

"Shush, Carol Burnett." Buzzy's command went unheard, and Carol Burnett persisted in barking at the bathroom door. "Carol Burnett is still trying to coax Maxine out of the bathroom and failing. How long will it take you to get over here, dear?"

"I should be there in twenty minutes." Norman looked around the living room for his car keys.

"The sooner the better. And, Norman, would you bring a blunt or two with you? Two. Bring two," Buzzy said without intonation or the expressiveness.

Norman stopped in his tracks, and the silence lingered for a moment.

Thirty seconds later, Buzzy said, "Maxine tells me everything, dear. Everything."

"Oh."

"Bring the good stuff, Norman. She needs a confidence boost, and only a good high will do it."

Norman determined that for all the *dearing* and *honeying* Buzzy espoused during their telephone conversation, she was not the sweet old lady she portended to be. The woman was a loaded pistol with on-point knowledge of weed and its effects.

"Maxine doesn't smoke and surely won't smoke two joints," Norman pointed out.

"She will smoke it once I'm through with her. She needs the stimulation. And the second joint is for me. It's been a while since I've indulged in the cannabis, but I can recognize a quality spliff. Understand?"

As Maxine described, the old woman was a pip, brash, blunt, uninhibited, and intrusive. Edith Morgan spewed what was on her mind without consideration for proper etiquette. Buzzy was coarse and could only be taken in small doses at a time.

Norman took a liking to Buzzy.

"Sure. Okay. I can do that, but you will be the one to talk Maxine into blazing it because I can't do it." Norman walked to the kitchen, reached into the tea canister, and rifled through its contents, searching for the bag containing the pot he confiscated from Dawson Metcalf. As the wealthiest boy in school, Dawson only bought the best quality dope.

"Yes, of course. I understand that Maxine wouldn't take kindly to the man bedding her, supplying the joint, or being a pothead. Her being the daughter of a Pastor and all."

"Wait. What?" Norman caught his breath and froze on the spot. "She's the daughter of a Pastor?

"Ah, she omitted to tell you that tiny detail while rolling between the sheets with you. Don't hold it against her, dear. She likely held back telling you because it might have psychologically affected your plan to violate her body tonight as you did this past weekend."

"Jesus! You know how to turn a phrase."

"Honey, at my age, time is of the essence. You can't waste time pussy footing around with the politically correct words your generation needs to communicate."

"Well, no one can fault you for pussy footing around anything." Norman pocketed the dope and rolling paper.

Buzzy broke into appreciative laughter. "I like you, Norman McDonnell. Anyway, dear, I would not dream of jeopardizing your odds of getting some tonight." Buzzy spoke in such an even and steady voice that Norman could not help but burst into raucous laughter.

"I appreciate your consideration in not thwarting my plans, Mrs. Morgan, ah, Buzzy."

"Now, enough chit-chat. Get that tight ass of yours over here, pronto."

At the command, Norman turned the car's engine over and squealed the tires out of his driveway. "On my way."

Buzzy flicked her eyes to Carol Burnett. "You, missy, can take pointers from Norman on how to heed orders."

Chapter 17

SITTING AT THE sofa, Buzzy sipped brandy and watched Norman in silence as he anxiously knocked on the door, doing his best to coax Maxine out of the bathroom.

The tips of Norman's dark hair, still wet from his shower, sexily curled. Behind the glasses sliding off his nose, his eyes were dark pools of anxiety. He wore a white shirt over a black T-shirt stamped with a *Black Sabbath* logo.

Buzzy approved of that sexy-geeky look Norman had going.

"Please come out of the bathroom, Maxine." Norman frantically begged as Carol Burnett, propped on her rump, scrutinized the stranger in the room. "Please, Maxine."

Buzzy sank back into the sofa and admired the fit of Norman's jeans on the firm behind. Buzzy thought of the tautness of youth and let out a wistful sigh. Picturing Norman naked, Buzzy concurred with Maxine's assessment that he looked good naked.

"No. I'm not coming out. I'm not going on stage," Maxine said in between sobs.

From next door, Bobo's barks blared at top volume and pierced Norman's concentration.

"Christ! That dog is loud. It's no wonder Maxine has been on edge for weeks," Norman said.

Buzzy raised her finger to her lips to silence Norman. "I would not dwell on Bobo's barking too much. It will make Maxine more anxious. Focus on the task at hand, Norman."

"Yes." Norman fiddled with the lock, hoping to unlock the door magically. "You don't have to perform if you don't want to, Maxine."

"She does have to. Steven, that's my son, bumped another performer on the roster at my request to give Maxine the slot. If Maxine doesn't appear, all hell will break loose. Comedians are a hostile lot when you appropriate their time slot." Buzzy sipped at her brandy.

"You can't force her, Buzzy. She sounds traumatized." Norman went through his wallet and pulled out his library card.

"That's just Maxine being Maxine. She's a dramatic one. She needs calming down." Buzzy made the gesture of sucking in smoke from the imaginary joint between her fingers.

Bobo's earsplitting barking persisted, agitating Norman, and he snapped. "That's not what she needs, Buzzy. Right now, she needs someone she trusts to talk to." Norman slid the credit card between the lock and the door frame. "She needs TLC and assurances and love."

Buzzy raised an appreciative brow at Norman's insight and skill at reading Maxine and determining her needs.

"That's not going to work, Norman," Buzzy said when Norman attempted to maneuver the library card to unlock the door.

Carol Burnett lost interest in Norman's shenanigans, trotted toward the sofa, and leaped up next to Buzzy. Her fruitless barking had taken its toll, and she needed a nap.

"Well, I'm open to suggestions." Norma retrieved his destroyed library card and looked around the room for an alternative tool.

"A knife. Only a knife will work on a door with privacy handles such as that. Insert it into the door's lock opening and jiggle it to trigger the lock open."

Norman raised an eyebrow. "You sound as if you've done it once or twice."

"More than that, dear." Buzzy ran a hand across Carol Burnett's coat as she slid into doggie dreams.

"Then why didn't you unlock the door earlier?" Norman looked at Buzzy with puzzlement in his face.

"Just got a manicure." Buzzy waved manicured fingers with red polish in the air. "I couldn't afford to chip the polish."

"Christ!" Between the barking dog, Buzzy's craziness and Maxine's breakdown, Norman was reevaluating the current state of his life.

Sex was not worth the insanity Maxine brought on, and Norman certainly did not need Buzzy's idiosyncrasy in his life. Until today, his life was primarily uneventful—as he liked. Norman might be willing to deal with Maxine's craziness, but the two women together were enough to drive a man to insanity. He was going to end up a basket case and in a hospital psychiatric ward mumbling gibberish. Women.

Norman was fond of Maxine. He would venture to say he was in love with her. Norman would do anything for Maxine. And the sex. Christ! Norman had to admit the catch-up sex with Maxine was fantastic. It was better than great. It was incredible. Maxine was adventurous, wild, insatiable, and very flexible. She was the most passionate woman he had had in his bed.

Maxine told Norman sex had not been a priority in her life for years. Maxine went as far as to tell Norman that Jesse had extinguished the flame in her and said nothing more. And Norman had not pressed her. Maxine was not prepared to tell her unpleasant story yet, and Norman would not force her to rake up the past. Maxine would tell him everything when she was ready. You hang your dirty laundry when you're prepared to show people your wounds and the real you so you can decide if they are worthy of your affection.

Norman was up for the challenge and would make Maxine see she was worthy of his affection.

What Norman had learned from their time together was that Maxine's sexless years had intensified her libido. Maxine's pent-up sexual frustration flared up in fiery flames at Norman's touch. Like boiling magma from deep within a dormant volcano, Maxine had detonated and made it for the best sex Norman had.

The sex with Maxine was memorable, better than the encounter he and Beth had shared at the teacher's seminar a few years back. Norman refrained from telling Maxine about his meaningless night with her best friend because it would be misunderstood and served no purpose. Maxine was too vulnerable and fragile from whatever Jesse did to her to deal with such information. There was a time and place for such a conversation, and now was not the time to share that information.

Besides, Norman's shared night with Beth was a one-off, a drunken mistake. Norman regretted it so much that when he woke up beside Beth, he snuck out of her hotel room without saying a word and hoped it would not become a topic of conversation. Whether because Beth was married and racked with guilt or was too intoxicated to remember, she never brought up their shared night. Norman attributed it to the latter rather than the former. Regardless, the veil of mystery was never lifted, and

Norman was pleased Beth had not broached the topic. Aside from not knowing how to deal with the aftermath of the horrendous mistake, Norman had no interest in Beth.

"Where's the cutlery drawer?" Norman said in as steady a voice as he could summon.

"The drawer next to the refrigerator. I'd choose a butter knife for the task." Buzzy's lip bent up in a sly smile.

"Of course you would." Norman scanned the neatly laid-out cutlery until he found what he sought.

"Insert the flat head facing forward into the hole and turn it clockwise," Buzzy instructed, and Norman did. "Do a sixty-degree turn in the lock. Et voilà. Honey, I'm as old as Methuselah and with as many experiences under my belt," Buzzy said when Norman looked over at her, perplexed.

Norman opened the door and let the light into the darkened bathroom. Maxine sat on the white tiled floor. Her back pressed against the bathtub, Maxine rested her head on her updrawn knees and hugged her legs tightly to her body. She was barefoot and wore a white terry robe.

Norman flicked the bathroom light on as Bobo's barks stopped. "Maxine, are you okay?"

"I'm not," Maxine said in an angry growl more rooted in fear than anger.

Norman maintained a steady tone to avoid fueling Maxine's instability. "You look uncomfortable on the floor. How about we get you out of here and onto the sofa?"

Maxine did not respond.

Norman sat at the bathtub's edge. "You don't have to go on stage tonight, Maxine. You don't have to do anything you don't want to. You're at the wheel of your destiny, Maxine."

Maxine did not look up.

Norman's hand moved to rest on her shoulders and felt the knotted ball of tension. "Maxine, let's get you out of here and get you a drink. It'll calm your nerves."

Maxine looked up at Norman but did not comment, even after he gave her a reassuring smile. Her glossy, dark hair fell around her mascara-tear-stained face in waves.

"You don't have to do anything you don't want." Norman sat beside Maxine on the floor. "It's your decision. You do what you want." Norman slowly held out a hand for her, and she met it.

Helping Maxine off the floor, Norman walked her to the living room and guided her to the sofa beside Carol Burnett. Smelling Maxine's scent, Carol Burnett woke up. Pleased to see Maxine, Carol Burnett smiled and thumped her tail.

"Hello, Carol Burnett." Maxine scratched the dog's head.

Carol Burnett gets an immediate reaction, Norman thought.

Reading Norman's thoughts, Buzzy's lips twisted into a grin. "Norman, get Maxine a tall glass of brandy." Buzzy pointed to the pantry.

"Yes, of course."

"The glasses are in the cupboard above the sink. You should pour one for yourself and top me up while you're at it."

Norman handed Maxine the glass. "Drink, Maxine. Slowly."

Maxine sipped without looking up.

"Feel better?" Norman topped Maxine's glass and his.

Maxine smiled for the first time. "Thank you, Norman." Carol Burnett lay her head across Maxine's lap and gazed at her soberly. "Thank you to you too."

"Great, I rate up there, along with a dog," Norman said sternly, but there was a crinkle in his eyes.

"Excuse me, but this isn't just any dog. It's Carol Burnett," Maxine said, making a smile spread across Buzzy's and Norman's faces. I'm sorry I went a bit…."

"Nutty, batty, foolish," Buzzy finished for Maxine.

"Thank you, Buzzy, for that. Have you ever considered availing yourself of a more diplomatic way of speaking?" Norman asked.

"No," Buzzy said swiftly. "Diplomacy takes too much time to decipher what you're trying to convey. Directness is simple and gets the job done."

"Yes. Well." Norman turned to Maxine. "As I said, Maxine, you don't need to do anything you don't want, regardless of what Buzzy says."

"I know." Maxine held the brandy glass in both hands.

"You are the author of your life." Norman watched Maxine stare into her glass quietly for a moment. The bland look on her face told him nothing. "Maxine, did you hear what I said?"

Maxine nodded. "The thing is, I want to go on stage. I was looking forward to Maxi Bass making her debut."

These words made Buzzy smile broadly, and she sat up straighter in her seat. "It's natural to be nervous, dear. Every performer experiences it. You're not alone. It comes down to not the anxiety of performing in front of people but the worry of how you will be judged. To which I say fuck them."

Norman's brow shot up. "Do you ever hold back?"

Buzzy shook her head. "Why? Eighty years old, remember? Do I need to explain myself again? I thought you were smarter than that."

"I know why you do it. My question is…."

"It's all right, Norman." Maxine interrupted. "I like that Buzzy's upfront and direct and speaks her mind. I know the material. I can deliver it, and I want to do it. I'm just too nervous and terrified."

"Well, Maxine, I know how to remedy that. If you're willing to do what I tell you." Buzzy said, and Norman polished off the brandy in his glass.

"I'll try anything, Buzzy."

Buzzy reached into her shirt pocket and pulled out the joint. "A few puffs will take the edge off."

Maxine's blue eyes got big. "Oh, I don't know, Buzzy. Smoke a joint. Aside from being against the law, I've never smoked. I don't know how to inhale, which I think is what I need to do. Isn't it?" Maxine looked over at Norman, and he glanced sideways, then away.

"Honey, you don't have to be a brain surgeon to figure it out. Inhale, hold and exhale. As I said, many performers do it to take the edge off. You'll feel so good and uninhibited afterward that you'll wander onto the stage and kill it."

"It sounds as if you speak from experience, Buzzy." Norman poured another two fingers of brandy.

"I do, dear. In the day, I blazed many blunts." Buzzy confessed without humiliation.

"You did?" Maxine's voice rose slightly, and Buzzy proudly nodded. "Well, if you do it and Norman does it, it can't be that bad. I'll do it."

Norman was mid-sip and choked out some of the brandy. "I don't toke."

"Yeah, you do, Norman. I smelled it in your house. I thought it was what made you so … empirical in bed." Maxine smiled to herself when she saw the hot embarrassment rise in him.

"You never said anything."

"Why would I complain about you being so … skilled?"

"Yay, Norman." Buzzy gave Norman a thumbs up. "If I were years younger, Normie, I would test-ride you and teach you a thing or two."

A deep red flush worked its way up Norman's throat to his cheeks. "Jesus!"

That made Maxine snort a laugh, and Buzzy joined in.

"Stop tormenting Norman, Buzzy. I have an hour and fifteen minutes before I'm due on stage," Maxine said after checking the time on the stove clock. "Let's get this show on the road. Both of you show me what to do with this joint."

Chapter 18

TONIGHT'S SHOW WAS sold out, leaving no bar stool or table unoccupied in Ba-Dum-Bump.

The first three performers had hit their comedic mark, and the energy in the room was electric. Servers dressed in black and white wound their way around the room, serving chicken wings, nachos, a selection of finger foods, and concocted drinks with tiny colourful umbrellas, which Ba-Dum-Bump was known for.

The room was alive, a symphony of laughter left by John Bixby as he walked off the stage. John, an amateur turned headliner after signing a deal with the Comedy Channel for a three-show special, was a crowd-pleaser. As always, John Bixby left the crowd electrified.

Buzzy told Steven to schedule Maxine to follow John's performance so she could benefit from the upbeat wave he left.

Norman and Buzzy sat at a front-row table as Maxi Bass calmly stood stage-right, waiting to be introduced.

Steven Morgan commanded the audience's attention on stage as he gripped a microphone in his right hand and a tumbler of whiskey in the other. Very à la Dean Martin.

Like his mother, Steven was gregarious, articulate, and suited for the emcee role. Steven stood six-one with a slim build. Steven looked athletic, blending rugged masculinity and refined elegance in designer jeans and a gray silk shirt under a black leather jacket. His waves of dark hair, flecked with silver at the temples, framed the strong jawline on his handsome face.

"Ladies and gentlemen, put your hands together for Maxi Bass." Steven led the audience in applause, and they echoed with enthusiastic claps.

The cheers from the men in the audience became deafening when Maxine stepped on the stage and walked toward Steven. The hits from the joint had put confidence in Maxine's step and a mischievous glint in her eyes. Four deeply inhaled drags were enough to transform Maxine into the poised, self-assured woman Norman saw before him. But then, Norman did not doubt Dawson's product would not. The Deadhead Kush strain was one of the best on the market. Just a small nug of the joint was a stimulating motivator.

"Here we go." Buzzy sat back in her chair with a tall brandy, although she did not need the stimuli. Buzzy was riding on the euphoric effects of the joint she had expertly inhaled.

"Fingers crossed," Norman said, reaching for his whiskey glass and drinking it in one gulp.

"Easy there, cowboy. You're my guest tonight, but there's no need to overdo it. Besides, Maxine's going to do fine. Look how relaxed and great Maxi Bass looks. Every eye in the room is on her." Buzzy stuffed her mouth with nachos. "Christ, I'm hungry."

Norman gave Buzzy a long, hard stare as she topped her nacho with guacamole and sour cream. "Yeah, I wonder why. But you're right about Maxine. She looks great. I'm not thrilled about how every guy in the room is eyeing her," Norman murmured the last part to himself.

Maxine looked stunning in her short red dress and tall heels, highlighting her long, shapely legs. The club's makeup artist made Maxine's long waves look windblown and her lips full and kissable. Her long eyelashes, artfully accented with thick mascara, framed eyes that shimmered with an even deeper blue under the drug's spell.

Norman watched Steven's gray eyes, bright with the stimulation of alcohol, and every male in the room, eye Maxine with a predatory, hungry look. Norman ached with jealousy, resentment, and, worse, an unhealthy possessiveness. Envisaging the vile thoughts filling their heads, how could Norman not feel as he did?

Norman reached up as far as his arm would stretch to get the server's attention and signalled for a whiskey refill. A double.

"There's no need to be bitter, dear. Maxine is crazy about you." Buzzy held up a silencing hand when Norman started to speak. "She is and has no interest in anyone here," Buzzy said, surprising Norman. "I'm high, not deaf. I heard everything you said." Buzzy snapped her fingers at her ears.

"I want you to show Maxi your love, not hate. Capiche? This is her first appearance, and she needs your support." Steven's smile exuded a timeless appeal that charmed every woman, including Maxine.

"She'll get my support, and I'm sure that of every horny man in the room." The man in the front row screamed with a lisp and followed the comment with a bottom-lip whistle that incited the hecklers to jump in with their remarks.

"You can have more than my support, baby." Someone sitting at a back table called out with a snorted laugh, and many of the men in the room agreed.

"Ditto, honey. Good performance or not, count me in," another said.

Norman immensely disliked the audience.

"Take it down a notch, you plebeians. Show some respect for the lady, or I'm throwing your asses out the door." Steven's warning settled the audience down. "Take that as a compliment and kick ass, Maxi Bass." Steven's confidence and quiet strength when he kissed Maxine's hand before handing over the microphone irked Norman.

Norman took an instant dislike to the man.

"I will, Steven. Thank you," Maxine said with a coy smile.

"I know you will, honey." Steven gave Maxine a flirtatious wink and walked off the stage.

Norman's loathing for the man grew tenfold, but he set it aside when the spotlight bathed Maxine in the bright light that made her look angelic.

The air buzzed with anticipation as the audience settled in to listen to Maxine. With confidence, Maxine delved into her monologue. Maxine's voice, sensual and full of character, was amplified by the silence in the room as everyone cast their eyes on her.

The broken, nervous woman Norman saw minutes earlier looked like she belonged onstage. Norman found himself watching her move around the stage with feline grace. Maxine's timing was impeccable, and the pride in Buzzy's face was visible.

Maxine's delivery was spot-on, and her wordplay razor sharp as she told her tale of her nonexistent relationships and the mundane she observed in her daily life with a lewd twist. After every observation, the crowd erupted into a chorus of laughter.

"You, Mither Lithper." Maxine pointed to the man with the lisp who incited the hecklers. "Have you asked yourself what kind of fucked up monster adds an S to the word lisp?"

The man said nothing, but the audience erupted into laughter.

"You thould write a sthern email to the Lithper Thothiety and demand reform. You have my thupport," Maxine commented with a wink.

The audience burst into laughter and cheered their support for Mr. Lisper, who let out a hollow laugh.

"And you, sir." Maxine pointed to the heckler who had followed Mr. Lisper with the inane comment. "That comment was genius. Has anyone called you a genius?"

"Not recently," he answered from the depths of the room.

"I doubt ever. And I'll put money down that it's going to be a long wait for anyone to see such a simpleton in that light," Maxine craftily said with a bite of snark in her voice that sent the room into peals of laughter. "And honey, I'd think twice about hitching my wagon to that misogynistic star. Rumour has it men like him use misogyny to compensate for the fact they can't find their way around a woman's body. Unless you want frustrated to become your middle name, I'd get a real man who can," Maxine said to his companion to the cheers and applause from the women in the room.

With the laughter bubbling throughout the room, Maxine gave one last wave to the audience before she walked off the stage.

Chapter 19

MAXINE LOUNGED IN the sun, her skin glistening with suntan lotion as she sipped a margarita. White sand dotted with palm trees was all around her. The air smelled of cocoa butter and salt carried by the ocean, which was as blue as the sky. The steady whoosh and waves slap lapped the shore, mingling with chirping birds flitting about.

Bobo's sharp barks shocked Maxine out of her idyllic dream. Maxine reached for her phone on the night table and read the time. It was five-forty-five a.m.

Maxine's belly tightened into the familiar ball of anxiety, frustration, and anger, leaving her unable to drift back into sleep. Hopping out of bed, she sat at the edge of the bed and covered her face with her hands. Maxine decided to work her anger, anxiety, and frustration off by going for a run.

Setting off on her run, dawn broke through the eastern sky as morning spread. The day promised to bring warmth and sunshine.

A plus of running at that early hour was that aside from a couple of early morning runners, Maxine was alone with her music. Maxine ran down the tree-lined neighbourhood with Technotronic pumping up the jam in her ears.

Having gotten in a ten-mile run, Maxine should be relaxed and ready for the day ahead. Maxine was neither relaxed nor prepared for the day ahead. The irritated state of mind brought on by Bobo's early morning barks was still seething in Maxine two hours later. Maxine decided a call to Animal Control was in order. Flipping the laptop open, Maxine checked the office hours. They opened at eight, giving her enough time for a shower and breakfast before heading for work.

Shedding her running gear, Maxine showered. She chose a yellow knee-length skirt and a matching blouse from her closet. She applied muted colour on her face and bound her hair into a ponytail. Maxine headed upstairs for breakfast.

Buzzy was at the stove, flipping sausages on the stove-top grill. The kitchen smelled of fried eggs, sausage, toast, coffee, and baked bread.

"Good morning, dear," Buzzy said when Maxine dropped into a chair at the table.

Buzzy wore white Capri pants and a watermelon-red flowing shirt, and her face and hair were done to perfection. She looked well-rested and ready to take on the day.

"Good morning is a stretch. That goddamn dog woke me up before the sun was out and from a fantastic dream. I may add." Maxine leaned down to scratch Carol Burnett's head. Carol Burnett did not acknowledge Maxine. She was too busy devouring the sausages Buzzy had placed in her bowl. "I'd like to have punched him in the face."

Buzzy's reply was to lift a brow. "Bobo is only a simple-minded dog."

"I know that. I'm talking about Miles. I heard him calling Bobo back to the house when he started to bark. Dense as a sloth, the man is to think letting his dog bark that early is acceptable." Maxine treated herself to the full breakfast of a sunny-side-up egg, sausage, and buttered bread Buzzy set before her as Buzzy looked on incredulously. "What? I couldn't get back to sleep and went for a long run. I can afford to eat all this."

"Well, enjoy. And I have to agree with you about Miles's obtuseness." Buzzy turned to Carol Burnett when she sat on her rump and gave her a beseeching look. "No, missy, you're not getting any more sausage. We have to watch your waistline. Go rest up before we head out for your morning walk."

Sulking, Carol Burnett trotted toward her bed by the sliding door.

"I was this close," Maxine showed a slight width between her thumb and forefinger, "to surfing the dark web for a hitman."

"Don't joke about that, Maxine." Buzzy topped Maxine's coffee cup.

"Who's joking?"

Buzzy's eyes held Maxine intently, wondering if she meant what she said. "Anyway, is there such a thing as a dark web?"

Maxine shrugged. "Norman mentioned it in passing. I don't know exactly what it is. I tune out when Norman goes off on his geek rants," Maxine said glibly, to Buzzy's relief.

"Calm down. Enjoy your breakfast, dear. That's freshly baked bread," Buzzy said, and Maxine stuffed her mouth with bread dipped in egg yolk, more out of stress than hunger.

Maxine did not hear a word Buzzy said. Her mind drifted, thinking about what she would say to the Animal Control supervisor when she called their office in three minutes.

"Maxine, are you with me?" Buzzy snapped her fingers, knowing forces were taking hold of Maxine's mind.

"I need to make a phone call." Maxine pushed off the table and walked to the kitchen counter. Retrieving her cell phone from her tote, she dialled.

"Who are you calling this early in the morning?"

"I need to strike while the iron is hot. Or while I'm hot. Marlene Rowan, please. Sure, I'll hold." Maxine said between clenched teeth.

"You're not calling the city again."

"I must. I need to vent to someone." Maxine opened the sliding door and gestured for Carol Burnett to step out. Carol Burnett did not budge. "What's up with her?"

"Carol Burnett won't go out. The summer heat heightens the scent of Bobo's shit, which Becca and Miles let to accumulate. They are filthy human beings and the worst neighbours this community has had in the decades I've lived here." Buzzy concluded her rant when she realized she had said too much.

"Thank you. Finally, you're saying the quiet out loud." Maxine held a finger up to silence Buzzy when Marlene Rowan came on the phone.

Pacing the room with nervous energy, Maxine laid into Marlene.

"Did you not hear the five-forty-five a.m. part?"

"I did, but as I said before, no by-law infraction was committed."

"Why? Why can't you do anything about his barking? Your by-law stipulates a dog cannot consistently bark all day." Maxine's voice banked down on the frustration she felt.

"That's open for interpretation unless the dog is consistently barking…."

"He consistently barks at dawn, dusk, and every hour in between." Maxine stalked the room as she spoke.

"They're only good at picking up roadkill, Maxine," Buzzy pushed to her feet. "Let's leave Auntie Maxine to her own devices and go for your walk."

At the word "walk," Carol Burnett raced to the front of the house with her tongue lolling.

"Let me speak. Consistently means for long periods." Marlene Rowan was full of attitude.

"So, you're telling me that a dog emitting an ear-splitting bark at midnight and five in the morning and shocking you out of sleep is fine with you."

"Is the dog barking for longer than fifteen consistent minutes?"

"No, but…."

"Is the dog barking all night and morning? Continually."

"No, but…."

"Then he's not doing anything illegal."

Maxine countered with. "Is the dog paying taxes?"

"No, but…."

"Is the dog paying your salary?"

"No, he is not, but…."

"Then the dog has no right to make a law-abiding taxpayer's life a living hell in their home, and you have a fiduciary duty to provide me with a good quality of life in my home."

"The dog has every right to his enjoyment, Ms. Basset."

"Jesus, fucking Christ. I'd have a more rational conversation with a meth head." Maxine murmured in disbelief.

"There's no need for rudeness or disrespectful comments," Marlene Rowan said in a rigid voice.

"You weren't supposed to hear that," Maxine said.

"And yet I did."

"Do you see how ridiculous this conversation is?" Maxine said.

"As I've mentioned, Ms. Basset, I can do nothing." Marlene's tone was emphatic.

"You're siding with a dog's ability to wreak misery on my life. I have an expectation of a good quality of life in my home, and your actions, or lack thereof, are preventing that from happening."

"Those are the rules. I can patrol the area and keep an ear open."

"Because driving by once a day for a few seconds will help you gather the necessary intel to address the boorish dog owners who believe the world revolves around them. Have you read in CSIS, the FBI, MI5, and every intelligence agency out there about your extraordinary tactics? They may be able to detain more terrorists."

"I'm hanging up now."

"That's the only thing you do well," Maxine said and hung up before Marlene could get a word in.

Several emotions crossed Maxine: defeat, hopelessness, and frustration. Once again, her hopes for a resolution had been in vain.

Chapter 20

BETH EASED HER hip on the edge of Maxine's desk and tapped a finger to her lips. Beth's flawless complexion had the healthy colour of a woman who spent every spare moment soaking in the summer sun. Her blonde hair was a stark contrast against her bronzed skin. Beth wore white ankle-high, slim-fitting pants and a floral blouse. A plated gold chain hung around her neck, and slinky drop earrings dangled from her ears. Her shoes were red, patent slingbacks.

Beth gave Maxine a pointed look. Maxine's knee-length skirt and blouse with a neck bow tie made her look matronly and ordinary. Maxine tried to conceal the dark circles under her eyes using a darker shade concealer than her skin tone. Maxine looked the same but was not the same woman Beth knew. There was a punch in Maxine's step that Beth had not seen before.

"You seem different," Beth said, closely studying Maxine.

"I don't know what you're talking about." Maxine smiled inwardly.

Days later, Maxine still rode high of her night with Norman and her stage performance. Maxine had not expected to do as well as she had or get the encouraging reaction she did from the audience. Maxine had not expected to enjoy the experience as much as she had. In one night, Maxine transformed herself into a seductive temptress, delivered a monologue in front of ogling strangers, intimidated a misogynist with confidence, and toked. And Maxine enjoyed every minute of crossing the line from prim and proper to wicked.

Maxine shuddered to think what her parents would think of her debauched behaviour. Truth be told, she did not care. The time had come for her to redefine herself.

"There's something different about you, but I can't put my finger on it," Beth said.

The classroom was bright, with afternoon sunshine spilling through the rectangular window, looking out on the school's playground. The alphabet, numbers, and colourful artwork the children made during past art classes hung from the white-painted walls, creating an atmosphere of comfort and safety for her students. The children's desks formed a circle, with Maxine's at the front and the blackboard behind her.

"You're letting your imagination run wild." Maxine capped the paint jars the children used to make their Father's Day cards and stored them in the paint caddy. "Make yourself useful and grab the Lysol bottle and paper towels." Maxine set the paint cans in the cupboard.

"I'm not wrong about these things." Beth continued her scan of Maxine. Her eyes went wide when it hit her. "You're getting some."

Maxine did not react to Beth's comment as she collected the brushes from the children's desks. Maxine placed the brushes into the water-filled Mason jars to soak. The paint on the brushes' hair spread in vivid colours in the water.

"Your silence and not looking me in the eye says it all. You are getting some." Beth pushed off the desk and embraced Maxine. "It's about time.

"I can't breathe, Beth."

"Yes, sorry." Beth released Maxine from her tight embrace. "I'm just so happy for you. How do you feel? Do you feel unfettered, limber, or both? Who is he? Did he push all the right buttons?"

"You assume much, Beth." Maxine took the paint-stained paper towels off the desks and tossed them into the garbage bin. "You know what they say happens when you assume."

"Yes. Yes. You make an ass out of u and me." Beth looked Maxine in the eye. "But I don't believe I'm assuming anything. I'm right about this. Who is he, Maxine?"

Maxine lowered her gaze to avoid eye contact with Beth and sprayed the desk surfaces with Lysol. She wiped the paint smears and fingerprints off until the desks gleamed.

"Spill, I'm-getting-some-Maxine." Beth took the Lysol bottle from Maxine's hands to get her full attention.

"Beth, I need that back. I want to leave the room spic-and-span for when the children come in tomorrow morning."

"Not until you tell me who has been heating your bed."

"No one has, Beth. Give that back." Maxine reached for the Lysol bottle, but Beth tucked it behind her.

"Not until you tell me whose body you've been wrapping your legs around."

"Jesus, Beth. I'm tired, and I want to go home. The kids were finger painting this afternoon, and I'm exhausted."

Maxine pointed to the cards set to dry overnight on the bookcase.

"Your energy isn't depleted from finger painting. It's drained from all the sex you've been having." Beth handed Maxine the Lysol bottle. "And here I thought I was your best friend and told me all."

Maxine wiped down the last desk and stored the Lysol bottle and the paper towel roll in the cabinet. "You are my best friend, and I have told you everything." Maxine ensured her tone remained sincere.

Beth did not get a ring of sincerity in Maxine's voice.

Beth stared into the sea-blue eyes that held secrets and read them with eyes that had seen all. The thought then popped into Beth's head.

"Oh. My. God. You're rolling naked between the sheets with geeky Normie, the man you said you would never, ever, ever, ever give in to."

The longest and most anxious few seconds of Maxine's life scrolled past as she debated whether to be honest with Beth.

"No, I'm not." Maxine's defensive tone confirmed Beth's suspicions.

"You have been getting poked by Norman McDonnell."

"Christ, Beth, do you have to be so crude?"

"Do you have to be so secretive? What's the big deal? Norman likes you, and you need poking. Well, you do," Beth said when Maxine's brow cocked. "You and geeky Normie are a match made in heaven. I'm happy for you, Maxine." Beth grinned and took Maxine into a tight bear hug.

"Jesus, Beth." The flush rose to Maxine's cheeks.

Beth held Maxine away and looked into her bashful eyes. "Why couldn't you tell me something so innocuous?"

"Because it's embarrassing." Maxine's eyes looked for someplace to settle, not from embarrassment but out of guilt and to cover her overt lie.

Maxine trusted Beth with her secrets, but she knew disclosing her involvement with Norman could expose Maxi Bass and her moonlighting job. It would require an explanation to Sister Fisk and colleagues, and Maxine was unprepared for it. Maxine was not ready to risk everything she knew and loved.

A successful first performance at Ba-Dum-Bump under her belt did not qualify as a success. The comedy-slash-performing business was fickle, and Maxine might fall flat on her face on her upcoming appearance. The last thing Maxine wanted was more people than necessary to know about her failures.

"It's me you're talking to, Maxine. You don't have to be embarrassed. You can tell me anything and everything. I'm your friend. I won't judge."

"I know you won't. It's still awkward talking about it." Maxine's voice carried a noticeable strain as she convincingly portrayed her unease.

Beth chained an arm around Maxine's shoulder. "Girlfriend, we've told each other everything. Haven't we?"

"We have, but…." Maxine became contemplative and ultimately acknowledged that she had to tell Beth something. Beth would press until she got the truth from Maxine. "You promise not to tell, Beth. If you do, I'll have to report our sleeping together, which is all it is, to Sister Fisk. And goddamnit, that's the last conversation I want to have."

When the world shifts too much under your feet, Maxine found her strength, thought Beth. "Maxine Basset, sex is making you sizzle hot."

"Stop, Beth. This is why I didn't want to tell you about Norman and me. So, can we stop talking about this now," Maxine said to end the conversation before she let out more than she should. "You won't tell anyone."

Beth raised the three fingers of the right hand. "Scouts honour. You can trust me. I have one question. How do you rate his performance in bed?" Maxine formed a silent wow with her lips.

"That good, hmmm."

"He was tender and caring and loving and…."

"Enough. You're making me very *caliente*."

Chapter 21

MAXINE FINISHED PUTTING the finishing touch to Maxi Bass. Maxi was scheduled to perform her set in the eleven-thirty slot tonight. It was a late-hour set, and everyone would be drunk and rowdy by the time Maxine made it onto the stage, but being her second performance, she could not be particular. It would take time to move up to prime time.

Maxine took a last look at herself in the mirror. Tonight, she wore a slinky, body-fitting dress with thin straps. Her glossy hair fell around her face, painted with the trademark ruby-red lips. Eyeing her reflection in the mirror, Maxine liked what she saw. She even liked who she saw. Maxi Bass was her alter ego, the woman trying to break out for years.

Maxine felt calmer than her first performance, but her nerves still pulsed. She needed a calming effect and inviting Norman and Buzzy to dinner and drinks before the show was a start. Blazing a spliff afterward would complete the nerve-easing impact.

Maxine checked the time. Norman and Buzzy were due in fifteen minutes.

Walking past the table, Maxine took a quick scan. The dollar store glasses and white china plates looked suiting beside the linen napkins on the salmon tablecloth her mother dug from the church's donation bin.

Giving the table setting a nod of approval, Maxine walked to the stove and opened the oven door. The smoky aroma of the roasting brisket, with hints of rosemary potatoes and carrots, permeated Maxine's apartment. The rolls and apple pie Buzzy had baked that morning sat on the island counter, and the garden salad was waiting to be dressed with Buzzy's homemade vinaigrette.

Maxine closed the oven door and turned to the ringing telephone on the counter. Guilt struck Maxine hard when she saw the caller's name on the telephone's screen. She sucked in her breath and stepped away from the counter.

The telephone continued to ring and would until Maxine answered it. Maxine did.

"Hi, Mom. How are you?"

"I'm fine, Maxine, but your father isn't." Georgiana's voice was cold and unemotional.

"What's wrong with Dad? Is he okay?"

"He has a head cold, but you know how men are. He makes it seem as if he's contracted a fatal disease."

"Yes, well, I'm glad he's fine. Give him my love." Maxine absently straightened the tulips in the vase at the center of the table picked from Buzzy's garden.

"I will. Take your aspirin, Barret. It's a headache. Not a brain tumour," Georgiana said with snark in her voice. "Honestly, he's like a child. Anyway, I'm calling to see when we can expect you home for summer vacation."

There was a tiny silence.

"The Lady's Church Committee are looking forward to a helping hand and the ideas from a city girl. Are you there, Maxine?"

"I'm here, Mom." Maxine reached into the pantry for the brandy bottle and poured a tall drink.

"So, when can we expect you? School should be out in a couple of weeks."

There was a moment of awkward silence between them.

Maxine drank half of the brandy in her glass. She swallowed hard before saying, "I'm not coming home this summer, Mom," with a quiver in her voice.

Georgiana dismissed Maxine as she always did. "Of course, you're coming home. You come home every summer. And I have many things scheduled for you to help with."

"I'm sorry, Mom, but I won't come home this summer." Maxine emptied the remaining brandy in her glass. "I have some stuff going on."

Georgiana took a quick, exasperated breath. "What do you have going on that's more important than seeing your father and me and spending quality church time?" Georgiana's voice was sterner now.

Maxine considered how to respond because telling her mother that Maxi Bass was scheduled to perform all summer at Ba-Dum-Bump was out of the question. Maxine could not tell her overly conservative mother about Ba-Dum-Bump, the comedy club where the audience drank to excess to escape the pressures of life. And Maxine's mother would certainly not understand her daughter performing on stage before that drunken audience.

Maxine could not say any of that to her mother. Everything Ba-Dum-Bump stood for was sinful and corrupt acts that paved the way to hell. Having a candid conversation with her mother was not in the cards. It never was.

Maxine's father was no better than Georgiana. A personal discussion with her father was an impossibility. Barret Basset only spoke to Maxine through Georgiana.

"I'm … ah, teaching summer school to make extra money because I'm, umm…." *Think, Maxine, think.* "Planning to buy Buzzy's house," Maxine said, her voice softer with the lie.

An audible gasp from Georgiana followed. Whether from shock or approval was indeterminate.

"You never said. When did this come about?"

"Buzzy and I have been discussing it for some time. I wanted to surprise you," Maxine said, waiting for her mother's response.

"That's wonderful news, Maxine."

Shit, Maxine thought when Georgiana's voice was suddenly eager. Maxine was digging herself into a hole she could not crawl out of.

"Is it, Mom?"

"It is. Your becoming a homeowner is impressive, Maxine."

The compliment came from left field, leaving Maxine stunned and speechless.

"Thank you, Mom," Maxine said when she gathered her thoughts.

"I only wished it wasn't in the city; too much temptation and depravity around you. There's no sense of morality in the city, Maxine, as there is in our small town. We hear so many stories from the city in the news. No, Maxine, your father and I want you to come home. Permanently." Georgina did a one-eighty turn, and Maxine's excitement flat-lined.

For a moment, Maxine thought she had talked her mother into believing the lie. The panic leapt at Maxine's throat at Georgiana's sudden reversal.

"Your father and I need you here, Maxine."

Maxine rubbed at the dull ache building at her temples.

"We need you home, Maxine, and that's that," Georgiana said, and Maxine communicated her disappointment through her silence.

Maxine looked gut-punched, and several emotions crossed her face before resentment and anger jockeyed to the front at her mother's assumptions she could pack her life in overnight to meet her demands. So typical for her mother to think of her life as inconsequential. Maxine had her own life. She had responsibilities, a job she loved, and students who depended on her. Maxine had a home she had made for herself and friends who cared for her. She had a good man who cared for her.

"Are you there, Maxine? Have you listened to what I've said?"

The suppressed anger bubbling up in Maxine soared into a frightful fury, and she found her voice. "I heard you, Mom, but I can't pack up my life on a whim."

As was always the case, Georgiana overlooked Maxine's comment. "Of course you can. You have a home and family here."

"I have a family of sorts here. Buzzy is like family. You said so yourself. I have friends at school, and I have responsibilities. I'm doing well here, Mom. I have a life." Maxine cut her mother off when she started to speak. "I'm not coming home, Mom." Maxine's resolute tone took Georgiana aback.

City life was corrupting her daughter and making her the defiant woman that would darken her soul. Georgiana thought she had put an end to that when she spoke her mind to Jesse and told him he should stop leading her daughter down the immoral, sinful path he set her on.

Georgiana might have been miles apart from her daughter, but she knew precisely what Maxine was doing and with whom.

Georgiana took a computer course at the local library, learned how to set up a fake profile on social media, and followed Jesse. Today, kids post their lascivious lives for everyone to see. Georgiana saw images of Jesse drinking, partying, and conducting himself in unsettling ways, and Maxine was there with him, sharing his depraved lifestyle.

Noticing Maxine pulled into the immoral life that Jesse introduced to her pure and unsullied daughter, Georgiana direct messaged Jesse. Under her pseudonym *thedevilslayer,* Georgiana sent several messages encouraging Jesse to save his soul and that of every person in his circle.

Jesse did not respond to *thedevilslayer's* messages, but after months of Georgiana's messaging, she got through to him. Jesse disappeared from Maxine's life, as did *thedevilslayer.* Maxine would never know of Georgiana's influence in her life because children could not distinguish between a parent's best interest for their child and meddling.

Georgiana had to stop and consider how she wanted to respond to Maxine so as not to turn her daughter against her.

"Mom, are you there? Did you hear what I said?" Maxine's voice broke the threads of Georgiana's thoughts.

There was the slightest hesitation before Georgiana said, "I heard you, Maxine, and your father, and I trust you to steer clear of debauchery."

Georgiana's response struck Maxine dumb. It was some time before Maxine said, "Yes. Yes, you can, Mom."

"Good. Good. Can you afford to buy Buzzy's home? Can you qualify for a mortgage? You haven't worked long and have minimal savings. And with your father being a pastor, money is tight with us. We can't help you financially."

"I don't expect you to help, Mom. Besides, I want to do this myself. It'll be tight, but I can manage it with the earnings I expect to make during the summer." Maxine sighed and closed her eyes briefly. She was piling lie on top of another lie, creating a leaning tower that could topple at any minute. She should stop now. "Buzzy offered me the opportunity to buy her house at a better than fair market price. The home is sentimental for Buzzy, and she won't sell it to an outsider. Buzzy has offered to take the mortgage on herself with minimal deposit, which means I don't have to qualify through a bank."

The lies flowed out of Maxine like a raging river, fast and effortlessly.

"Why would she do that? Is Buzzy all right? She's not sick, is she? I will pray for her," Georgiana interrupted with the thought when it came to her.

"No, Mom. It's nothing like that. She's getting older, and the house has become a burden." Maxine lied some more. Her voice did not break or sound dubious now.

Maxine never imagined she had it in her to lie as easily as she did. She supposed it was a byproduct of her new persona, Maxi Bass.

"Where will she live?"

"Here. Buzzy will live here with me. Rent free. It's why she's offered the generous price," Maxine said, astounding herself at her plausible lie.

"Makes sense. That being the case, your father and I forgive you for not making it home this summer. I said, we understand why Maxine cannot come home this summer, Barret. No, she's not coming home. Be quiet, Barret. I'll explain later."

"Thank you for your understanding, Mom." Maxine could not help feeling guilty, and her eyes turned bleak. "I have to go, Mom. I have to check on the brisket I have in the oven."

"All right, Maxine. I'll pray for you."

"Thank you, Mom." Maxine ended the call.

Although she did not feel as guilty as she should, Maxine's thin shoulders hunched. There was a touch of Maxi Bass's brassy character surfacing in her and staying permanently.

"So I'm old, am I?"

Maxine looked up to see Buzzy standing by the front door with Carol Burnett by her side. Tongue lolling, Carol Burnett sniffed the brisket-scented air, ran toward the stove, and plopped down before it. Carol Burnett wore a Dolce and Gabbana silk scarf around her neck today.

"Shit," Maxine murmured under her breath. "How long have you been standing there eavesdropping on my telephone conversation?"

"Long enough," Buzzy said.

Buzzy wore Capri pants with large pockets and a sunflower print. Her short hair had been blow-dried and styled into soft waves. Her tan Roman sandals matched the cross bag hanging off her shoulder.

"What have I said about that?" Maxine said.

Buzzy dismissed Maxine's comment. "I'm so old and frail I can't take care of my home anymore, let alone remember what's been said."

"It's not what I meant." The dull ache at Maxine's temples was turning into a throbbing headache.

"It's what you said. How much am I selling my home for?"

Carol Burnett stretched out on the floor and stared at the oven window with hopeful eyes.

"You're not. I had to say that." Maxine looked regretful.

Buzzy waved her hand in an airy dismissal. "I'm teasing, dear. I know you lied to your mother because you want to fulfil the slotted performances I got you at the club."

Maxine took a calming breath. "Christ, Buzzy, you couldn't tell me that from the onset."

Buzzy shook her head. "You're too easy to play with, dear. So, what did Mom have to say?"

"Oddly enough, she understood, but I feel terrible having to lie to her."

"It's for a good cause, dear. It's for you." Buzzy raised a hand to Maxine's chest. The gold bracelets at her wrist jangled with the motion.

"Would you appreciate Steven lying to you?"

"He does all the time, even at his age. The only difference is I know when he's lying. In contrast, your mother's judgement is clouded by an irrational religious doctrine that has deluded her into believing everyone has good in them. Spoiler alert: we do not. Human beings are a spawn of the devil."

Maxine's dark brows lifted. "Norman is right. You do know how to turn a phrase."

The few lines around Buzzy's gray eyes creased when the smile flickered on her face.

Chapter 22

THE SATURDAY NIGHT crowd that filled every seat in the club was as rowdy. Men and women dressed in casual weekend attire—jeans, T-shirts, and running shoes—expected to be entertained. The smells of fried foods mingled with expensive perfume and spicy cologne.

When Maxine stepped onto the stage, many in the audience stopped mid-drink to stare. Maxine looked breathtaking in tonight's Maxi Bass costume, a killer gold cocktail dress with a low cowl neckline and thin shoulder straps that underscored her smooth, dark skin.

She looked gorgeous and sexy, Norman thought, admiring how Maxine's stiletto heels shaped her muscular calves. Whether it was due to the effect of the Deadhead Kush strain that filled his head or the surge of lust that Maxine ignited in his gut, Norman thought he could detect her perfume above that of every other woman in the room.

The three men sitting at the table to Maxine's right lobbed lewd comments. The men were in their twenties, drunk, and belligerent. Within seconds, Joey, the bouncer, sprinted into action and walked to the table where the group of men sat.

With a raised hand, Maxine stopped Joey as he was about to toss the men out of the club. "It's all right, Joey. They're projecting what psychologists refer to as TDE."

"And what's that, hot babe?" With a crooked smirk, the blonde, sitting between his friends, slurred his words.

"It's a scientific acronym for Tiny Dick Energy." Maxine waved her pinky finger. "They can't help being size-challenged or playing at being men. Isn't that right, boys?"

The audience roared with laughter, and Joey raised an appreciative dark brow as the three men went from cocky to cowering in their chairs.

Maxine powered through with confidence. "And to no one's surprise, they're alone. You know what that means, ladies. You can trade spit with them." Maxine made a heart sign with her thumb and forefingers.

Many of the women in the room guffawed, some ewwed, and others expressed their disgust more effusively.

"I don't own a magnifying glass," said the brunette sitting on a bar stool.

"You couldn't pay me enough," said the stunning black woman sporting a leather jacket and skintight leather pants, provoking uproarious laughter.

"I haven't gotten any in months, and I'd still turn them down." The fiery redhead called out.

"Gentleman, do you want to stick around for more abuse?" Joey asked.

Heads bowed, the trio of men rose from the table and skunked out of the club. Joey followed them to ensure they exited the club without incident.

Maxine raised her hand to wave at the exiting men. "All we need is a fat kid with a tuba following them out the door. Money on the table if they did a colonoscopy, they'd find their heads up their asses." Maxine ad-libbed the lines with the ease of a seasoned comedian to the applause and cheers she grew to crave. "Now, with that carousel of nonsense brought to a screeching halt, let's get this show on the road."

"Smoking that bong rip before heading to the club works wonders for her." Buzzy stuffed her face with chicken wings smothered in hot sauce.

Norman's brows drew together in a frown. "You're an author of poetry with words."

Buzzy reached for the napkin and wiped the barbecue sauce staining her mouth. "It is a special talent of mine."

"Right. Well. You're right to say that a few hits boost Maxine's confidence." Norman agreed.

With the hecklers out of the way, Maxine dove into her monologue. The laughter and continual applause reverberated in the warm club air throughout Maxine's fifteen-minute set.

Steven dashed onto the stage. Over the cheers and applause, he said, "Ladies and gentlemen, Maxi Bass." Steven leaned into Maxine and whispered. "They love you, honey. If you keep this up, I'll move you to prime time soon enough."

Maxine felt Steven's hand lower down her back down to her butt. "And if you continue to paw me like a dog in heat, I'll make sure you're moved to the emergency room."

"Damn, you are a feisty one." Steven gave Maxine's butt a suggestive squeeze.

"I'm not joking, Steven. Get your hand off my ass, or I'll break it. Right here on stage," Maxine murmured the threat with a warm and sincere smile aimed at the audience.

Steven removed his hand and gave Maxine's behind a sweeping glance as she sauntered off the stage with a confident, sensual swing of her hips. "A whirlwind with a great ass," Steven murmured, smiling.

Chapter 23

MAXINE KICKED HER stilettos off. She fell onto Norman's sofa and stretched her legs on the coffee table. "I kicked ass tonight."

"You did." Norman made his way to the kitchen and reached into the refrigerator. "Did you write tonight's monologue? It sounded more like you than the last one." Norman waved the bottle of wine at Maxine. She nodded.

"Buzzy helped some, but I wrote most of it. Did you like it?" Maxine accepted the offered glass of Merlot.

"I did. It was well written, and your delivery was on point. Like that of a pro. You'd never know this was only your second performance." Norman sat beside Maxine on the sofa. "You were terrific, Maxine. I have a feeling you will achieve great success."

"Thank you, Norman, but I had a good teacher and great support." Maxine touched her wine glass to his. "Steven said if I keep it up, he'll move me to a prime slot."

The house was quiet and smelled of the popcorn Norman had for lunch. Out the living room window, stars flickered in the darkened sky, and a full moon burst in radiance across the skyline. Music from cicadas in the stillness of the night and the scent of lilac poured from the open windows.

Norman fastened his eyes on Maxine's face. "Is that what he told you at the end of your set?"

"That, and he put his hand on my ass. The goddamn nerve. The entitlement." Maxine's voice, bristling with anger, rose a few decibels.

Norman paused and glanced at Maxine.

"Are you all right?" Norman contained his anger not to fuel Maxine's, but what he wanted to do was punch something, anything.

Maxine nodded. "I told him if he didn't take his hand off my ass, he'd end up in the emergency room. I would have kicked him in the balls so hard on stage he would have, too." Maxine's eyes turned a darker shade of blue as angry heat spit out of her eyes.

Norman was sure she could assert herself and effectively keep the wolf in sheep's clothing at bay. Still, he would keep a watchful eye and stay close to Maxine when she was around Steven. Norman knew men like Steven. Their good looks, smooth ways, and wealth got them all the women they wanted and came to expect it. A feisty, aloof woman like Maxine became a worthy challenge to men like him.

"You should tell Buzzy. She'd want to know how her son behaves around women. I guarantee you you're not the first and won't be the last." Norman said, playing on her uncontained animosity toward Steven.

Maxine tipped back her head. "I know, but I haven't decided yet if I should speak to her. Buzzy knows her son well. She knows what Steven is made of. Besides, he doesn't seem to be the type who will listen to what mommy has to say."

"I will if you don't," Norman said, allowing his simmering anger to overtake him. "I don't like him pawing you. I know Steven's type. A mere threat won't stop a man like him."

Maxine suppressed her anger from surfacing.

She could take care of herself and intended to make that clear to Norman. However, the strain in his voice and the emotions etched on his face stopped her. Norman genuinely wanted to take care of her, which was not a bad thing.

"You don't need to worry about me, Norman," Maxine said.

"I know I don't, but…."

Maxine silenced Norman with a kiss. "I like you. A lot. More so than I like Steven."

Norman's anger drifted away. "You do?"

"Mmm-hmm." Maxine leaned into him and kissed him. They kissed long and deep, their tongues dancing and tangling together. "Proof enough?" Maxine said when they both came up for air.

"Yes. I'm sorry. I'm not usually a jealous jerk. It's just where you're concerned. I turn into this crazy person," Norman said, spilling emotions.

Along with jealousy, despise, and anger for Steven, Maxine saw the love in Norman's eyes for her. Maxine had sensed Norman's feelings for her were strong, but until now, she was unsure how strong.

What did she do with this information? The question was a whisper in her head.

Acknowledging Norman's feelings meant reciprocating, and she could not do that. Maxine's feelings for Norman had not reached the I love you stage. She was not ready to return the "I love you" words. Not yet.

After some consideration, Maxine decided to shelve it—for now.

"That's sweet, Norman, but you have to trust me." Maxine reached out her hand for his and held it tightly. "I can handle myself."

"I know you can. I don't trust Steven. There's a look in his eyes I've seen too often in entitled, manipulative pricks like him who aim to use and hurt."

"I know that." Maxine rose, walked to the counter, and picked up the wine bottle.

"Then you should stop the performances, Maxine." Norman held out his glass for her to pour a refill. "Don't dangle the carrot in front of the donkey."

That made her eyebrows lift in mild amusement. "I can't stop performing, Norman. Performing has freed me from my hamster wheel life, living rent-free in my head. When I'm on the stage, I feel … empowered, a sense of accomplishment. And I hate to admit that the adulation grips me. Maxi Bass is the rebel woman in me, trying to escape for some time. Maxi Bass helps me forget the past and move on."

"I see that. A blind person can see that, but you shouldn't give Steven the access he wants."

Maxine poured wine into her glass. "You're clearly not a woman."

"I should hope not, or God fucked up."

"Sardonic humour. I like it." Maxine tucked her legs under her on her sofa. "Women have been enduring men like Steven since the beginning of time and will continue to do so for all eternity. It's the curse we live with."

"Does my penis automatically make me a part of the problematic club? If you blame it for the world's evils, don't hold it against me. I'm nothing like Steven, nor do I believe or condone his tactics."

"I don't, and no, he,"—Maxine's eyes flicked to Norman's crotch—" doesn't automatically make you a member of the Asshole Club."

"Oh, good, because he's served me well, and I'm very fond of him."

"We're still talking about your penis, right?"

Norman echoed the smile on her brilliant blue eyes. "We are."

"Then I will submit that I, too, have become very fond of him." Maxine knocked the wind out of Norman's sails when she reached out to stroke his crotch with her foot.

"Oh, geez." Norman's voice came out as a squeak.

"That's what performing has done for me. I'd never have dared to do anything so…."

"Pleasant, stimulating, exciting. Provoking."

"Bold was what I was going to say, Mr. Thesaurus. I grew up in such a puritanical environment that merely glancing at a boy felt immoral and inappropriate. And here I am, stroking your crotch with my foot and enjoying it."

"Not as much as I am," Norman said with a winning smile, and her eyes lit with laughter.

"The old Maxine would have never done anything that daring. Maxi Bass has allowed me to perform a natural, physical act to a man without feeling like I'm going to hell. It's allowed me to step beyond my comfort zone."

Norman leaned into Maxine and fastened his eyes on her face. "Acting out on your physical urges and needs is nothing to be ashamed of, Maxine. It's not as if you're being promiscuous, and even if you were, as long as it was your choice—which I hope is not the way you want to go—it's fine. Your choice, Maxine." Norman emphasized.

"I know, but knowing and acting out are two different things. And you're right. I'm not the promiscuous type." A smile brushed over Maxine's lips when Norman blew out a breath. "I understand everything you said now that Maxi Bass has liberated me. It's the reason I can't give up performing. Ambivalence is no longer a factor in my life because of her."

Norman gave Maxine an understanding look. "I just hope you don't mind me watching over your shoulder."

"I don't. I like someone looking after me. I like you looking after me."

"Good. Because you can't get rid of me that easily."

"I'm glad. All I ask is you only step in when I ask you to."

"All right." Norman Pinky swore. "Why the glum face?"

"I feel guilty for not telling Mom about you or Beth about my moonlighting job."

"And toking." Though Norman curled his lips, Maxine's did not.

"Yeah, no. That we're taking to the grave."

"Your secret is safe with me. I understand you want to be seen as a true moral crusader." Norman vowed when Maxine's eyes urged him. "I understand and don't mind you not telling your mom about me. I don't mind," he said, meaning it.

Norman was the kindest, most loving, and understanding man. Norman supported her when she told him about Maxi Bass. Norman did not judge her. Norman stood by Maxine through the craziness in her life. It was why Maxine thought she was falling in love with him.

"I don't understand why you can't tell Beth about your performances?" Norman said.

"Because if I fail, I don't want her to feel sorry for me. She's my best friend, but deep down, she sees me as this lost, naïve puppy dog who can't find her way alone."

Norman reached for the loose strand of hair around her face and casually wound it around his finger. "She doesn't think of you in that way. Even if she does, you know that's not who you are. I like you just as you are if it counts for anything."

"You're just saying that because you want to get lucky tonight."

"I do hope to get lucky, but I mean what I say. I think you're amazing just the way you are."

"Now, you're quoting Billy Joel." Maxine sipped on her wine.

Norman shook his head. "He quoted me. I mean what I say, Maxine."

"Just for saying that, I'm going to let you do what you like to me." There was mischief in her face as she held his eyes. "And without a Bobo around, we can do the nasty all night and sleep in tomorrow morning."

Eagerly, Norman pushed his hands under her body and lifted her off the sofa. The wine in the glass in her hand sloshed to the edge.

Norman paused and glanced at Maxine. "Wait. Is that Maxine or Maxi talking?"

She leaned in so their faces were inches from each other. "It's me talking. Now, take me upstairs before I change my mind."

"Yes, ma'am," Norman said, sprinting up the stairs.

Chapter 24

SUMMER SLID INTO fall and fall into spring, and before long, it was fall again. Maxi Bass had become a regular on the Ba-Dum-Bump stage and earned a prime-time spot on the roster. Maxi Bass was filling seats and making money for Steven, hand over fist.

As tired and anxious as Maxine felt due to Bobo's relentless barking, she met the gruelling appearance schedule Steven set. But teaching, planning her classroom activities and lessons, and writing her stand-up monologue were taking their toll on Maxine. Even her daily runs were down from five weekly to one.

Exhausted and bleary-eyed, Maxine sat at Buzzy's kitchen table. Unable to keep her eyes open, Maxine rested her head on the polished wood of the kitchen table. Maxine was still in her pyjamas. Her dark hair was dishevelled, and last night's makeup stained her cheeks.

Buzzy set the coffee cups with a thump on the table. Maxine instantly snapped her eyes open. Raising her head with a jolt, Maxine picked up her rant where she had left off.

"Over one year, Buzzy, of Bobo barking all hours of the day and night, and all those goddamn people at Animal Control can do is tell me they'll patrol the area to keep an ear open on his barking. As if. That was code for 'Shut the fuck up already, lady.' I pay their salaries." Maxine's pulse galloped as tense nerves and anxiety pressed down on her chest like a boulder.

"More so I do. You know, through property taxes," Buzzy pointed out.

"Don't joke about this," Maxine said coolly, glaring at Buzzy with weary eyes.

It was six in the morning. As the moon gracefully slipped away, the sun's ascent transformed the horizon into a breathtaking display of gold and rust as it heralded the arrival of a new day. The well-lit kitchen was filled with the delightful aroma of freshly baked biscuits.

Buzzy had been up since five thirty when Bobo was let outside to relieve himself in the backyard and barked. Bobo's three loud barks shook Buzzy out of sleep. Sleeping with headphones was not as comfortable as Buzzy led Maxine to believe, and she had removed them in the middle of the night. Buzzy thought it wise to keep that to herself.

"Apologies." Buzzy wore tan Capri pants and a loose teal shirt and smelled of French perfume.

"I've sent dozens of emails, along with the barking log they requested to the so-called Animal Control Supervisor under your name since it had to come from the homeowner to no avail."

Barry Manilow's soothing voice flowed from the radio, and Carol Burnett lay still in her bed by the sliding door. With keen eyes, she watched the squirrels scurry over the fallen leaves carpeting the ground beneath the trees. Carol Burnett wore a stylish Dior aquamarine silk scarf around her neck today.

"You never told me about the log." Buzzy retrieved the baking sheet from the oven with gloved hands and set it on the stove for the biscuits to cool.

"I'm telling you now. I had to do something, Buzzy. You're too nice to do anything. I am not. Anyway, it was a waste of time. I doubt Ms. Animal Control Supervisor reviewed the log or read the emails. She promises to do something but does nothing." Maxine paced, her wool-socked feet stomping on the floor. "They do nothing to stop Bobo barking and still make us take down the ultrasonic device I made you buy because it's outlawed in this god-forsaken city. That's three hundred dollars down the drain. I'm sorry about that, Buzzy."

Buzzy opened her mouth but closed it when Maxine kept going.

"Bobo and his idiot parents can lawfully keep me up at night or wake me early in the morning without repercussions. Animal Control only exacerbates the problem by justifying Becca and Miles's unreasonable belief that because Bobo barks three or four times each time, it disturbs no one. These inconsiderate, self-centred dolts are allowed to live in a civilized society when they have no idea what the definition of civilized is." Maxine reached into the cupboard for the bottle of brandy and poured a generous amount into her coffee. She drank deeply.

"Easy with that, dear. You have school this morning. Sister Fisk will not be very pleased if her kindergarten teacher shows up to class three sheets to the wind at nine a.m." Buzzy flitted about cleaning up bowls and putting away ingredients.

"Jesus C., over one year of this bull shit, Buzzy. Over. One. Miserable. Fucking. Year." Maxine gave each word separate weight before she clamped her lips shut.

"That Maxi Bass potty mouth is getting pottier." Buzzy flipped the cooled biscuits into a basket.

"I'm serious, Buzzy." Maxine's pacing became brisker. "I can't take it anymore. Look, I'm losing my hair." Maxine ran her fingers through her hair, but they got stuck in the thick knots. "Okay, so I'm not losing hair, but I'm losing sleep and my sanity. I have PTSD. I hear Bobo's bark in my head when it isn't there."

"I'd keep that to myself, dear." Buzzy set the basket on the table along with butter and jam. "Sit down and eat a biscuit while it's warm."

At the word biscuit, Carol Burnett rose and ran so fast toward the table that she slid across the shiny tile into the wall. It took her a few seconds to recover and reach the table.

"They're too hot for you, Carol Burnett. You'll have to wait a few minutes," Buzzy said when Carol Burnett looked up with her feed-me-human stare.

Disappointment came over Carol Burnett's face, but she was a patient dog. Carol Burnett spread out on the floor beside Buzzy to wait.

"I don't want biscuits, Buzzy. I want peace and quiet. Is that too much to ask?" Maxine's shoulders slumped in defeat, and she fell back in the chair.

Buzzy shook her head. "It's not, dear, and I am sorry."

Buzzy's patience, too, was wearing thin for Becca and Miles. Buzzy had not been able to do her gardening. The stench wafting from Bobo's urine and the feces left to fester under the burning sun was overpowering. Several times, Bobo almost sent Buzzy into a coronary episode when the unexpected barks came at her, and she gave up spending time in her garden in her backyard.

Buzzy had made every effort to go the lawful route to rectify the issue but failed miserably. The neighbours were unwilling to get involved, and Animal Control's willingness to address Bobo's barking was zilch. Becca and Miles refused to listen to reason, and there was no point in talking to them. Now, Buzzy feared Maxine would consider moving out of her home. Buzzy saw Maxine as a daughter and friend, and she and Carol Burnett enjoyed her company.

"Steven said he has someone to get rid of the dog." Maxine picked at her biscuit.

Buzzy's eyes levelled on Maxine, considering the offer. Ultimately, common sense kicked in, and Buzzy dismissed the thought.

"No. No, we can't, Maxine. I'm an animal lover."

"Jesus, Buzzy, no. We're not ordering a hit on Bobo. I'd order one on Becca and Miles before I did the dog," Maxine said and watched Buzzy's eyes cock high. "I'm joking, of course." Maxine's side-eye look said otherwise. "Steven meant to kidnap the dog and take him far away from here."

"One, that's impossible to do. The dog is never out of Becca and Miles's sight. Two, have we become insane?" Buzzy spread butter and jam on a cooled biscuit and fed it to Carol Burnett.

Bobo's bark blared, and Maxine walked to the window and pressed her back to the wall as she cast spying eyes out. Bobo pressed his nose to the fence slats sprayed with citronella oil. Bobo's tail wagged vigorously. As inconspicuous as Maxine was, Bobo taunted her with a series of loud barks.

Maxine was about to sprint into the backyard to spray Bobo with the water hose when he let out several more barks. Before she could make it past the sliding door, Becca summoned Bobo into the house.

"Fucking Bobo," Maxine grumbled as she slid the door close.

"If you want to move out, Maxine, I'd understand. I'll help you with the first and last month's down payment," Buzzy said reluctantly.

There was a tiny silence. "Is that your polite speak for telling me I'm complaining too much? I'll tone it down, Buzzy."

"It's not your complaining, Maxine. Bobo is driving me to insanity also." Buzzy waved Carol Burnett away when she looked up, expecting a second biscuit.

Carol Burnett gave Buzzy an indignant look before ambling to her bed.

"So, you're not getting rid of me?"

"Of course not, Maxine. I and Carol Burnett like you being here. Don't we, baby?" Buzzy said, and Carol Burnett barked her wordless agreement.

"Good, because I'm not going anywhere. This is my home. You're my family, and so is Carol Burnet. Besides that, I can't afford the rent anywhere else. I live on a teacher's salary. Remember?"

Buzzy watched Maxine set the brandy-laced coffee aside and walk to the coffee pot. "Are you saying Steven hasn't paid you for your performances?"

Shaking her head, Maxine poured coffee into a cup. "Why would he? I'm still an amateur."

Aghast by what she heard, everything about Buzzy went hard, and her eyes turned cold.

Chapter 25

BUZZY'S ANGER TOOK over. "Why didn't you tell me Steven wasn't paying you, Maxine? You've put in dozens and dozens of performances to packed houses. Steven's been raking in the money on your appearances. You're no longer doing open mic shows. Your appearances are scheduled and advertised. You deserved to be paid."

Maxine held her cup in both hands, staring into it quietly. "I haven't made as many appearances as that, Buzzy. Bobo has been keeping me from getting a good night's rest, clouding my mind, making it impossible to write coherently, let alone comedy."

Bobo let out several booming barks at a squirrel, the sky, or a floating leaf that startled the women and woke Carol Burnett.

Buzzy's anger rose and icily said, "Stop deflecting, Maxine, and answer the question."

"You heard that, right?" Maxine waved a hand toward the window, but Buzzy remained defiant. "Steven's paid me for the handful of corporate shows he booked for me."

"How much?" Buzzy said with an impatient hiss.

"The last one, Steven paid me one thousand dollars for the hour and paid for my dress, shoes, makeup artist, and the hair stylist."

Heat flashed in Buzzy's gray eyes. "He made ten thousand dollars on that booking. Did you know that? No, of course, you didn't," Buzzy said when Maxine's jaw dropped and her eyes widened. "Steven, my son whom I taught better, is profiting from you and probably many others, and I will not stand for it. Profiting from struggling performers is not what Ba-Dum-Bump is about." Buzzy's face was a mixture of anger and disappointment.

"It's not important, Buzzy. Calm down and think of your blood pressure."

Buzzy dismissed Maxine. "That goes against everything Morty and I believe in. We compensated our performers fairly, even when financially struggling, and garnered their loyalty. It's why every comedian wanted to perform at the club and what made it today's acclaimed venue."

It shattered Buzzy to think of her son's lack of integrity and purposely taking advantage of struggling comedians. Integrity and honesty are the measures of an honourable person, and her son had neither. It was not how Steven was raised, but it was who he had become.

"You should have said something to me, Maxine."

"It's no big deal. I don't need the money."

Buzzy's brows lifted high. "That's the best you can do?"

Maxine looked down at her kneaded hands. "I don't want to come between you and your son, Buzzy," Maxine said, hoping Buzzy would end the conversation there. A continuance of the conversation might lead Maxine to spill her guts and tell Buzzy her son was a lecherous womanizer on top of everything else.

But the conversation did not end there, and Buzzy pressed Maxine to tell her everything. Maxine remained tight-lipped.

"You've been performing at Ba-Dum-Bump without compensation because the club affords you the status, which allows you to get gigs in the rival comedy clubs. Isn't that right?"

Maxine looked up from her kneaded hands with genuine surprise on her face. "You knew about my appearances in the other clubs?"

"I know everything, dear. I have friends everywhere." Buzzy checked on the second batch of biscuits in the oven. Another five minutes, Buzzy decided and closed the oven door.

"I'm sorry, Buzzy. I've let you down."

"Why would you think that?"

"You introduced me to comedy, concocted Maxi Bass, and provided the first costumes. You taught me everything I know, and here I go and use that knowledge to perform at competing clubs." Maxine watched Buzzy remove the tins from the oven and place them on the rack to cool.

"I did all that." Buzzy removed the oven mitts before swivelling to face Maxine. "But I don't blame you for capitalizing on what I taught you."

"It's not so much capitalizing, Buzzy. It's that I've come to love every aspect of performing. I love being on stage and losing myself in Maxi Bass. I enjoy the adulation. Christ! I enjoy it all. I've even come to enjoy the risk of failure with every performance. It's a…."

"Rush, a high," Buzzy finished.

Maxine nodded.

"I also understand that performing is costly. Costumes, makeup, and travel don't come cheap. Are the clubs paying for your sets?"

Maxine's guilt swallowed the words. Without meeting Buzzy's eyes, she nodded.

"Are you selling out?"

Maxine huddled more into herself as she nodded.

"Well then, I hope you're making sure they pay you scale. You deserve it, Maxine. You've become very good at the trade."

"I'm making enough to cover the expenses, and I've been able to send some money to my parents. It's the least I can do after not having gone home for the past few summers. Mom hasn't been happy about it, and I can sense she's questioning the veracity of my telling her I'm working summers at the school."

"Why would she suspect anything? You haven't posted anything about your side job on social media, and I certainly haven't breathed a word. As for Norman, your parents have no idea he's in your life and wouldn't have a reason to speak to them or vice versa. Aside from Norman, you, and me, no one knows about Maxi Bass," Buzzy said.

"That may be, but my gut tells me she's suspicious. Anyway, I'm not completely lying to Mom. I have been able to set a bit of money…."

"To pay for the mortgage on the home you bought from me." Buzzy jumped in to say.

A lopsided grin glanced across Maxine's face. "For the home, I will eventually buy."

"Hmmm." Buzzy picked up the dirty dishes off the table and put them in the sink as her mind considered the angles.

Steven was unfair and wrong in what he did to Maxine, and where there was one Maxine, there were others. Buzzy did not know when Steven went down the wrong road. She had not raised Steven to be opportunistic, greedy, or a womanizer. Buzzy was aware of the rumours regarding Steven's inappropriate behaviour with female performers and firmly confronted him. Steven denied it even after

Buzzy again expressed her disapproval when she saw Steven take liberties with Maxine.

"I don't like that you've taken to pollinating the city's female population to Olympic sports level, but you're a grown man, Steven, and it's not my place to interfere. However, when you engage in lecherous behaviour with the female performers at the club, I will not hold my tongue. I have taught you better than that. I have taught you to treat women with respect," Buzzy said to Steven and saw the dismissal in his eyes.

"Mom, you're being your overly dramatic self." Steven walked behind the Ba-Dum-Bump stocked bar, chose the bottle of Canadian Club fifteen-year-old sherry and poured himself a double. He did not offer Buzzy a drink.

"I'm not being overly dramatic, Steve. I saw what you did to Maxine on stage. Everyone with eyes saw."

"What did you see exactly, Mom? You were high as a kite." Steven rounded the bar and sat at a bar stool across from Buzzy, who sat at a front-row table. "Really, Mother, a woman of your advanced age high on—what?—coke, oxy, Adderall, ecstasy, dope. All of the above."

Buzzy disregarded the jab. "You do not handle Maxine or any woman under this roof in that manner. Ever. Understood?" Buzzy's face went taut, and Steven was cornered into nodding.

"This Maxine girl is tight with you. Are you sure she doesn't have ulterior motives? You're a wealthy woman, Mom," Steven said bluntly.

Buzzy closed her eyes briefly, adjusting the anger Steven sparked. "You would be a rich man and not need Mommy to bail you out as often as I have if you weren't squandering away your money faster than it's deposited into your account."

Steven anxiously tapped the side of the glass with the gold ring on his pinky finger. A sure sign Buzzy touched a nerve.

"Don't make me regret my decision to make you the club manager, Steven."

Mortimer was right. My excessive indulgence of Steven as my only child has fostered a troubling sense of entitlement in him that is now impossible to overlook.

Buzzy had to right this wrong for Maxine, the performers who deserved better, and to salvage the reputation of the iconic club she and Mortimer had built.

"Well, Maxine, home ownership may come to you sooner than you think," Buzzy said, but Maxine had fallen asleep on the table.

Chapter 26

THE TENSION IN the room mounting, Buzzy watched Steve's pace become fast and furious as he stalked the room.

"Have you lost your fucking mind, Mother?" Steven sucked back cigarette smoke before he chased it with a deep swallow of his favourite whiskey.

"You're not allowed to smoke in here, Steven." Buzzy calmly walked away from the bothersome smoke to the red velvet upholstered sofa and sat. She looked elegant in red silk and smelled of expensive Chanel. "There are laws against it."

Steven momentarily stopped pacing to touch the lit cigarette to a new one he fished from the pack on his desk. "I can do what I want. It's my fucking office."

Sunlight streaming from a clear, blue sky reflected off the glass of the large picture window overlooking Ba-Dum-Bump's rear parking lot. The lot was empty but for a handful of staff-owned cars. On College Street, traffic was heavy but moving at a steady pace.

"I like what you've done with the place." Buzzy's eyes scanned the office on the club's second floor.

Steven transformed the office Buzzy and Mortimer shared for years into a pornographic den of gold, red velvet upholstered furniture, shag rugs, dim lighting, and mirrors. Lots of mirrors. Framed posters that had hung on the burgundy walls of renowned comedians that Buzzy and

Mortimer bought at various flea markets were replaced with pictures of busty women in scanty lingerie. A couple of questionable nudes that Steven deemed art hung amongst them.

"It is my office." Steven inhaled deeply and let it out in a quick stream.

Steven was dressed in Armani Jeans with a crisp crease, topped with an Italian light brown leather jacket over a blue silk shirt, and finished with Ferragamo loafers. He had neatly combed hair and a clean-shaven face. The fragrance of his musky cologne infused the office.

"Not for long, dear," Buzzy said.

Steve abruptly stopped pacing. "What's that supposed to mean?"

"You haven't been holding up your end of the bargain, Steven. You promised me you would stop being a lecherous womanizer, and you haven't. On top of that, I find out you're cheating Maxine out of her hard-earned stipend in addition to stealing money from her corporate performances." Buzzy sipped on her brandy as she stared at Steven over the rim of her tumbler.

Steven was silent.

"When she remained silent, you continued to take advantage of her, and I'll venture to say many other performers." Buzzy gave Steven some time to process what she said.

Biting his bottom lip nervously, Steven remained silent.

"Goddamn it, Steven. We make thirty percent of the bookings that come through the club. But that's not enough for you. You have to avail yourself of as much money as you can from Maxine because she's inexperienced with navigating the complicated maze of our business and inexpert at negotiating." Buzzy's tone had an unmistakable chill, reflecting her disappointment and anger toward her son.

"Well, you're making it up to her by endowing her your home, which belongs to me, your son. Your flesh and blood," Steven spat back.

"My home belongs to me, Steven, and I can do as I please with it. And after your duplicity, which has been going on for over one year that I know of, I believe Maxine deserves it."

Steven felt the dagger of betrayal sinking deep into his back. Buzzy was choosing a stranger over him to inherit his childhood home.

"Aside from the house having sentimental value to me, the home is worth hundreds of thousands of dollars," Steven said through a cloud of smoke.

Buzzy scoffed at her son's blatant lie. Steven could deliver a lie convincingly, but Buzzy, as his mother, could read him like a book.

"Who are you kidding, Steven? You and I know you feel no sentimental attachment to the home besides its dollar value. I know you've already valued the home and plan to put it on the market when you take possession." Buzzy's eyes did not leave Steven's face.

"That's a blatant lie," Steven said, feigning indignation to mask his shock that Buzzy knew about the valuation he had done on the home.

Buzzy quirked her brow in response.

"I might owe Maxine, at most, seventy-five thousand dollars, which I'll gladly pay her."

The lack of remorse in Steven's expression made Buzzy's chest constrict. Buzzy's gray eyes held the man's before her intently. When had Steven become the self-centred, selfish man who stole money from a struggling artist? Those were not the values she and Mortimer instilled in him. Steven might be her flesh and blood, but Buzzy no longer knew him.

"How many artists have you cheated out of their rightful earnings?" Buzzy spoke calmly, but anger rode in her eyes. "That's fine. I'll find out when Lester gets here."

"What's Lester got to do with anything?" Steven fell back into the high-backed chair behind his desk when his knees weakened. "You're auditing me."

Steven had never been one to overthink anything or hover in Einstein-intelligence-level territory by any stretch of the imagination. Still, Buzzy credited him with quick foresight.

"Yes, Steven. At my request, Lester's accounting firm will audit the club's books."

"You can't do that." A nauseating wave of panic rolled through Steven, momentarily stunning him. "I'm your son, and this is my club."

"I own sixty percent of this club. If my math is correct, sixty percent makes me the majority owner, and I can do what I please."

"I've been making you lots of money since taking over the management of Ba-Dum-Bump."

"You have, but it isn't my money now. Is it? When Lester's done reviewing the books, I'll use it to pay those you've cheated out of their fees. I have a feeling there will be many payouts to make. Am I right?"

Steven did not say anything momentarily, groping for the correct response. "Why waste your time on a problem that hasn't reared its head?"

A deafening few seconds of silence followed as Buzzy looked at Steven closely. Over the years, Steven had learned to read the subtleties in Buzzy's facial expression and body language. He saw deep disappointment in her eyes.

"Have you listened to anything I've said, Steven?"

"I have. I'm telling you, there's no need to poke a sleeping bear. And I promise to refrain from upsetting you further, but you have to stop this auditing nonsense," Steven added, his gray eyes staring at his mother from above the rim of his glass.

"Lester will be here in a few moments. I want you to round up the books for him," Buzzy said firmly and before Steven could refuse came the knock on the door.

Steven gave Buzzy a defiant stare. "I'm not doing that. I'm busy. Go the fuck away," Steven barked, believing Lester was the knocker at the door.

Annoyed though Buzzy was with her son's superior, offensive tone, she bit her tongue and said nothing. But the disappointed look she gave Steven spoke volumes.

"I thought you'd say that. It's why I'm bringing in an assistant manager until the audit is complete and I decide how to proceed." Buzzy rose and opened the door before Steven could challenge her decision. "Come in, Jack. Jack Sievers, my son Steven Morgan."

Jack stepped forward, hand extended. Steven did not reciprocate the pleasantry.

Jack was in his sixties with a short, thick gray hair crown. He looked dapper in a burgundy three-piece suit with a pink shirt and silk tie. There was a pink silk square in his left jacket pocket. Behind the round glasses, his eyes were hazel, friendly, and radiated intelligence. He had bushy Groucho Marx-style brows, thick and gray.

"Jack is an old friend. He will be stepping in as the assistant manager. Guy will assist Lester with his probe and take over the scheduling and booking for the performers.

Guy will also look after the payroll and accounts payable. Anything money related."

Steve got a sick look on his face. "And what the fuck am I supposed to do?" Steven snapped like a pit bull.

"Language, Steven. You will do what you do best, emcee. You have stage presence. People gravitate to you," Buzzy said.

Steven's eyes went to slits. "Don't patronize me, Mother."

"I'm not. I'm telling you the truth. I should have never overwhelmed you and given you so much responsibility. I should have gone with my gut and insisted on an assistant manager when you took on the management role."

Steven gave Jack a cagey stare, feeling judged by his silence. "And you trust him more than your son at handling the back of the house?"

"I do," Buzzy said simply. "You will not be hostile toward Jack or Lester, Steven. You will give them access to everything they want and will follow Jack's guidance."

"I'm not here to replace you, Steven. I'm here to help," Jack spoke for the first time. His voice was commanding and authoritative.

Steven stared at Jack, his expression hostile. "The fuck you are. What if I refuse?"

"Honey, you forget I own all this. The building is mine. The club is mine. I control the company's bank accounts. You're merely a co-signer. I will cut off your overly generous salary at the knees if you don't do as I say. The ball is in your court, Steven." Buzzy's calm voice grated on Steven's nerves.

"You wouldn't dare." As menacing as Steven's tone was, it did not intimidate Buzzy, nor did she dignify the challenge with a response.

As much as it hurt Buzzy to do and say what she did to her only son, she let her serious face speak for her. Tough love, Buzzy told herself, was something she should have done long ago.

"Fucking Maxine. You're going to pay for this," Steven murmured as he stormed out of the office.

Chapter 27

MAXINE DISMISSED BUZZY'S talk of gifting her her home as a spurt of profound disappointment in Steven and put it out of her mind. No further words were exchanged until today.

The dinner plates had been washed and were now neatly stacked in the dish rack. Buzzy joined Maxine at the kitchen table, bringing two glasses of sherry. Buzzy set a glass of sherry before Maxine.

"I invited you for dinner for a reason, Maxine. I have documents I want you to sign." Buzzy wore a Burgundy flowing shirt with large purple flowers stamped all over and burgundy Capri pants. Even after making a pizza from scratch, her face and hair were flawless.

"What documents?" Maxine had changed from her school attire and wore black leggings, an oversized sweatshirt, and ankle socks. Her hair was loosely tied in a ponytail.

Buzzy reached for the Manila folder, flipped it open, and reached for the pen. "I've already signed it and dated it. You need to do the same."

Maxine looked over the document. Maxine stared at Buzzy, stunned and puzzled, when she finished scanning it.

"The Post-it arrows indicate where you must sign, dear." Buzzy handed Maxine the pen.

The perplexed look lingered, and Maxine did not take the offered pen.

"Take the pen and sign, dear."

"You were serious about that," Maxine remarked when she found her voice.

"Of course I was. I am. I'm sorry it took so long. I was waiting on the papers from my lawyer." Buzzy set the pen on Maxine's hand. "Don't you want to sign the documents, Maxine?" Buzzy said, watching Maxine absently continuously click the pen's mechanism.

"I do, Buzzy. I do. I just need some time to get my head around the idea." Maxine took her sherry in one gulp as she glanced from Buzzy to the documents and back to Buzzy again. "I didn't imagine you were serious. Are you sure about this, Buzzy? Steven won't be happy when he hears about this."

Maxine feared Steven's reaction when the news Buzzy chose to give his rightful inheritance, his birth home, to her reached him. And the news hitting Steven so soon after the withholding-payment debacle and subsequent audit was bound to garner Maxine a lot more hate.

The whispers at Ba-Dum-Bump were that Buzzy forced Steven to relinquish the club's management to Jack Sievers. Steven blamed Maxine for the setback and everything that came with it. That stopped being a rumour when Steven confronted Maxine and told her she would pay for her loose lips.

Now, Maxine was about to become co-owner of Steven's childhood home. Maxine sensed she was in for the fight of her life. Steven was not the type to stand down and readily accept it. Steven would not let go of the home as easily as Buzzy assured Maxine he would. Of that, Maxine was sure. Maxine had come to know Steven as a selfish, entitled man who held tight to what was his and expected what was not, be it property, money, and women.

Maxine had escaped Steven's grubby hands and his demands for sexual favours off her by forfeiting her hard-earned money to him. Not wanting to cause Buzzy further distress, Maxine kept that information to herself because no mother needed to know such distressing news about their son. Maxine had also kept Norman in the dark, although he suspected Steven's lecherous ways and had broached the topic a few times. Tension rose when Maxine denied Norman's assumptions, fueling his suspicions about her relationship with Steven.

Steven had nothing to lose now that the secret was out of him, skimming her pay and Buzzy taking action for the reparations. Maxine could only sit back and wait for the repercussions.

"This is my home to do as I wish." Buzzy sipped on her sherry.

"Still. I don't feel right about this, Buzzy."

"I do, and don't you worry about Steven? I'll deal with him. Sign, Maxine." Buzzy's commanding voice left Maxine with no choice but to sign. "No need to feel guilty, dear. As I said, this is my home, not Steven's." Buzzy stacked the papers in the folder and flipped it close. "Now, I'll have the lawyer register the papers to make it official. In a week or so, you will be the co-owner of this home. When I die…."

"Don't talk like that." Emotion choked Maxine's voice.

Buzzy reached across the table and closed her hand over Maxine's. "I'm not going anywhere anytime soon, but this property will be yours when I do. I would transfer it to you now outright, but Lester, my accountant, suggested we do it this way to avoid a hefty capital gains payment. Lester hasn't steered me wrong in sixty years, and he won't now," Buzzy said.

Maxine clicked the pen close and set it down on the table. "I don't know how to thank you, Buzzy."

With a sweep of the pen, Maxine's life took a one-eighty turn to a future she had dreamed and hoped for but never imagined would become a reality.

"Fulfilling our agreement is how you can thank me."

"You have my word that I'll meet my end of the bargain. You're my family, Buzzy, and I wouldn't dream of casting you out of your home. You living upstairs and me remaining in the basement apartment is exactly what I want. And I will pay half the expenses: taxes, hydro, water, etc." Maxine held a silencing hand when Buzzy started to speak. "I insist."

"I was going to say that right you will. After all, you're now half-owner of this palatial estate. But you will no longer pay rent, so it balances out." Buzzy rose and walked to the stove to take out the apple pie from the oven when the timer dinged. Its scent and the oven heat poured around her when she opened the oven door.

Carol Burnett came racing from the backyard into the kitchen when a trace of the apple pie fragrance reached her overly sensitive nose. Carol Burnett slid across the floor to land in front of the stove. She wore a Burberry black and white chequered scarf.

"Not yet, Carol Burnett. It's too hot. Get your butt outside and return in twenty minutes," Buzzy said, and Maxine laughed inwardly at the idea of Buzzy reasoning Carol Burnett could tell time. "Another thing I want to say, Maxine."

"Sounds ominous."

"It isn't, dear. I've decided to spend some of the wealth I've amassed." Buzzy cut two slices of hot apple pie. "Get the vanilla ice cream."

Maxine pushed to her feet and walked to the refrigerator. "What do you mean?"

Buzzy took from Maxine the tub of ice cream and signalled for her to get the scoop. "I've decided to travel."

"That's wonderful, Buzzy. When? Where are you planning to go? I hope you're going with friends," Maxine added with concern.

"Are you saying I am an old biddy and can't manage on my own?"

"I'm saying that a woman should not travel alone in foreign lands."

Maxine's reply caused Buzzy to lift a brow. "You don't think I'm wise enough to know that. I have decades of experience more than you," Buzzy said with scorn, but there was a soft smile on her face. "I've decided to take up a friend's invitation to a Mediterranean cruise. We plan to visit Greece, Sicily, Venice and other Italian cities."

The excitement for Buzzy flashed on Maxine's face. "That sounds amazing, Buzzy. I'm so happy for you. It's about time you lived a little. Which friend? Ava, Mia, Sofia, or Barb?"

"Lester," Buzzy said, topping the pie slices with vanilla ice cream.

Taken by surprise, Maxine straightened in her chair. "Lester. As in Lester, your accountant."

"Uh-huh." Buzzy set the plates with pie on the table.

"But Lester is a boy."

"Uh-huh."

"I'm going to need more information than an uh-huh." Maxine looked at Buzzy with interested eyes. "Spill, Buzzy. Now."

"You are a nosy one."

The slash of dark eyebrows rose. "I learned from the best."

The smirk twisted Buzzy's lips. "Touché, dear. As you must know, Lester and I have been friends for a long time. Having recently connected, we got to talking, and him being a widow like myself, I accepted his invitation to join him on the cruise when he asked."

Maxine's blue eyes stayed focused on Buzzy's face, assessing. "Nah, there's more to the history between you than that."

"There is, but that's all you're getting."

"How come you can meddle in my life, and I can't get answers to simple questions from you?"

"You're young and need the guidance and moral support of a woman who has lived life. I do not."

A sigh trickled out of Maxine. "Fine, be like that. Still, I think that's wonderful, Buzzy. I'm so happy for you. I've told you again and again you should travel and live. Spend that money you worked hard for to pamper yourself. And doing it with someone you like—you do like Lester. He's a good man?"

Buzzy regarded Maxine's questions as one of concern rather than meddling, and she said, "I do like Lester, and he is a good, honourable man. He's two years younger than me, but…."

"You cradle robber," Maxine interjected with a teasing smile.

"As I said, Lester is looking for companionship, and I am happy to provide that and more."

"Does that intent look on your face mean you'll be sharing a cabin on the ship?"

Buzzy glanced sideways at Maxine. "And a bed."

"I'll provide you the necessary protection as a going away gift." Maxine's mouth twitched with hidden laughter.

Buzzy overlooked the comment. "While I'm away, you will mind the homestead."

Maxine rose and crossed to the coffee machine when it stopped spurting. "I'll take good care of your home."

"It's your home now as much as mine." Buzzy accepted the coffee cup, added sugar and cream, and stirred. "And this being your home, you can have boys overnight to copulate with whenever you want."

Maxine stared back at Buzzy, knowing what she meant. "Norman and I are still at odds with one another. So, he won't be around anytime soon to copulate or otherwise."

"Honey, why are you two at odds? Norman is a good boy, and you are good together."

"Because he's an asshole."

Buzzy rose and walked to the sliding door. "Carol Burnett, come get your apple pie." Before Buzzy finished her sentence, Carol Burnett was in the house like a bullet and glided across the kitchen floor toward the table.

"Difficult to tell if she wants pie or not." Buzzy put a small piece of pie on Carol Burnett's dish and added a dollop of ice cream. "Eat slowly, Carol Burnett. You'll get a brain freeze if you don't. Back to Norman. Men are all assholes, dear, but he's your asshole and a sexy asshole at that."

Maxine set the spoon down on her plate. "He is that, and I miss him, but...." Maxine left the unfinished thought hanging.

"What did I say about brain freeze, Carol Burnett," Buzzy said when Carol Burnett's gaze froze into an aimless stare. Buzzy turned to Maxine when Carol Burnett regained her composure. "Finish your but, Maxine."

Maxine told Buzzy about Norman missing her performances, his ongoing neglect, and his blaming Steven. "Translation, he's bored with me, tossing me aside, or possibly intimidated by my success, or …."

"It's neither of those things," Buzzy leaped in to say. "That's not at all like Norman."

It was like Steven, however, giving Norman the wrong performance times or lying to him to come between them, Buzzy thought.

"I didn't think so either, but here we are." Maxine absently stuffed her mouth with pie and ice cream. "I don't want to talk about Norman anymore. Good riddance, I say."

"Don't dismiss him so quickly, dear. I have a feeling he'll be back on hands and knees."

"I don't care if he does come back on all fours. I don't want him to. I'm done with his bullshit. Eat your pie, Buzzy," Maxine said, indicating they'd exhausted the topic.

"I have another piece of news to share with you."

"I don't know if I can take more news, Buzzy," Maxine added sweetener to her coffee and stirred.

"I got you a twelve-minute spot on the upcoming Lisa Lampanelli roast on Comedy Central. A ten-minute standup set on a late-night talk show can follow if that works out," Buzzy said and saw Maxine spoon more pie and ice cream. "Did you hear me, Maxine?"

Maxine said nothing.

"I'm serious, Maxine. I still have many contacts in the business and was able to pull this off for you. What do you say?"

There was a moment's pause as Maxine stared at Buzzy and let herself study her, evaluating the veracity of her statement. The earnest look on Buzzy's face led Maxine to deduce she was serious.

"You're dead serious."

"Of course I am, dear." Buzzy set more pie on her plate and Carol Burnett's dish.

Maxine dropped the spoon in her hand on her plate with a clang. "You're shitting me. The Comedy Network? Lisa Lampanelli? Letterman?"

"Yes. Yes, and yes. So, are you in?"

"Shit, yeah. My belly button is puckering and unpuckering, thinking about it."

Chapter 28

MAXINE COULD HARDLY believe that Buzzy would present such a bold proposal, and days later, she remained in a state of shock. The idea struck her like a lightning bolt, leaving her exhilarated and terrified.

"Maxine Basset, homeowner," Maxine repeatedly said to herself, endeavouring to wrap her head around the idea.

Maxine considered Buzzy the motherly figure Georgiana was not. Buzzy provided the emotional support Georgiana did not. Buzzy was the level-headed, rational mother Georgiana could never be as long as her head was clouded by irrationality. Maxine often turned to Buzzy over her mother for advice.

As much as Maxine considered Buzzy, her family, she never imagined what had transpired would.

Still dizzy, Maxine had a faraway look when Beth walked into her classroom. Beth got a dose of the faint aroma of freshly sharpened pencils and the fruity smells of banana and orange from the children's afternoon snack. As Maxine had taught the children to do, low shelves were neatly organized with picture books, educational toys, puzzles, and games.

"Earth to Maxine." Beth snapped her fingers to draw Maxine out of her trance.

Seated behind her desk Maxine turned her attention toward Beth who took a seat on top of the closest desk. "Sorry, yeah."

"I asked if you were up for dinner at the Blue Plate Diner. My treat." Beth brushed luxuriant blonde hair over her shoulder and crossed her long legs.

Beth wore a teal pantsuit with a marine blue silk blouse. Even after a gruelling teaching day, no hair was out of place, and her makeup was perfect.

"Sure. Okay, but are you sure? It's a miserable night. Wouldn't you rather head home?" Maxine said, turning her gaze toward the window. Beth joined her.

The rain came down in a thick sheet of water on the roar of thunder and slammed against the windowpane and everything in its path. The last vestiges of gold leaves dangling from tree branches fell onto the wet ground. In the dark, the night gleamed under the lamppost lights.

"Head home and do what? Settle in with a good book in front of the fireplace. No. I've been knee-deep in the classic Animal Farm all day, and what Mama needs now is a stiff drink, dirty or otherwise. Drinking is in my horoscope today."

Maxine snorted a laugh. "Horoscope or not, every day of the year is a drinking day for Beth Caplan."

Maxine wore a lilac dress with a lace collar and three-quarter sleeves. Her hair was tightly tied back in a bun.

Beth reached for the tube of lipstick in her purse and touched it to her lips. "It's a byproduct of being the teacher of hormonal teenagers with limited attention spans, immature brains, and snappy retorts. They drive you to exhaustion, which in turn drives you to drink. It's a vicious cycle, Maxine, but one I'm happy to placate with alcohol and steamy sex. Tonight, I'm flying solo, so drinking it is."

"I'm your backup plan. That makes me feel special."

"Did you miss the part where I said it's my treat?"

Maxine gave it a quick think. "I can certainly be bought."

"I know." Beth looped the gold chain draped at her neck around her finger.

"That's stunning, Beth," Maxine said when she caught sight of the white gold Gucci chain. The diamond solitaire pendant that hung from it looked expensive.

"I'm not going to tell you what I had to do for it, but I can tell you it was well worth it." Beth winked at Maxine and gave her a smile.

Maxine made a little snorting giggle. "I should say so. It's beautiful, Beth."

"So, are we doing dinner?"

"We are, but can we go to Shrimpos instead?"

That garnered Beth's full attention. "Still, tepid on Normie."

Maxine's silent shoulder shrug set off warning bells for Beth.

"Sounds serious," Beth replied, sounding concerned.

Maxine glanced at Beth and murmured, "Not so much."

The pained expression on her best friend's face told Beth otherwise. Beth gave Maxine a dubious look.

"Norm's good for you, Maxine. And vice versa. What did he do or not do to piss you off?" Beth said that knowing from experience, it was always what a man did not do more than what he did.

"We've had another tiff, and I need to give myself some space for his safety," Maxine effortlessly deflected, something that came easily to her now since Maxi Bass came to be.

Guilt weighed on Maxine's conscience, but telling Beth the truth was still not an option. Opening up to Beth about her growing disagreements with Norman would force

Maxine's hand at telling her about Maxi Bass. The story of her life and the people in it were interwoven.

Maxine had concealed Maxi Bass from Beth for too long, and it had crossed over into the long overdue line that, once crossed, made it difficult to correct. Telling Beth now would raise resentment and bitterness in her best friend. Norman's knowledge of her alter ego added to the turmoil Maxine created by secreting Maxi Bass from Beth. Best friend or not, Beth would begrudge Maxine for bringing Norman into the fold of her covert life and leaving her out.

Maxine wished she could talk to Beth about her growing arguments with Norman. Beth knew men and their mindset better than anyone. Beth could counsel Maxine on Norman's growing resentment toward Steven and his relentless lying.

Norman not showing up for Maxine's appearances and claiming Steven purposely misinformed him of the performance times caused friction between them. Maxine could not accept Norman's excuse that Steven refused to sell tickets to Norman for her shows and had the club's staff turn him away at the door. Maxine's skepticism that Steven could be so duplicitous and her refusal to accept Norman's begrudging jealousy rearing its head caused a rift between her and Norman.

Beth could help Maxine find the answers she needed.

Returning Maxine's steady gaze, Beth said, "You need to sort things out between you and Normie, Maxine. You work in the same school."

"You don't think I know that."

"Seeing him every day isn't going to help matters."

"I know that too. So far, I've managed to avoid him."

"You can only hide in your classroom to avoid facing him for so long. Do you want me to talk with Normie?"

Maxine shook her head. "Thanks, but things will sort themselves out. They always do between us."

"Okay, but let me know if you want me to chat with Normie-Boy. I'll give him a swift slap on the head to set his tiny brain back in place," Beth said, and both women laughed.

Maxine glanced at her watch. "If we leave now, we'll get to Shrimpos in time for happy hour and half-price shrimp cocktails, and you know how much you love both."

"What are we waiting for?" Beth hopped off the desk.

Maxine reached into the bottom desk drawer for her handbag. "I'm driving."

"Yeah, you are. You're the official designated driver." Beth shouldered her handbag and started for the door. "Hey, what were you daydreaming about when I first walked in?"

Maxine had a big smile when she said, "You won't believe it, but Buzzy is gifting me her home." Saying it out loud made Maxine's heart beat a little faster.

Beth stopped at the door with her hand on the knob and stared right at Maxine. "You're shitting me."

"That was my reaction when she showed up with the deed with my name on it. It knocked the breath out of me. It took me a while to realize she was serious. I still can't believe it." Maxine reached into her handbag for the car keys. "I'll tell you all about it over a cosmopolitan and jumbo shrimp," Maxine turned the lights off and closed the door behind her, wishing she could tell Beth about her television performance.

Chapter 29

BUZZY WAS ON her Mediterranean cruise with Lester, and the house was quiet. Too quiet. At least Carol Burnett was there to keep Maxine company.

Carol Burnett was not pleased to be left behind, and for the third day, she spread out on Maxine's sofa, sulking. Carol Burnett barely mustered the interest to watch Maxine pace her apartment with the excitement that infused her.

"I'm up for the challenge. I am Carol Burnett, but it's not going to be easy. Crafting jokes for a twelve-minute performance will take me days, if not weeks, because my routine has to be flawless. You know? It's the roast of Lisa Lampanelli on the Comedy Network. We're talking about television, Carol Burnett." Maxine stopped and took hold of Carol Burnett's face. "Television, Carol Burnett. Do you know how huge that is? I'm going to be on the fucking television, Carol Burnett. Me, a small-town girl with a population of ten thousand, including cows and pigs."

Carol Burnett raised one eye and the other.

At Buzzy's request, because Carol Burnett could not care less, Maxine put on Carol Burnett a gold Gucci scarf that cost four times more than Maxine's outfit.

"It's not even so much that I'm going to be on the tube with Lisa fucking Lampanelli on the Comedy fucking Network. It's not even about the great paycheque. It's that Buzzy, the queen of comedy, thinks I'm good enough to do it." Maxine fell back on her sofa, causing Carol Burnett to bounce on the cushion.

Maxine's apartment smelled of the buttered cinnamon toast she and Carol Burnett had shared for dinner.

"The fact Buzzy left me alone to cope with this pissed me off at first. This is a huge deal, and the only thing on Buzzy's mind is getting some. Could you imagine at their age thinking of sex? Let's try to unsee that image." Maxine shook her mind clear. "Anyway, after a clear mind kicked in, I realized Buzzy left me on my own because she believed I could do it alone. So, I'm not pissed off anymore and intend to make her proud." Maxine reached for her laptop on the coffee table and flipped it open.

Maxine had not changed after her run and swore the black leggings and neon pink tank top.

"This is Lisa Lampanelli." Maxine turned the laptop toward Carol Burnett. Carol Burnett peered at the image of a bubbly, smiling blonde woman for five seconds before becoming disinterested.

Carol Burnett hopped off the sofa and walked toward the television, planted her butt, and woofed. Maxine set the laptop aside and walked to the television. Tuning into the taped episode of *One Hundred and One Dalmatians*, Carol Burnett's favourite movie, Maxine read Lisa's Wikipedia page. Maxine had read it many times before, but rereading it would not hurt. Research was essential to tailoring content for a well-crafted set.

"Lisa kicks ass and is hysterical. Her comedic timing, writing, and everything about her is seamless, and I need to be as good," Maxine told herself.

Carol Burnett gave a low-throated growl when Cruella de Vil made her appearance on the television screen. The growling persisted until Cruella left the screen.

Lisa was one of the comedians Maxine had modelled Maxi Bass after. Still, Maxine spent all her free time on the internet reading all she could find about Lisa's likes, dislikes, and political views.

Maxine had YouTubed every past performance she could find on Lisa to study and learn. Maxine did so again and made pages of notes. Note-making on the subject was imperative to writing the ten minutes of gripping comedy expected from the producers and audience.

"I need to write my best jokes ever. I will be the only unknown comedian performing alongside names like Garofalo, Silverman, Romano, and Ansari," Maxine said each name reverently.

The sudden rising flutter of nerves in Maxine's belly struck, and she set the laptop down. Maxine's nerves winding tighter than a guitar string was not from the idea of performing alongside A-list comedians or the television appearance but from its dangers.

Maxine's television performance was bound to open a massive can of worms and upended her life when certain people saw her.

Maxine was not so worried about her mother seeing her. Georgiana did not own a television and refused to allow Barret or herself to listen to anyone who brought up the wickedness displayed. Beth, however, was another story. There was a high probability Beth would see the television special, and telling her beforehand did not fare any better. Then there was the staff at St. Boniface. No one at the school knew of Maxine's moonlighting job or her alter ego. They would come to know all once Maxine appeared on the popular network.

Everyone would know about Maxi Bass, including Sister Fisk. Maxine's teaching position at St. Boniface was at risk, and she was not sure putting it at risk without a steady income from her comedy work was the smart thing to do.

Nerves bouncing, Maxine paced. Too engrossed in the movie, Carol Burnett paid no mind to Maxine.

The human mind could conflate what it saw to fit your viewpoint, and many in Maxine's circle had tunnel vision. Maxine risked everything if she proceeded with the television appearance. But how could Maxine not? It was her big break—the biggest. Maxine's future depended on it. Maxine could become the next Carol Burnett, Gilda Radner, Lucille Ball, or Tina Fey.

Maxine's thoughts were focused away from her growing worry toward the sound from Becca and Miles's backyard. Bobo's bark was its usual deafening pitch, and as he always did, he did it standing by the fence a few feet from Maxine's apartment.

From the basement window levelled with the ground, Maxine watched Bobo's wagging tail. She heard his idiot owner, Miles, praising the dog as he barked at a squirrel, the sky, or the wind.

Maxine could feel her stomach tighten. "Goddamn dog, and goddamn his moronic, irresponsible, clueless owners. They are going to be the death of me," Maxine said, letting her mind roll over the various schemes she had concocted to silence Bobo once and for all.

Maxine smiled a little at the ideas rolling through her head.

In the cold night air, Bobo went on to bark, on and off, at a piercing level for the rest of the night. Unable to concentrate, Maxine put the laptop away. She was about to throw on Buzzy's noise-cancelling headphones when there was a knock on the door.

When Maxine answered the door, Steven stood on the other side. The smell of whiskey on his breath filled her head. Steven wore jeans and a black shirt under an Italian leather jacket. All looked to be designer and expensive. His clean-shaven face had a healthy, tanned look from the weeks spent under the Tahitian sun where he had been since Jack Sievers took over the management of Ba-Dum-Bump.

As centrefold handsome as Steven looked, Maxine's nerves tightly coiled.

"Buzzy's not home, Steven. She won't be for another three weeks."

"I know." Steven struggled to connect the lighter to the cigarette between his lips. "She's off gallivanting and doing God knows what with Lester while his accounting firm audits my company." Steven's words came out slurred through a haze of cigarette smoke.

Buzzy's company, Maxine refrained from pointing out for fear of antagonizing Steven.

"I'll let Buzzy know you were here looking for her, Steven." Maxine smiled a cautious smile.

Steven stuck his foot out to block the door from closing and lost his balance. Falling forward, Steven took hold of Maxine by the shoulder.

When he regained his composure, Steven pulled back and said, "I'm not here to see Mommy Dearest. It's you I'm here to see."

Maxine's nerves coiled tighter. "Me? Why?"

Steven leaned a shoulder against the doorjamb to steady himself on his feet and let himself study her. He did not see sensual Maxi Bass in the plain, unpainted woman before him. But Steven could see the long, curvy lines under the body-hugging leggings and tank top she wore. He let his mind wander.

Maxine was the only woman who had rejected Steven, and he could not deny it made her more desirable. Try as hard as he did, Maxine made it clear she wanted nothing to do with Steven. Steven was not the type of man to take rejection well. That Maxine chose a simpleton like Norman over him made Steven resentful and vengeful.

"Do I make you nervous, Maxine?" Steven let out a mouthful of smoke in a quick stream.

The general sense of unease Maxine felt was palpable, and her reaction was an uneasy laugh. "No. Why would you?"

A feeble smile surfaced on Steven's face. "Then invite me in. It's freezing out here, Maxine."

Maxine realized that keeping Steven out would only escalate the situation. Despite her reservations, reluctantly, she stepped aside and let him in.

Chapter 30

NORMAN PULLED HIS SUV into Maxine's driveway. Norman said, killing the engine and turning off the headlights.

"I don't know about this, Beth." Norman bore the look of a heartbroken man.

He wore an old ratty jean jacket over a chocolate-brown polo shirt and jeans. His hair was unkempt, and his jaw was covered by days of beard growth.

"You can do this, Normie," Beth put her hand on Norman's shoulder.

"She's been pissed at me for weeks. She thinks I'm lying to her about...." Norman stopped himself before he said something he shouldn't.

Frustration rising to the surface at Maxine's stubbornness and inability to talk openly to Beth, Norman raked his finger through his hair. Everything was a secret with Maxine lately. Don't say this, only say that, and be careful when you speak. Norman always felt as if he was always walking on broken glass.

"What does Maxine think you're lying to her about?" Beth squeezed Norman's shoulder in encouragement.

Norman was silent.

If Norman could tell Beth everything, he would. Norman would tell Beth his suspicions that Steven had sabotaged him by purposely passing on Maxine's wrong performance times and venues. It was as if Steven wanted

Norman to look like he was abandoning Maxine to build a wedge between him and her. And Steven had succeeded. Norman and Maxine's relationship had been strained for weeks.

Maxine's silence was stifling Norman. Norman needed to talk to someone, Beth, anyone about his predicament, but he could not. Norman needed reassurance he was not going crazy. He needed to be told he was not misreading Steven's actions as those of a man doing his damndest to jeopardize his relationship.

Norman doubted himself and welcomed the unbiased input of a neutral voice as to whether Steven intentionally deceived him to come between him and Maxine. But Norman could not talk to anyone about Maxi Bass, Steven, or the club. Promises were made, and Norman would not compromise Maxine's trust. Besides, doing so would only exacerbate the mess he was already in.

"It doesn't matter that Maxine thinks I'm lying to her, Beth. The point is she believes I am." Norman flicked his eyes from Beth out the car window.

The night air was crisp and cool, filled with the smells of a not-distant winter. Up and down the quiet street lined with tall oaks and maple trees, their branches almost bare, streetlamps blazed and cast cones of light.

"Whatever is going on with you two, you and Maxine need to talk it out. I hate to see you and her so miserable," Beth said.

Beth wore black leggings, a teal silk blouse, and a down jacket. Her strawberry-blonde hair floated in shining waves around her face.

"I'm miserable. I miss Maxine. I tried to talk to her several times. She refuses to return my calls. She doesn't miss me as much as I do her." Norman gazed at Beth helplessly.

Beth met Norman's despairing eyes. "Well, we've come all this way, and I'm here with you. I will force Maxine to sit and listen to you if I have to tie her down to the chair. We're not going anywhere until you talk to her."

Norman had reservations about Maxine being forthcoming and exposing Maxi Bass, Steven, and the club with Beth present. But Norman would prod Maxine because she would have to open that Pandora's Box herself. Norman was desperate. He missed Maxine enough to have her expose her secret life and put her relationship with Beth at risk. Mending his relationship with Maxine was foremost in Norman's mind.

"I'll give it another go. Maybe Maxine will talk to me with you here," Norman said, sounding hopeful. "Let me give this a try on my own first. Wait here until I tap you in."

Beth nodded. "I'm not going anywhere. I'll be right here, Normie."

When Norman opened the car door, cold air hit his face like a hard slap. He walked along the walkway alongside the house leading to Maxine's apartment door. On hearing the murmur of a man's voice, Norman suddenly stopped. Stepping between the tall cedars flanking the house, Norman fixed his gaze on the man's silhouette on Maxine's stoop.

From the shadows, Norman watched intently. Norman could see the man's back and reasoned that his height matched Steven's, as did the neatly combed short hair and trademark leather jacket. Norman thought he smelled the spicy scent of Steven's cologne.

Norman's breathing came rapid and shallow as his hands clenched and unclenched.

Bobo's barking broke the neighbourhood's calm. Bobo continued to bark, preventing Norman from hearing what was said between Maxine and the man at her door. Norman hoped the dog would be called back into the house soon.

Bobo continued to bark.

Hot rage burning on top of cold fury, Norman barked, "Shut the fuck up, you stupid mutt," remaining well-hidden in the bushes when Maxine scanned the area for the shouter.

Bobo barked more and louder.

Jesus, fucking, Christ. It's a fucking wonder Maxine hasn't done you harm.

Seeing no one, Maxine returned her attention to the man standing on her stoop. Norman closely watched the exchange between Maxine and the man.

Anguish and dejection bubbled into anger when Norman saw the man wrap his arms around Maxine's shoulders and press his body to hers. Norman's heart deadened with pain when he saw Maxine step back to let the man into her apartment. There were no excuses, no ifs, ands, or buts anymore. Norman had lost Maxine to Steven.

Feeling the world around him narrow, Norman got back into his SUV. Ignoring Beth's many questions, he shifted the car into drive and peeled out of the driveway.

Beth thought she saw tears in his eyes.

Chapter 31

MAXINE STOOD STARING at Steven, who had seated himself on the sofa and stretched his legs out on the coffee table. Carol Burnett, too engrossed in her movie, paid no mind to Steven or Maxine, who walked behind the kitchen island to mark a safe distance between them.

"How about pouring me a drink, darling?" Steven stared at Maxine keenly, making her spine stiffen.

"I don't keep alcohol in my home." Maxine's voice faltered under Steven's gaze.

"Yes, it is your home now, isn't it, Maxine?" Steven's eyes, bright with the stimulation of alcohol, froze Maxine with his hard stare.

Maxine made no response.

"I have to hand it to you, Maxine. You play the game well. You befriend my mother, move into her home and take advantage of her by paying her next to nothing in rent. Then you entertain her idea and become a comedian to please her yet endearing yourself more. Until, bam!" The word came out forceful enough to heighten Maxine's anxiety and startle Carol Burnett, who turned to Steven and barked. "Shut the fuck up, you mutt," Steven growled, sending Carol Burnett scurrying into Maxine's bedroom to hide under the bed.

"Was that necessary? Carol Burnett didn't do anything to you."

Maxine moved closer to where her telephone sat. Slyly, she slid it into her jacket pocket and speed-dialled Norman's number. Safety trumped pride. Maxine hoped Norman would hear her exchange with Steven and come to her aid. At odds with Norman or not, Maxine could count on him.

"She's an annoying mutt. You and my mother spoil her. Mommy Dearest loves that dog more than she does me."

"That's not true," Maxine said.

"Pfft. I always assumed Mom would leave the house to that mutt and probably would have until you stepped into the picture. But then you are smarter than that mutt. You talked Mommy Dearest into signing over her home to you. Do I have it right, Maxi Bass?" Steven's glower could have melted the ice caps, and instinct told Maxine it was best not to say much.

Maxine kept quiet and wondered how Steven had found out about Buzzy adding her name to the house deed. Buzzy had left on her trip shortly after both signed the documents and had not spoken to Steven about it. Maxine thought briefly about who the informer might be, and she always circled back to Terri Masters, Buzzy's lawyer. Buzzy once mentioned that Terri and Steven had a brief fling. Solicitor-client privilege was not a consideration when you are rolling in the sheets, Maxine thought. Confide a secret to one person, even a lawyer, and it is a secret no more, Maxine concluded.

"That's right, Maxine, say nothing because what is there to say about taking what rightly belongs to me? This house is my…." Steven stared at nothing for a split second when he lost his thought. "I need a drink. Give me a drink, Maxine. And don't give me this bullshit about not having alcohol because, knowing Mother Dearest, she would have stocked your cupboards."

Steven pushed off the sofa when Maxine did not budge, but he could not lift himself. Watching Steven unable to maneuver to his feet bolstered Maxine's confidence, and she found her voice. "You're drunk, Steven. I'll make coffee."

"I don't want any fucking coffee. Stop playing the innocent simpleton because you're not, and get me a drink."

"You're not getting a drink, Steven. Not here, not from me." Maxine's defiant response made Steven cower.

All bravado and no backbone, Maxine thought, but then that's how it usually goes with bullies.

Steven brushed Maxine's comment aside and circled back to his earlier thoughts when his mind cleared some. "As I was saying, this is my home. I rightly deserve it. It's mine. I want it." The slurred words did not convey the flex Steven wanted to communicate.

Maxine took a close look at the man glaring at her through alcohol-glazed eyes.

Here was a man with everything anyone could want: handsome, good looks, fame, money, and women lining up for his attention. In his intoxicated state, however, Steven appeared weak, and his good looks lacked its usual allure. The confident Steven that Maxine knew with the world at his feet at that moment looked like a pathetic mess.

Seeing Steven for who he was made Maxine wonder why she had felt threatened by him, and she said, "I want you to go, Steven."

"I'm not going anywhere until I get my drink," Steven said as the telephone in her jacket pocket rang.

"It's my mother calling. She calls at this time to check up on me. I need to answer. She won't stop ringing if I don't," Maxine lied with a straight face.

Steven looked grudgingly at the interruption but waved a hand, indicating to answer the call. Maxine reached into her jacket pocket for the telephone and concealed her setback when the caller I.D. displayed her mother's number, not Norman's.

Where the hell was Norman? Why had he not answered her S.O.S. call? She needed him. Although drunk and unsteady, Steven was volatile and erratic when he had too much to drink. As unstable on his feet as Steven was, Maxine could not predict what he would do. Aside from the perfect opportunity at her feet to prove to Noman that she had no interest in Steven, Maxine relied on him to safeguard her. The disappointment in Maxine at Norman letting her down was immense.

Keeping up the lie for Steven's benefit, Maxine answered the phone rather than blowing off the call as she wanted to.

Maxine screwed up her face and said, "Hi, Mom. How are you?"

"I'm fine. Your father says hello. He survived his cold and is well. He's in his office, working on Sunday's sermon. It's about deterring our children from taking the wrong path of lying and deception," Georgiana said, washing Maxine in guilt seconds into the conversation. A new record for her mother, Maxine thought.

"What's up, Mom? I'm a bit busy right now." Maxine brazenly lied, hoping to get her mother off the telephone.

Since Maxi Bass appeared in her life, lying has come easily to Maxine, and she used it to its full effect where her mother was concerned. Lying was easier than enduring the doom-and-gloom conversations Georgiana delighted in. Maxine could not recall the last time she had an enjoyable conversation with her mother.

"Busy doing what?" Georgiana's voice was sharper than usual.

"I'm planning tomorrow's lessons for the children."

"Or you have a drunk man in your apartment, and that's unacceptable, Maxine."

Stunned by Georgiana's words, Maxine stared dumbfounded. She surveyed her apartment for the cameras. She saw none.

"Why would you say that, Mom?" Maxine had yet to perfect the art of the follow-up lie.

"Your hesitation tells me it's true."

The silence that followed was deafening as Maxine worked the angles.

"You shocked me with your implication, that's all. There's no one here, Mom." Maxine said in an attempt to regain her footing and prayed Steven would not make a sound.

"Are you telling the truth, Maxine? I figured the mouse would play with Buzzy gone, and I thought I heard someone stirring in the background. Who is he, Maxine? Answer me. Having a man in your apartment and a drunk one at that. Your father and I will not condone such immorality, especially when Buzzy is away."

Maxine looked over at Steven. His eyes flickering shut, he fell asleep and was snoring. "What you hear is the television and Carol Burnett snoring. I'm dog-sitting while Buzzy's on her Mediterranean cruise."

Maxine looked around her apartment again. She saw no signs of cameras.

Maxine was paranoid and justly so. Too many coincidences were adding up for her not to become suspicious. Maxine would swallow her pride again and ask Norman to scan the apartment for listening devices and cameras.

"Don't lie to me, Maxine." Bobo's bark sounded like a bullhorn just then, and for once, Maxine was grateful for the mongrel's bark. "Dear God, what is that?"

"It's Bobo, the next-door neighbour's dog."

"But it's," Georgiana checked for the time, "Ten o'clock at night."

Maxine looked out the window to see Bobo's wagging tail as he wandered his backyard. Relieving himself against the fence, Bobo then set off barking for thirty consecutive seconds, and for once, Maxine appreciated the mutt's bark for derailing her mother's attention.

Maxine exhaled an exaggerated breath. "It goes on all hours of the day and night. Sometimes, he's let out past midnight to bark at his pleasure."

Georgiana's force-of-nature attitude softened. "How do you get any sleep?"

"I don't. I'm tired most days, anxious, nervous, and stressed," Maxine said just before Bobo let out several more loud barks.

"Have you called Animal Control?"

"They've been useless. They're more pro-dog than preserving the sanity of the people who must endure the ear-piercing barking. Buzzy and I have emailed and telephoned the Animal Control supervisor and Service Officers umpteen times to no avail. When Buzzy insisted a Service Officer be sent to speak to them, the Service Officer told Bobo's owners the dog had a right to live and from spending time in his yard. So you know what happened then?"

"The owners let the dog out to bark day and night. We had a similar situation happen to Mrs. Livingstone. She was at her wit's end, sleep-deprived, and on an emotional roller coaster. The woman was in tears when she begged your father to intervene and help her. Your father is a pastor, not a dog whisperer. We prayed for her, and your father made the necessary calls to help the poor woman. Animal Control proved ineffectual and counterproductive."

"Our Animal Control people, too, have been both and I, too, am at my wit's end. I'm ready to commit murder."

"I will overlook your claim to violate the sixth commandment only because Mrs. Livingston, too, expressed the same sentiment after enduring her next-door neighbour's barking dog for months. It broke her, and I see it's breaking you, Maxine. We are a fragile species because God made us so. But God also gave us a brain, and I devised a scheme that saved Mrs. Livingston's sanity and will save yours, too. Let me share it with you."

Maxine listened intently to Georgiana and made the notes in her head. "That's very devious, Mom."

"Sometimes we have to be more, shall we say, creative to resolve our issues." When Georgiana spoke this time, her voice was subdued. "Do exactly as I said, dear. It will take some time to lay out the scheme to work properly, but when it does, you will have peace again. And remember, tell no one of your plans, especially not Animal Control."

The phone went quiet, leaving Maxine wondering who the woman she had spoken to was. Georgiana sounded unconventional, radical, broadminded, and even

Machiavellian. Yet, there was a normalcy to her that was strangely captivating.

Chapter 32

NORMAN DID NOT come to Maxine's rescue. Maxine felt as alone as when Jesse left. The crushing weight of aloneness was more than Maxine could bear, and she determined she would not allow herself to love anyone again.

Maxine needed a long cry, but there was no time for that. Maxine had only herself to rely on and gathered herself to deal with the issue at hand.

Steven was fast asleep on Maxine's living room chair. Maxine seized the chance to coax Carol Burnett out from under her bed. Cradling Carol Burnett in her arms, Maxine quietly made her way out of her apartment.

Dead tired, Maxine passed out in Buzzy's guest room, in her clothes, with Carol Burnett by her side until Bobo startled awake when he barked at six in the morning. Sprinting out of bed, Maxine went to the window. Maxine poked her head out. The cool air hit her face. The sky faded from darkness to light, and Maxine could see Becca in the backyard, watching Bobo relieve himself.

Tension running high, Maxine growled like a rabid dog, "Do you think it reasonable to let your goddamn dog bark at this hour on a Sunday, nonetheless? He startled me out of sleep."

A physiotherapist, Maxine wondered why Becca could not apply her intelligence to improve her self-awareness.

"He's a dog. It's what they do." Becca said in her whining voice without remorse or regard. Bobo barked his tacit agreement when he lowered his back leg.

"I know that the world revolves around you and your goddamn dog, but news flash, you live in a community. With. Other. Human beings. Be respectful of your neighbours who work all week and would like to sleep in on the weekend." Maxine pointed out, and Becca squished her long face as Bobo barked and wandered around the urine and feces-laden backyard. "You shouldn't have a dog if you don't have time to walk him. You shouldn't be visiting your ineptitude on us."

Becca was tall with dark eyes behind the wiry frame. Her dark hair was stark against the papery white long face with a pointy nose. Becca was rarely seen wearing anything other than jeans and a tank top, which she was wearing at the time.

"Your dog is the only one in a neighbourhood full of dogs that barks day and night. He's annoying, and his bark intrusive." Temper whipped colour into Maxine's face.

Bobo barked and set off, every dog within hearing range barking from inside their home. Becca's response to that was, "See, they're barking too."

Stunned by the absurdity of Becca's words, Maxine gaped at her sheer idiocy. "Bobo's barking is what set them off. None were barking until he started howling. Goes to show you how loud your goddamn dog is."

"I don't agree," Becca's high-pitched, whiny voice grated on Maxine's frail nerves.

"You are the worst neighbours Buzzy's had in the fifty years she's lived here. She's now forced to wear noise-cancelling headphones to sleep."

"That's your opinion," Becca said.

Bobo continued to bark, and every dog in the neighbourhood responded to his calls with their bark.

Maxine sighed and hissed in frustration. You can't fix stupid, and Becca was the embodiment of stupid. Or was it inconsiderate, selfish, or uncaring? Maxine decided it was all of the above,

"If you have no time to care for a dog, you shouldn't have one. How is it mine and the neighbour's problems that you cannot cope with your responsibility?" Maxine shouted and watched Becca stroll into the house, signalling for Bobo to follow. "That's right, walk away with your noisy fleabag," Maxine murmured as she turned to head into the bathroom to shower her anxiety away.

After slipping back on her slept-in clothes, Maxine fed Carol Burnett and made herself a cup of coffee and toast. Minutes later, Maxine walked around the house to her apartment.

The morning turned to an overcast, sunless December day, cold and leaden. Maxine wrapped her arms around herself to keep warm.

Biting down on her lip, Maxine nervously opened her basement apartment door. The apartment was ablaze in lights, and the spicy scent of Steven's cologne lingered in the air. Poking her head in, Maxine scanned the room for Steven. The last time Maxine saw Steven, he was slumped in her chair, snoring in his drunken stupor. Maxine did not see Steven in the chair, so she took a few steps into the apartment and listened. Maxine waited for the sound of a toilet flush or running water from the bathroom sink.

A loud few seconds of silence followed.

Maxine slowly and quietly took a few more steps into the apartment until she reached the bathroom door. Peeking through the wide open door, Maxine breathed a sigh of relief when she saw no sign of Steven. He was gone, and Maxine was glad about it. The last thing Maxine wanted to deal with was an awake Steven in the post-morning, hungover fog.

Maxine gathered her laptop and a change of clothes in her arms and closed the door to her apartment behind her. If Steven decided to return, she would not be there. Although she thought he would unlikely show his face, it was better to be safe than sorry.

Locking the door to her apartment, Bobo ran out of his house into the backyard and let out his usual booming bark, startling Maxine and making her jump. Maxine almost lost her grip on her laptop and the clothes in her arms.

Maxine's anger rising to the surface, she shouted, "Jesus, fucking, Christ!"

Bobo's dark eyes peeked through the gap between the fence slats. Maxine stared at him, her eyes blazing with pure contempt. Maxine was sure Bobo laughed at her before letting out a few more barks and triggering her anxiety.

"Shut the fuck up. Shut up, shut up, shut up." Maxine's infuriated scream made Bobo bark more and louder.

"Get back in the house, Bobo," Miles called, but Bobo ignored him.

Maxine tried to calm herself by envisioning the various ways to get back at Bobo and his parents. It did not work.

Maxine screamed, "Get control of your goddamn mutt." Whether Miles did not hear Maxine over Bobo's barks or purposely ignored her was up in the air.

Bobo was left outside to continue barking.

Maxine's mouth twisted into a nonverbal Jesus before she stormed away with Bobo's barks following her into Buzzy's living room.

Bobo's bark persisted, on and off, all weekend, heightening Maxine's already tightly coiled nerves.

Maxine shut her laptop, strode to the kitchen, and poured herself a generous glass of brandy—her third of the morning. Carol Burnett watched Maxine drink and pace the kitchen from her bed by the sliding door.

"Goddamn dog." Maxine drank the remaining brandy in her glass in a single pull.

Carol Burnett let out a bark of displeasure.

Maxine walked to Carol Burnett and affectionately stroked her neck. "I don't mean you, Carol Burnett. You have been raised right. I meant the horrible mongrel next door. Look at what Bobo does to me." Maxine held her shaking hand out for Carol Burnett to see. "Bobo does that to me. He makes me nervous, crazy, and anxious. I can't write. I can't think."

Maxine returned to the counter, picked up the bottle, and emptied the remaining brandy into her glass. Maxine sipped in contemplative thought. After last night's unsettling encounter with Steven and Bobo's relentless barking, Maxine found her nerves frayed and her creativity stifled.

"How am I supposed to write my set for Lisa's roast when my brain is in a fog and I can barely string two words together?"

Disinterested in Maxine's babbling, Carol Burnett rose and scratched the door to be let outside. That is until Bobo walked into his backyard and started barking for the umpteenth time that day. Hearing Bobo, Carol Burnett turned and headed out of the kitchen toward the living room.

That broke the camel's back, and Maxine dashed out into the backyard and proceeded to spray citronella oil on the fence and mist the air. The pungent smell stung the air.

"That's for Carol Burnett, you stupid crossbreed. She can't enjoy her stroll in the backyard because of you." Maxine screamed for all it was worth.

To Maxine's delight, the citronella smell sent Bobo to the other side of the backyard, and he barked noisily in Mrs. Livingstone's direction.

"Enjoy, you old bat. The dog's bark doesn't bother you, my ass." Maxine headed into the house and to the living room, where Carol Burnett was stretched out on the sofa.

Maxine walked to the bar cart. She poured a double shot from the brandy decanter into a snifter.

"I have one thing to look after. Afterward, how about you and I watch a Lassie flick, Carol Burnett, and zone out?"

Carol Burnett fixed her smiling black oval eyes on Maxine and woofed her approval.

"Sometimes, for your sanity, you must check your mind out of the moment," Maxine murmured, feeling her mind slide into a gray mist of despair.

The writing for Lisa's roast would have to wait until Maxine's head cleared.

Part III

The End

Cherish the victories in life, no matter how minor or few.

—M.L. Lexi

Chapter 33

MAXINE'S HEAD DID not clear the following day, the day after, or the day after. Maxine's nerves were frayed as her anxiety and irritability grew worse each day with Bobo's barking.

Maxine stepped out onto the porch and closed the door behind her after seeing the uniformed man on the security camera wandering outside her home. "May I help you?"

"Do you have any illegal devices in your backyard?" His voice was unwavering and impatient.

In his sixties, the man was about five-four but exuded an attitude suited for a more imposing figure. His pot belly bulged noticeably between the seams of his navy blue uniform jacket and pants. Gray wings at his temples peaked from beneath the blue cap. His eyebrows were thick and bushy above his hard hazel eyes. On his round, cherubic face, he had an authoritative look he could not carry off.

Maxine called her inner Maxi Bass after reading his confrontational body language and tone. Maxi Bass outmatched it when she said, "I'm not answering any questions until you identify yourself and tell me what this is about."

"I'm Officer Pope, a bylaw officer with the city." Pope retrieved his identification card and flashed it with authority. "There's a report by a neighbour that you have an illegal ultrasonic dog device displayed in your upstairs window," Pope said in a clipped tone, making it clear he was the law.

As if. "And who might this neighbour be?"

"That's not of concern." Pope's voice dripped with impatience. "Ultrasonic devices harm dogs and wildlife. It's why a bylaw doesn't permit their use." Pope cited the code and paragraph of the violation from memory.

"Ah, my next-door neighbours called in the complaint, and you took it as seriously as if I had stolen the nuclear codes. And here you are." Although Maxine spoke calmly, there was a bitter edge to her tone.

Maxine gave Officer Pope a long, sweeping glance. After months of enduring Bobo's barking and complaining to Animal Control, the man who did nothing to help stood at her front door attacking her. Maxine reacted like an alligator snapping at fresh meat.

"Officer Pope, where were you after my numerous emails to your office complaining about my neighbour's dog barking at ear-piercing levels day and night? Where were you when I begged you for help when that ear-piercing bark outside my bedroom window shocked me out of sleep or kept me awake? Where were you when I sent you the bark log your office requested, showing the barking timeline? That dog barks at midnight, at three-thirty in the morning. My inconsiderate neighbours let that horse out at six, six-twenty, and six-forty-five in the morning to pee and poo in the backyard because their life is too demanding to take that poor dog out for a walk as a responsible dog owner does." Maxine stopped to catch her breath.

"Where were you when I sent you photos of the feces-flowing backyard, which made it impossible for us to enjoy ours because the sweet smell of their dog's shit perfumed the air on hot summer days?" Maxine waited for Officer Pope's response. None came.

"They call you with a report of a device that doesn't exist, and you're here faster than a Japanese bullet train, which, based on your girth, was somewhat of a challenge. To top it off, you show up with attitude, and your mind is already made up. Well, Officer Pope, one, you shouldn't be here with this attitude." Maxine put one hand up, palm out and circled it. "And two, your question shouldn't be laced with flawed accusations. Your question should be, why do you need to use an ultrasonic device? And are you even a real policeman?"

Officer Pope's inflated ego swiftly deflated like a punctured balloon, and he wisely said nothing.

"To answer your question, Officer Pope, I have an ultrasonic device propped on the window ledge overlooking the neighbour's yard." Maxine saw his eyes lit up at the admission. Victory! "Don't look as if you found the Holy Grail. You can't pull it off. The ultrasonic device is a decoy. It doesn't work. I put it out hoping they would report me so I could get you here to listen to my side of the story, which you haven't bothered to do after all these months." Maxine said, ensuring she followed her mother's script to the letter.

"I'm nervous and anxious, my blood pressure is up, and I don't get enough sleep, which makes Maxine very cranky and brings out the super bitch in me, which is what you're enduring now. I'm usually a delightful person." Maxine's mouth lifted at one corner.

"The bitchy Maxine, who has determined you're going to be as useless as your entire department has been to date, says to get off her stoop. Oh, and by the way," Maxine opened the door, called Carol Burnett, and picked her up when she appeared. "I have a dog. Say hello to the pretend officer, Carol Burnett."

Carol Burnett let out a low-throated growl.

"As you can see, I'm a dog lover, which is more than I can say for you based on Carol Burnett's reaction," Maxine said, slamming the door behind her.

Maxine leaned back against the closed door, filled her cheeks with air, and exhaled. "Shit. Here's hoping he doesn't have grandchildren. It would be a bitch if I taught any of them."

Carol Burnett let out a soft bark.

"I know. The Maxi Bass in me is trouble. Anyway, phase one of the Georgiana Basset barking-dog-be-gone plan is complete. On to phase two."

Chapter 34

THE HIGH MAXINE rode on from telling her story to Officer Pope, swiftly deflated like a punctured balloon when Celia, Sister Fisk's secretary, knocked on the classroom door. The children and Maxine turned their eyes toward the door.

"Hello, children." Celia shuffled into Maxine's classroom.

"Good morning, Miss Tosh," the children said in unison.

"Sister Fisk wants to see you," Celia said in a low voice, making her way to Maxine's desk.

Celia was as portly as she was cherubic and smoothed out Sister Fisk's hard edges.

"What does she want to see me about, Celia?" Maxine's mind raced, and little flickers of fear danced along Maxine's spine. Being asked to Sister Fisk's office never ended well.

Maxine's first thought was that one of her students was Officer Pope's grandchild, and her brash approach was coming to bite her in the ass in the form of Sister Fisk.

"She didn't say, but don't look so worried and certainly don't look that fearful when sitting before Sister Fisk." Celia put a hand on Maxine's shoulder. "She hates weakness."

Maxine got the worry line between her eyebrows. "I'm in the middle of my morning class, Celia."

"I'll cover your class. Sister Fisk wants to see you now." Celia leaned in to say.

Feeling childlike, Maxine sat at one of the green padded chairs that lined the front office wall and waited to be called into Sister Fisk's office.

The front office, bright with light from the fluorescent ceiling fixtures, was a hive of activity. Telephones rang incessantly, and the constant hum of conversations from the clerical staff and teachers filled the office. At the front desk, students told centuries-old excuses for their tardiness.

Maxine had been a good student, obedient, and polite as a child. Maxine had never been summoned to the principal's office and felt a wave of nausea coming on.

Thoughts rolled in Maxine's head like a ticker tape. What did Sister Fisk need to communicate in person that could not be said through an email? Maybe it was about Officer Pope or Sister Fisk found out about her and Norman. Perhaps it was her tired appearance and zombie-like state. Sister Fisk had expressed concern about her tired state and nervous fidgeting. If that was the reason for being summoned to the scary office, how could Maxine explain that a dog was the cause of her fatigue? Sister Fisk would not believe such a sad ass excuse.

"I'm going to lose my job over a fucking dog," Maxine screamed in her head.

Sister Fisk emerged from her office, and Maxine thought she heard "The Imperial March" follow her out.

Sister Fisk's navy jacket over a shin-high skirt made her look boxy. The silver cross around her neck gleamed against the white, high-collar blouse, and her black rubber-sole shoes were buffed clean.

Sister Fisk walked young Marielle to the front desk and instructed the secretary to write her a late arrival slip. "Don't let it happen again, Marielle."

Marielle's hair was pulled back, highlighting her anxious eyes as she looked at Sister Fisk. "I won't, Sister Fisk. I promise it won't."

"See that it doesn't, Marielle. Now, get yourself to class."

"Yes, Sister Fisk." Mariella ran out of the office, her backpack bouncing with every step.

Sister Fisk turned to Maxine. "In my office."

"Yes, Sister Fisk." Maxine stood out of her chair and followed Sister Fisk step for step.

Sister Fisk's office was austere: a gray filing cabinet, a sideboard, a desk, and three guest chairs—for the parents and their misbehaving child. The office was orderly and neat as a pin. The manila folders on her desk were evenly lined, as was the pen beside them, and the laptop, at one corner, was precisely at a forty-five-degree angle. The desk was maple and polished to a gleam. Sister Fisk dialled up the cleanliness next to godliness credo to eleven.

Maxine did not believe Sister Fisk was a bonsai tree person, but the one on the sideboard below the unblinded window thrived.

Maxine remained standing across the desk from Sister Fisk until told otherwise. Nervously, she straightened the bow on her long-sleeve blouse and smoothed the front of her black pleated pants.

"Sit, Maxine." Sister Fisk ordered.

Maxine sat. "What did you want to see me about, Sister Fisk?"

"Sit up straight, Maxine," Sister Fisk commanded, and Maxine straightened her hunched shoulders.

Maxine watched Sister Fisk silently and slowly tap on her laptop keyboard with her index fingers. The thundering silence made Maxine's stomach churn.

Maxine opened her mouth to speak, and Sister Fisk raised a finger to silence her. Maxine pursed her lips.

Sister Fisk pressed play on the laptop screen and turned it toward Maxine without saying a word. Maxine watched Maxi Bass on the stage at Ba-Dum-Bump come to life. It hit Maxine like a backhanded slap on the face. Maxine felt the warmth of shock spreading into her body.

In the video, Maxine wore an off-the-shoulder red sequin dress with a seductive low cleavage. Her hair flowed in waves around a face painted in bronze eye shadow, blushed cheeks, and fire-red lips.

Maxine was genuinely surprised by this and said, "Shit," under her breath.

Of all the reasons for being called into the office, this was not what Maxine imagined. There was an unsettling feeling of nausea in the pit of her belly.

The silence in the room amplified Maxine's voice as she delivered the set about sexually frustrated nuns, leading with the joke of how they secretly satisfied their urges at a sex club called Sweet Jesus. Jesus was said with a Spanish inflection. The sound of roaring laughter from the audience followed.

The room became icily silent, and Maxine slid lower in her chair.

"Is that you, Maxine? Or should I say, Maxi Bass?" Sister Fisk looked from the frozen image on the screen to Maxine. "I see the resemblance. Barely."

Maxine lowered her gaze in the ensuing silence.

"I was sent this, and much to my dismay, had to watch the entire performance—that is what you call it?—because I didn't believe it was you."

Maxine's mind raced. Norman sent it. He did it out of pure spite. Or maybe it was Steven in retaliation for taking his home. It could also be any of the men she humiliated during her performances at the number of comedy clubs she performed.

There were so many suspects.

Maxine asked the first question that came to her mind. "Who sent it to you?"

"That's your concern after I tell you I was forced to watch this sexually explicit video?" Sister Fisk sunk back in her chair and stared at Maxine, whose body language said she wanted to die there and then. "You know there are a million words in the English dictionary to express ourselves. This is how you decide to string your words together. And the outfit, Maxine. Does your mother know how you present yourself to a drunken audience? You, a pastor's daughter."

The dreadful feelings of guilt, fright, and remorse settled inside Maxine.

"Does the staff here know about this?" Sister Fisk asked.

Maxine did not hesitate to answer Sister Fisk this time. "No. No one here knows. I kept that part of my life from everyone here," Maxine said with a straight face, looking Sister Fisk in the eyes.

"Hmmm." A shadow of doubt that Maxine was lying crossed Sister Fisk's face. "I understand you have been moonlighting as Maxi Bass for months. Is that correct, Maxine?"

Maxine nodded.

"Why, Maxine? Money, notoriety, attention, boredom. Why risk your job and spotless reputation."

Nothing Maxine could say would justify her actions to Sister Fisk, and she held back from responding.

"Well, Maxine, you have left me no option but to terminate your employment."

Maxine was immediately crestfallen on hearing this.

"Please don't fire me, Sister Fisk. I'll stop performing. I won't do it again. I won't, Sister. I promise I won't." Maxine sounded much like Marielle had minutes earlier.

"You leave me no choice, Maxine. St. Boniface cannot be associated with the likes of Maxi Bass or the crudeness you spew. What would our children's parents say? I couldn't in good conscience defend your actions when the topic is raised. I received the video in strict confidence, yet one individual has already uncovered your identity. It's a matter of time before your alter life is made public when that rabble-rouser sees you and starts flapping their gums. The blowback will be substantial then, and I'm not inclined to defend you or deal with this. I must nip it in the bud. Please pack your things."

The words filled Maxine with genuine regret—and relief. Her secret was out, as was the burden of carrying it and keeping it hidden from Beth. Maxine could tell the world about the alter ego she took on to forget Jesse and get on with her life.

"What about my class, my kids?" Maxine said when the terrible feeling of hollowness came over her.

"Celia will take over until I find a suitable replacement."

Maxine's weakened legs made it hard for her to get to her feet. When Maxine finally managed to rise from the chair, her head bowed and her face filled with sadness and regret, she walked out of the office.

Chapter 35

WITHOUT THE CONSTRAINTS of a job, Maxine was free to do what she wanted when she wanted. Maxine could concentrate on her stand-up career and prepare for her upcoming television appearance.

But Maxine did not. She could not.

Too many thoughts tumbled around Maxine's head. Maxine thought about her beloved job, the children she missed, and her struggle for survival. Without a reliable income, Maxine lived in a constant state of anxiety about her finances. What Maxine had thought to be a plentiful pot of gold of savings was not. The funds required for her daily existence and the house expenses quickly depleted her savings.

When thoughts of money, or the lack of it, did not fill Maxine's head, the aftermath that would befall her television appearance did. Maxi Bass had become a burden rather than her salvation, and marking a safe distance between her and her alter ego was what Maxine did.

Carol Burnett, wearing a silk red scarf and a red and green elf hat, lounged comfortably in front of the crackling fire of the living room fireplace. Uninterested, Carol Burnett watched Maxine decorate the Christmas tree she picked up from the local farm that morning. Outside, in the flash of sunshine, snow drifted to layer the existing white blanket that fell the previous day. From Maxine's playlist,

Miles Bublé's baritone voice flowed with a smooth rendition of "Santa Claus Is Coming to Town."

Maxine added tinsel to the tree branches where colourful lights and gold ball ornaments hung. The silver angel at the tree's top caught a quick strike of sunlight spilling from the living room's picture window and sparkled.

Fresh pine scent from the tree mingled with the aroma of applewood from the crackling fire in the fireplace. On the mantel hung three stockings stitched with Carol Burnett, Buzzy, and Maxine's name. The blond wood bookcase built into one wall matched the wood floors. It was filled with Buzzy's books and many awards. The key to the city, awarded by the mayor to Mortimer and Buzzy for their contribution to comedy, was on display.

There was a long pink upholstered sofa with colourful pillows and two burgundy wing chairs. Rosewood tables and a yellow area rug complemented the look. Buzzy loved colour; the bolder, the better.

The crystal vase on the console table overflowed with fresh roses, as Buzzy liked, and the bar cart was restocked with her favourite brandy.

"There, that's the last of the decorations." Maxine wore black leggings and a black hoodie with white trim. Her hair was wound into a bun, and she was makeup-less. "That looks great and very Christmassy. Buzzy is going to love it," Maxine said when she made the lights on the Christmas tree come to life.

"It certainly does, and I do," Buzzy said, walking into the living room. Buzzy looked healthily tanned and had a vacation glow on her face.

Under the faux-fur coat, Buzzy wore bright yellow Capri pants and a shirt with pelicans and toucans. Around her neck, she wore an exquisite ruby necklace Maxine had not seen before.

"You're home," Maxine said with genuine surprise.

With a massive grin, Carol Burnett bolted to her feet. Yapping excitedly, Carol Burnett raced forward and lunged into Buzzy's arms.

"Hello, my beautiful Carol Burnett. I've missed you." Buzzy kissed Carol Burnett on the head. "Mommy is never leaving you behind."

Carol Burnett's tail swished in excitement as she lapped Buzzy's face.

"She's missed you. Welcome back." Maxine hugged Buzzy affectionately when she set Carol Burnett down on the sofa. "You look great."

"As do you, dear. You look…." Buzzy looked Maxine up and down, "Relaxed?"

"A lot has happened since you left." Maxine gave her glasses a quick polish with a tissue. "A lot," she murmured.

"Well, you'll have to tell me about it over a hot cup of coffee." Buzzy breathed in the scented air, "Is that baking I smell?"

Maxine nodded. "I made a carrot cake for your homecoming with cream cheese frosting."

Buzzy's brow cocked. "You baked? And a cake with frosting nonetheless. There must be tons to tell."

"There is, and you have to tell me about that." Wide-eyed, Maxine reached for Buzzy's hand to look closer at the blinding diamond she saw on Buzzy's finger.

"In due time. How about that coffee and a slice of delicious carrot cake," Buzzy said, and Carol Burnett raced out of the living room in the direction of the kitchen. Buzzy smiled and linked her arm through Maxine's. "As great and as eventful the trip was, it's good to be home."

Over coffee and cake, Maxine told Buzzy about Sister Fisk firing her over the video she received. "As much as I hate losing my job, I feel free from the burden of the secret I've carried for months. A heavy weight lifted off my shoulders when I told Beth about Maxi Bass and explained why I hadn't done so sooner. Better than that, Beth said she understood why I kept Maxi Bass from her, but I could tell it was a lot to take in, and she was hurt. I'm giving her some time to digest it."

Buzzy set her cup on the table. "I'm sorry, dear. Do you know who sent Sister Fisk the video?"

Maxine shook her head. "Sister Fisk claims not to know and is a sixty-three-year-old nun and not so computer savvy."

"Unless she's surfing for porn," Buzzy tossed in.

Maxine's brow shot up. "You think?"

"She's human. I wouldn't be surprised if she screams his name," Buzzy pointed a finger upward, "As most do, as she's climaxing."

Maxine winced. "Christ, that's a disturbing image, Buzzy."

"Anyway, back to who sent Sister Fisk the video."

"It could have been anybody. It could have been…." Maxine stopped short.

"You think it was Steven."

Maxine gave Buzzy a stunned look. "Why would you say that?"

"Security cameras, dear. They're a wonder. Did you know you can access the video anywhere in this big world? I got an alert and saw the video from the night Steven showed up at your door. As much as the exchange looked cordial, I don't believe it was. Was it, Maxine?"

Maxine hesitated for a moment. She had already caused enough tension between mother and son and did not want to add to it. After some prodding from Buzzy, Maxine shook her head.

Instinctively, Buzzy lifted a hand and closed it over Maxine's. "I'm very sorry about that, Maxine. I only got to see the video from the stoop since there are no indoor cameras. So, you must tell me what Steven said that led you to invite him into your apartment."

After some prodding from Buzzy, Maxine laid out every detail of her exchange with Steven.

"I don't know who would have told him about our transaction. Only you, me, and my lawyer knew about it. I said nothing, and I know Terri Masters wouldn't either. She may have had a fling with Steven, but she's professional through and through. Did you tell anyone, Maxine?"

Maxine thought back, and only then the thought came to her. "I told Beth. My brain has been so fogged I forgot about that. She wouldn't tell anyone. She's my best friend." Maxine shook her head when she thought of her best friend plotting against her. "Besides, she doesn't know Steven."

Buzzy put away that information in her mental file for future reference. "What about Norman?"

"No. No, he would never betray me." Maxine watched Buzzy cut a slice of cake and set it on Carol Burnett's dish. "That's it for you, missy."

Carol Burnett lapped the cake and licked her lips before she strode to the backyard when Buzzy opened the door.

"I know Norman would never betray you. What I meant is, have you and Norman patched things up?" Buzzy closed the sliding door, reached for the pot of coffee resting on a hot plate, and walked it to the table.

Maxine shrugged her shoulders. "He hasn't called or come by."

"Oh, Maxine. If the mountain will not come to Muhammad, then Muhammad must go to the mountain."

"What's that supposed to mean?"

"It means suck it up, Maxine, and call him already. Talk to the boy."

Maxine creased her face into doubtful lines. "Since when do you believe women should bow to a man?"

"Since I realized that life is too short and you're not bowing to anyone when the decision to act is yours. It's why I proposed to Lester, and he accepted by giving me this ring." Buzzy raised her ringed hand in Maxine's face. "He and I got married on the ship. The captain married us before one thousand people. I'll show you the pictures later."

Maxine's face filled with delight. "Oh, Buzzy, I'm so happy for you. And it's so nice of you to make it a spectacular event. I just wished I'd been there, and I know Carol Burnett, too, feels the same."

Buzzy rose to let Carol Burnett in when she appeared at the sliding door. Buzzy waited for Carol Burnett to stroll out of the kitchen to say, "I know, dear, and don't let Carol Burnett know. I don't know how she will take us moving in with Lester." Buzzy watched Maxine over the rim of her cup for a reaction.

"I'm so happy for you, Buzzy." Maxine forced a smile to surface on her face.

"Are you, Maxine?"

"I am. I'm sad for me. You're leaving me." Maxine fought down tears that threatened to well up in her eyes.

Norman was gone, Beth had pulled away, and now Buzzy was leaving her. Maxine was as alone as could be.

"I'm not leaving you, dear. I'll be a short drive away, and you can visit me and Carol Burnett anytime. This is your home now, Maxine. I want you to make a life here."

Maxine shook her head sadly and opened the self-pity spigot. "I don't think I can without you, Buzzy. You've been like a mother to me. I love you."

Buzzy curled her hand tightly around Maxine's. "And I love you, dear, but it's time for you and me to make a life for ourselves with the men we love."

"How can you say that? You just met Lester, and suddenly you're in love with him," Maxine snapped, but Buzzy understood it was out of fear of change that she had.

"Honey, I've known Lester for as long as I knew Morty. They were friends. I'll admit I love Lester like a friend. Lester knows I could never love anyone as much as I love Morty, but at this age, what we both want is companionship. And the sex doesn't hurt. Lester's a tiger in bed."

Maxine squished up her face. "Jesus, Buzzy, too much information."

Buzzy sputtered out a laugh. "I know, but I had to brag."

"I'm happy for you and Lester, and you're renewed— you know?—bedroom life. But is it wrong that I'm sad for me for losing you?"

"You haven't lost me or Carol Burnett, dear," Buzzy said as reassuringly as she could. "If anything, you've gained a friend. Lester has lived a colourful life and could be a great source of information on the male species."

Maxine held up a hand when Bobo's bark intruded into their conversation. Buzzy watched Maxine pick up the remote off the counter and click it, emitting a beeping sound.

"Listen," Maxine said, flashing a Cheshire Cat grin at Buzzy when Becca called Bobo back into the house.

Buzzy glanced at Maxine quizzically. "Don't keep me in suspense."

Chapter 36

MAXINE COLLECTED THE dirty dishes and walked them to the sink. "Aside from the barking you heard a few minutes ago, have you heard Bobo bark since your arrival?"

Buzzy thought about that. "Now that you mention it. No, I haven't."

"Believe it or not, it was Mom's idea." Maxine ran a soapy sponge over the dishes. "Since doing what she told me, Bobo barks ninety percent less."

"Yay, Georgiana." Buzzy handed Maxine her empty coffee cups. "And what has Georgiana told you to do?"

Maxine rinsed the dishes and cups and set them on the dishrack. "She told me to display the ultrasonic device in full view for Becca and Miles to see, which I did. Mom said they would call Animal Control to report me when they saw the device. They did. Mom also said Animal Control would have a by-law officer appear at my door the next day because a dog's welfare eclipses everyone else's."

"That doesn't sound like a winning outcome." Buzzy covered the leftover carrot cake with the glass lid.

"I'm not done. The device wasn't operating, so the Wannabe Officer couldn't charge me. While the Wannabe Officer was here, I set him in his place for his office's incompetence and sent him off with his tail between his legs. Phase one of the plan was completed, and I moved to phase two. That night, in darkness, I placed three key-finder receivers in strategic locations around the backyard. I click on this every time Bobo barks." Maxine held up the remote for Buzzy to see. "Setting off a random receiver so the noise travels, and Becca and Miles can't pinpoint where the sound originates. Each click emits a loud beep, which Becca and Miles assume to be an ultrasonic device that will hurt Bobo."

"But it's not a dog bark deterrent. You know I'm not a fan of those gadgets. I only permitted you to purchase one because my frustration at Bobo's constant barking trumped my moral code." Buzzy reached into the pantry for the brandy bottle and gestured for Maxine to get two glasses from the cupboard.

"I know, and I'm sorry I talked you into that. The FOBs are key trackers. Not illegal. If the By-Law Officer shows up, we won't get into trouble. Although I suspect he won't arrive at our door soon."

Buzzy poured a finger of the amber liquid into the two glasses Maxine set on the table. "What makes you so sure?"

"It's been several days since I've been clicking away, and he hasn't shown up. This leads me to believe that Mom was right: Miles and Becca were warned about Bobo's barking and possibly threatened with a fine if it continued. Becca and Miles don't want to risk it by calling him. Bobo's barking hasn't completely vanished but has decreased to a bearable level. With inconsiderate it's-all-about-us neighbours such as Becca and Miles, I call it a success. Carol Burnett has been able to enjoy the backyard, and I've been able to get a restful night's sleep for the first time in months. I'm not anxious or as stressed anymore."

"Yay, Georgiana and her spawn."

"To me and Mom, indeed."

"And how deliciously Machiavellian. If the Pavlovian effect doesn't work on the dog, turn it on its owners," Buzzy said admiringly. "I told you every good person has a little bit of bad in them. We all have a touch of Lucifer in us, even Georgiana."

"It seems we do."

"Here's to Georgiana, you, and Beelzebub." Buzzy tapped her glass to Maxine's.

Chapter 37

AS STEVEN PUSHED open the office door and walked in, he came eye-to-eye with Norman sitting behind his desk, tapping on the computer's keyboard. Steven's expression went steely.

"What the fuck are you doing here and on my computer?" The anger pulsed in Steven's voice.

Norman's startled eyes flew from the computer screen to Steven. "Jesus! You startled me."

Norman wore jeans and a brown-navy plaid shirt over a white T-shirt. Norman's hair, mussed around his face, looked almost blue under the sunlight streaming from the window behind the desk. The office was not as tidy as Steven liked, but the new occupant, Jack Sievers, unlike Steven, put in a full day's work.

"That's the reaction of a guilty man, so I ask again. What the fuck are you doing at my computer?" Steven said, his voice rising, hardening

From where he sat, Norman thought he could see Steven's neck vein pulse. It greatly pleased Norman.

The one-hundred-dollar haircut, Ferragamo shoes, Italian leather jacket, Gucci jeans, and expensive cologne did nothing to conceal the asshole Steven was.

Norman hated Steven with every fibre of his being. Steven was the man who came between him and Maxine and caused their rift.

It had been weeks since Norman heard or spoke to Maxine because of Steven's lies and manipulation. Norman was angry at Maxine for not believing him and taking Steven's word over his. But Norman loved and missed Maxine enough to overlook her disbelieving him and take Steven's side.

"I don't believe this is your computer anymore, and I have permission from Buzzy and Jack Sievers to access the club's security camera files." Knowing it would irk Steven, Norman's voice lingered on Jack Sievers's name.

Jack Sievers's name drew scorn and outrage from Steven. "I don't give a shit what Mom and Jack told you. It's my office, and that's my computer."

From downstairs, the sounds of clinking bottles as the bar was restocked, scraping chairs, the drone of a vacuum cleaner, and chat between the staff as they prepped the club for tonight's show were heard.

"It's neither your office nor your computer, dear," Buzzy said, walking into the office. She thought she could smell the testosterone permeating the air.

Buzzy wore lavender Capris, tan ankle boots, and a bright lemon-yellow shirt. Her face glowed with honeymoon bliss.

"Get the fuck away from me, you mongrel." Steven kicked Carol Burnett away when she snarled at him. Fast on her feet, Carol Burnett moved far enough to avoid Steven's swinging foot.

"Carol Burnett adores everyone but you, Steven." Buzzy set one of the two cups of coffee on the desk before Norman. "Why is that?"

Outside, a fire truck went screaming by, and a police siren followed.

"Who cares? She's a dog, Mother." Steven snarled back at Carol Burnett.

Carol Burnett did not cower as Steven aimed to do.

"Your brother didn't mean that, Carol Burnett. Still, you best get away from him." Buzzy waved Carol Burnett to the sofa, and she hopped onto the soft velvet and stretched out.

Carol Burnett wore one of the many silk scarves with a nautical motif that Buzzy brought back from her Mediterranean cruise.

"I've told you before, don't refer to me as her brother," Steven told Buzzy, who rounded the desk and stood behind Norman, watching the video play on the computer screen.

"Anyway, this office and everything within its four walls, including the computer, is temporarily Jack's property," Buzzy pointed out and watched Steven's lips close in a long, firm line as he walked to the tray of glasses and bottles on the sideboard. "It's ten o'clock in the morning, dear," Buzzy said when Steven generously poured Irish whiskey into his glass.

"Like mother like son." Steven's eyes laser-focused on Buzzy as he polished off half of the whiskey in his glass.

Buzzy lifted her coffee cup in a half-salute. "Touché, dear."

"What the fuck are you looking for?" Steven glared at Norman.

Buzzy rested a hand on Norman's shoulder to stop him from reacting to Steven's bait. Taking a deep breath, Norman twisted his jaw and remained silent.

"Language, Steven. I didn't spend a small fortune on your schooling to speak so vulgarly." Buzzy nodded at Norman when he pointed a finger at the image that surfaced on the screen. "To answer your question, this is what my computer whizz Norman was looking for at my request."

With a gotcha smile, Norman happily turned the computer screen for Steven to see. The image of the woman and him, sitting at the secluded table by the corner, lustfully eyeing each other, blindsided Steven.

"How long have you known her, Steven?" Buzzy asked.

Steven waved his hand in an airy dismissal. "She was a one-night stand."

Buzzy creased her face into doubtful lines. Steven and the woman looked as intimate with one another as two people sharing secrets that bound them as more than acquaintances.

"How long, Steven?" Buzzy repeated.

"Several weeks." Steven finished the last of his whiskey.

"What did you get in return for the expensive jewellery you gifted her? Aside from warming your bed, of course." Buzzy sat on the sofa beside Carol Burnett, who had fallen asleep. Too much drama.

"That's rich, Mother. You judging." Steven eyed the diamond ring on Buzzy's finger. "That's a great necklace and ring. Expensive. How is stepdad?"

Norman followed the direction of Steven's eyes and, for the first time, saw Buzzy's wedding ring.

"Don't be so crass, Steven. And I should think you'd be happy I married Lester. His fortune is far greater than mine."

"It's not as if I'm going to see any of his money." Steven took out a pack of cigarettes and shook one out. Buzzy was about to point out the no-smoking rule but thought that whatever she said ended up on deaf ears. "I mean, you, my mother, are denying me access to my entitled trust fund and a decent lifestyle. Christ! You've given your house, which I'm entitled to, to Maxine."

Norman's eyes suddenly filled with shock, and he gaped at Buzzy. "You what?"

Steven took in a deep lungful of smoke and exhaled it as his eyes scanned Norman. The look of disbelief in Norman's eyes was genuine. "You didn't know. And here I thought you'd be cashing in on Maxine's windfall."

Norman's brow lifted scathingly at Steven before he turned to Buzzy. "When did this happen?"

Buzzy crossed her legs. "I'll deal with you after I'm done with my son," Buzzy said, and a terrible sense of impending trouble snaked down Norman's spine.

Norman fell silent.

"You're receiving a very generous stipend for doing nothing, Steven. Why do children assume they automatically own their parents' money and holdings? Whatever I own is mine to do as I wish. And Maxine has been more of a daughter than you have been a son."

Steven crushed out his cigarette with one quick thrust. "Jesus, Mother, you've known her for a few months. I'm your son."

"You are, and it's why I'm being tough on you, Steven. Your father was right when he said I was too soft on you, and I'd live to regret it."

"So, now you're regretting me." Steven snatched the whiskey bottle and poured another shot. Polishing it, he refilled his empty whiskey glass.

"I'm regretting spoiling you, Steven. I don't like the person you've become. I don't appreciate your disrespect for women. I don't like your taking advantage of the performers relying on the cheque to survive. Your father and I would go out of our way to help them, but you have been stealing from them to the tune of one million dollars."

Steven did not look surprised nor gave Buzzy a remorseful look.

"But then you knew that, didn't you, Steven?" There was a moment of silence as Buzzy studied her son's guiltless face. "I don't like how you assume the world owes you a comfortable living and how you'll take it by any means. Well, Steven, I will do now what I should have done long ago."

Steven laughed a sneering laugh. "Be a real mother?"

Feeling awkward, as if he did not belong there, Norman rose to step out of the office to give Buzzy and Steven the privacy they needed.

"I think there's more footage for you to dig up, Norman," Buzzy said, and Norman sat back down. Buzzy turned to Steven. "I'll admit I wasn't the cuddly mother type when you were growing up you would have liked, Steven. Your father and I had more pressing issues, like putting a roof over your head and food on the table." Buzzy waved a hand to silence Steven as he opened his mouth. "It's not an excuse. It's a fact, and all I can do is apologize. I and your father could have devoted more time to you, but then you would have blamed us for not providing for you. It's a fine line poverty has a parent walking."

Steven took another pull of his whiskey.

"Everything your father and I did, we did for you," Buzzy said. "You were never short of love. You knew you were loved."

"Sounds like a seventies song." Steven put a fresh cigarette in his mouth, lit the cigarette, and inhaled deeply.

In the background, Norman tried his best to focus on the footage on the screen rather than the unfolding family drama.

Buzzy went on. "Guilt, however, had me providing you with anything you wanted without expectation. I now realize that was another mistake that contributed to the man you are today." Buzzy's eyes held an expression of regret. "As much as it pains me, Steve, I must correct this. You're too old to change your ways, but I hope the experience will teach you a lesson."

Steven stopped his cigarette half raised to his lips and stared at Buzzy for a minute. "What does that mean?"

Chapter 38

STEVEN SLAMMED THE glass on the sideboard. "I asked what that meant, Mother." Steven watched Buzzy walk to the sideboard, pick up the brandy bottle, and pour it into a crystal glass. "I asked you a question, Mother?"

"Patience was never your strong suit. Was it, dear?" Buzzy walked around the desk and looked over Norman's shoulder at the screen when he pointed to it. "First, you tell me how long you've known Beth Caplan? You know? The blonde woman in the security footage." Buzzy sipped on her brandy, waiting for her son's response.

Although Norman did not look away from the computer screen, he listened intently

"A few weeks," Steven admitted after a short silence.

Buzzy's and Norman's brows cocked simultaneously.

"Was that so difficult, dear? And what did you get from her?"

Steven hesitated.

"Did you know she set you up?" Buzzy stared at her son for his response.

Steven's face took on a dismissive look. "What are you talking about? She would never use me. She thought she was in love with me."

Norman threw back his head and laughed raucously. "You're such a smug bastard. Beth says that to every man."

"Shut the fuck up," Steven growled.

Buzzy turned to Norman. "No need to get too cocky. She played you, too."

Startled on hearing this, Norman sat up straight in his chair. "What are you talking about?"

"Beth played both of you like a fiddle. You'd be smart to remember that women are more cunning than men. They know best how to manipulate you to benefit their interests. Hell hath no fury like a woman scorned. The question is, how did you scorn her, Norm? I know how Steven did it, but how did you?" Buzzy said.

Norman shrugged his shoulders when he cast his mind back and could not come up with a plausible answer.

"Did she tell you that she loved you after an amorous encounter?" The look Buzzy aimed at Norman was sharp enough to stir his memory.

Steven scoffed. "Why would she be interested in him?"

Norman let out a small sigh and shook his head, now remembering. "It was a long time ago. We were both so drunk. She never said anything after that night. I didn't think she remembered. We were both so drunk," Norman repeated in a murmur.

"Well, she did and decided it was time for payback. I'm guessing for your neglect. It's always like a man to be neglectful after getting their itch scratched. In getting back at you, Steven and Maxine became targets." Buzzy rolled her eyes to the ceiling when she saw Norman and Steven's eyes filled with confusion. "Men are so dense." Buzzy walked to the sofa and sat in the seat she had vacated. Carol Burnett stirred, looked at Buzzy, Steven, and Norman and returned to sleep. "We could propound a theory."

Steven fell back into the wing chair, but not before refreshing his drink. "Propound away, Mother. You always did have a great imagination."

"Listen closely and learn, boys. Steven saw Maxine as a challenge and was eager to add her to his list of romantic conquests. Your ego couldn't stand it when she rebuffed your advances and pursued her harder when Maxine wanted nothing to do with you, Steve. Your repeated attempt to win over Maxine failed, and you decided to take revenge because of your wounded ego. Do I have that right, Steven?"

Steven said nothing.

"I haven't pieced yet whether you pursued Beth or if serendipity played a part in bringing you together. Although knowing Beth as I do now, she likely made it so your paths crossed. Which one was it, Steven?" Buzzy sipped on her brandy as she waited for his response. "I'm waiting, Steven."

"She was in the audience and bumped into me at the club one night," Steven said.

Buzzy shook her head. "No, she didn't. It was all calculated on Beth's part. Beth must have seen Maxine perform at the club and caught your interaction with her. You were brazen with her on stage. A blind person could have seen your act, Steven. Beth must have seen you there, too, Norman. Beth likely resented you and Maxine for not telling her about Maxi Bass and her moonlighting job. Although I sense Beth resented Maxine more so than she did you. Maxine was her best friend, and you don't keep secrets from your best friend."

Steven's attention was as riveted on Buzzy as Norman's.

"As I said, hell hath no fury like a woman scorned by her best friend or a man. Hurt, angry, and resentful, that's when the plot formed in her head," Buzzy said.

"You do have a wild imagination, Mother."

"Maybe, but follow the thread to its logical conclusion, boys. You were with Beth the night you showed up at Maxine's door drunk to harass her because Beth told you about me gifting Maxine my house." Buzzy signalled Norman to turn the computer screen toward Steven when he remained quiet. "That's you and her at the club. Notice the time stamp. It was an hour before you appeared at Maxine's door. You look pretty inebriated there, Steven. Were you?"

Steven lifted his shoulders in a shrug.

"I'm going to take that as a yes. You must learn to control your drinking, Steven. I will not have you stumbling through the club or anywhere like a drunken fool." Buzzy held up a silencing hand when Steven began to speak. "Riled up by the revelation of Maxine's inheritance, you had to confront her and set off to her place. I only hope you didn't drive yourself there."

Shoulders hunched, Steven shook his head.

"Hopefully, you're not lying to me because, Steven, if you are and I find out you sat behind the wheel drunk, I will have Jack confiscate your car."

In a surge of fury, Steven barked, "You can't do that."

"I can, dear. That Maserati you so love is a company car, and since I own this company, I can take it away anytime I like." The Cold, steely glint of Buzzy's gray eyes told Steven she meant what she said.

Steven thought it best not to press his luck and remained quiet.

"Back to Beth's scheming. Knowing you were on your way to Maxine's apartment, Beth got Norman there to witness the interaction that she hoped would be misconstrued by him. Her plan worked perfectly when you pushed your way into Maxine's apartment, and Norman's jealousy had him imagining all sorts of scenarios except the actual one." Buzzy looked over at Norman. "If you had stuck around long enough, you would have seen Maxine leave Steven in the apartment when she went upstairs to the main floor. Maxine slept in the guest room that night. Alone. Well, not completely alone. Carol Burnett slept beside her."

A rueful expression settled on Norman's face.

"You, dear, are the poster child for assumption."

Norman frowned. "What do you expect? Maxine took his side when I told her he was manipulating her and not allowing me entry into the club."

"Yes, she did. However, she was manipulated by Steven, who in turn was manipulated by Beth. And round and round we go. Imagine if you people put that angry energy toward more productive purposes. You wouldn't be a depraved drunk who believes the world owes him, and you, Norman, would still have the most important person in your life with you. Life is too short to be expending energy on nonsense. Carpe diem, boys. You'll be carried away in a box before you realize it."

"Jesus, Mom. You're a ray of sunshine."

"This is wisdom from a woman who's seen a lot and done much," Buzzy said. "That being said, Norman, I suggest you go off and beg Maxine for forgiveness so that she takes your sorry ass back."

Norman exchanged a pointed look with Buzzy. "Why do I need to do the apologizing? It takes two to tango."

"You silly, boy. I'm going to say this once. Hopefully, you will etch it in your thick skull. Accepting that the man is always at fault sustains a happy relationship, whether true or not. Go, get your girl. Apologize your ass off to Maxine. She'll take you back."

Norman sighed and rubbed his hands over his face. "What if she doesn't? She doesn't even trust me enough to tell me what Jesse did to her."

"I know she won't turn you away and will tell you her secrets when ready. Maxine misses you as much as you do her. I will deny saying that if you tell her I said so." Buzzy smiled at Norman warmly. "Go."

Norman jumped to his feet when commanded and ran out of the office.

Buzzy looked at Steven, lighting his fourth cigarette, and said, "Now, on to you, son."

Steven plucked the cigarette from his mouth. "What about me?"

Chapter 39

NORMAN GOT ON his hands and knees and begged Maxine for forgiveness. Norman accepted responsibility for causing the rift between them. He went as far as admitting to lying to Maxine, although he had not. Steven had, but as Buzzy said, if Norman wanted Maxine back, it was what he had to do.

Norman swallowed his pride and pleaded with Maxine to take him back. Norman reached deep into his heart and said what he had not before.

"I love you, Maxine. It's always been only you. My heart is yours if you'll have it," Norman said, and Maxine's wall of anger and resentment crumbled.

After Norman uttered those three lovely words and everything that followed, Maxine's heart filled to overflowing, and the wall she had erected came crashing down.

Norman sat with Maxine on her sofa, sharing a bottle of wine, when Buzzy let herself into the apartment. A cold draft that carried the sharp tastes of winter followed Buzzy in before she closed the door behind her.

"Boundaries, Buzzy. You can't just let yourself into my apartment," Maxine said. "What if Norman and I were … occupied."

Buzzy set Carol Burnett on the floor and tossed her handbag, coat, and keys onto the closest chair. Buzzy had a weary look on her face and a worn-out look in her eyes.

A look borne out of the disappointment for the callous, selfish man her son was. For the man, she blamed herself for creating.

"As you always say to me, TMI. Besides, Carol Burnett and I announced ourselves before walking in." Buzzy fell back into the chair opposite Norman. "You two look cozy."

"Norman and I have patched things up. He's accepted responsibility for the misunderstanding." Maxine made air quote signs with her forefinger around the word *misunderstanding.*

Buzzy was happy to hear no resentment or anger in Maxine's voice anymore. "Has he now? It's a wise man who takes responsibility for his mistakes," Buzzy commented with a wink.

Carol Burnett ran toward the cupboard where Maxine stored her treats and barked for service.

"Will you join us in a celebratory drink of wine?" Maxine walked to the cupboard and tossed Carol Burnett a Milk-Bone, which she caught midair and got busy chomping.

"My baby is hungry. I haven't had a chance to feed her lunch yet." Buzzy kicked her patent ballerina shoes off and flexed her feet.

"Follow me to the laundry room, Carol Burnett. Auntie Maxine will set you up with a food and water dish." Maxine did not finish her sentence when Carol Burnett made a mad dash toward the laundry room with the Milk-Bone in her mouth.

"After you do that, I'll join you in that celebratory drink, but I'd prefer a shot of brandy," Buzzy called out to Maxine.

"When Maxine was out of hearing range, Norman murmured, "I didn't tell her about Beth's duplicity or uncovering she sent Sister Fisk the Maxi Bass video."

"Best you didn't. She may have misread it as you throwing Beth into the mix to save your butt. Besides, now's not the right time to bring it up. Leave it to me to break it to her. I want to have a woman-to-woman chat with Beth before telling Maxine. I have a suspicion she's not only been manipulating Steven and you but also filling Georgiana's head with her brand of bullshit. I'll tell Maxine when the time is right. You, however, must tell Maxine about your liaison with Beth."

"It wasn't a liaison. It was a drunken mistake, and I told Maxine. She saw it as that and history. The fact Beth hasn't called her worked in my favour."

"Good. Did Maxine tell you everything?" Buzzy said.

"If you're referring to Jesse, she did," Norman said.

"So, you understand that Maxine didn't believe Steven's lies about you no more than she doubted you."

Norman nodded. "I think so. When your fiancé takes his life, and you find him spread out in your shared bed, it leaves you with the overwhelming guilt and the belief you caused it. On top of her grief of loss, Maxine is still struggling to cope with that guilt. By Maxine's grief-stricken logic, walking away from me when our quarrels and disagreements escalated was her way of protecting me from doing what Jesse did. By her logic, Maxine walked away from us to protect me."

"You're not just a pretty face, Norman McDonnell," Buzzy said, impressed with Norman's compelling observation. "Maxine has been through a lot, and although she looks well put together, she has much to sort out."

"I understand that now," Norman acknowledged.

"You need to be committed to supporting her plight, Norman, if you're going to marry her. Yes, Norman, I saw the diamond ring on her finger. Very tasteful, by the way."

Whoever said vision deteriorates with age did not know Buzzy Morgan, Norman thought. "Thanks."

"Maxine needs an understanding shoulder, a strong one to cry on to help her get through the trauma she's dealing with. Maxine will need a listening ear. More than that, she needs unconditional love."

Norman turned to look Buzzy in the eye. "And I will give it to her. I will give Maxine all that. I love her, Buzzy. Deeply."

"I know you do, dear, and I'm glad to hear your dedication to her because you'll have me to deal with if you deny her what she needs. I may be old, but I'm a force to be reckoned with." Buzzy warned, but her voice was light.

"What are you two whispering about?" Maxine reached into the pantry for the brandy bottle and poured it into a glass.

Buzzy took the offered brandy glass. "I'm telling Norman how happy I am to hear you two are back together. You belong together." Buzzy stretched her tired feet on the coffee table and crossed them at the ankles.

"Not only are we back together, but Norman proposed." Maxine held her ringed hand out for Buzzy to see.

Buzzy feigned genuine surprise as she eyed the ring. "It's beautiful, Maxine. Our boy has great taste in jewellery."

Maxine sat back in her seat, surprised. "You didn't help him pick it out?"

"I did not. I didn't know Norman was proposing, but I'm thrilled for you. For both of you." Buzzy embraced Maxine and Norman. "You're soulmates meant to be together. So, have you discussed any plans? I mean, aside from doing the tango tonight. You have some catching up to do." Buzzy winked at Norman and made his face turn bright red.

Maxine bit back a smile. "Stop teasing Norman, Buzzy."

"Let me enjoy it. I missed doing that." Looking more relaxed now, Buzzy sipped her brandy.

With a satisfied look, Carol Burnett entered the room and leapt onto the vacant sofa cushion. Carol Burnett put her head on her front paws and settled in for a nap.

"I've made a decision, which I'd like to share with both of you now." Maxine turned to Buzzy. "Don't get upset, Buzzy, but I decided to step away from Maxi Bass and walk away from the television gig. Please don't be angry with me."

Automatically, Buzzy reached for Maxine's hand. "I'm neither upset nor angry, dear. It's your life. I want you to be happy, as I know Norman does."

"Ditto," Norman said.

"Thank you. For days, my stomach tossed and turned at the idea of telling you after all you did for me." For the first time in a long time, Maxine experienced a feeling of calm and peace flowing through her.

"Honey, I don't ever want you to feel nervous about telling me what's on your mind," Buzzy said, and Norman echoed the sentiment. "We, Norman and I, love you and want you to feel you can talk to us about Jesse, your doubts, your fears, your dreams, or anything weighing you down. Understood?"

"We're in this together, Maxine," Norman's hand closed over Maxine's.

"I'm glad you said that because I have another announcement. "I'm unemployed…."

"We know that, dear." Buzzy rested her head on the back of the chair and closed her eyes.

The time had come for her to redefine herself, and Maxine said, "What I meant to say is with the club and TV work behind me, I have plenty of free time now. So, I've decided to write a children's book. It's going to be called Sir Barks-A-Lot. It will be about a golden doodle dog with white curly hair and inconsiderate, selfish parents who make him the pariah of the neighbourhood. Sir Barks-A-Lot doesn't like his name and wants to be accepted by the neighbourhood children and his animal friends, so he sets out to become a likeable dog. The book's underlying message is to teach children with dogs to be thoughtful and respectful of their neighbours."

"That sounds wonderful, dear, and with first-hand knowledge, you should have a best seller on your hands," Buzzy said just as Bobo's bullhorn-loud bark pierced the afternoon silence.

Casually, Maxine reached over for the remote, which she kept close by and clicked. Two loud beeps went off, followed by another two when Bobo barked again. Miles's irritating, nasally voice beckoned for Bobo to return indoors.

Maxine went on. "This is where you and your patience come in, Norman. I have some money left, but not enough to pay house expenses and live on. I thought about finding a part-time job. It will generate some income and allow me to write by day and work a few hours nightly. So, I won't be able to spend much time with you right now."

"If this is what you want to do…."

"It is, Norman."

"Then, I fully support you." Norman's hand closed tighter over hers. "You don't need to take on a part-time job. We're a team. I'll financially help you."

Maxine shook her head vehemently. "No. I can't have you do that. This is something I want to do for myself."

"I know, and I want to help you accomplish it. I want to be a part of your success."

"I don't know about success." Maxine pushed herself out of her chair and paced the room. "Writing a book is risky business, and a children's book, from what I've read, is the riskiest. It'll take time to get sales. That is if I even get any."

Norman's eyes volleyed back and forth as Maxine paced the room. "I know that, Maxine. Your dreams are my dreams, and I'll be by your side every step of the way."

Maxine's throat choked up, and tears ran into her eyes.

"I would expect you to do the same for me," Norman said.

Maxine bent down and touched her lips to Norman's. "And I would do it without a second thought."

"Then what's the problem?" Norman said.

Buzzy sighed heavily. "I feel like I'm in the middle of a bad Mexican novella. Maxine will write her book, and you, Norman, will not need to support her financially." Buzzy turned toward Maxine. "Steven owes you eighty-five thousand dollars, including penalty fees I tacked on for cheating you out of money you rightly earned."

There was a short silence among them.

"I need a refill." Buzzy held out her glass to Norman. "While there, see if you can round up a sandwich. I'm starving."

Norman hauled himself to his feet. "I'll see what I can do."

Buzzy gave Maxine her eyes. "The theft was discovered during the forensic accounting that Lester's firm performed on the club's financial records. As it turns out, and as I suspected, Steven has been defrauding performers. The investigation is ongoing, but as I suspected, Steven's been bilking performers of their hard-earned money."

Speechlessly, Maxine pinned her eyes on Buzzy and stared.

Norman walked to her the refreshed glass of brandy, which Buzzy needed. "I found pork chops, potatoes, and the ingredients for a salad in the refrigerator," Norman said, not knowing why.

Carol Burnett snapped out of sleep and barked at the mention of pork chops.

"Carol Burnett and I think that sounds heavenly. Buzzy took a sizeable, numbing gulp of brandy. "Get to it, Normie boy. We're hungry."

With a nod, Norman returned to the kitchen and got to work on peeling potatoes and marinating the pork chops. Carol Burnett followed Norman, plopped her butt on the floor, and looked up at him with an anticipatory look in her eyes.

"Steven will transfer the funds into your account within a week," Buzzy told Maxine when the brandy smoothed her out some.

Disinclined to come further between mother and son, Maxine only slightly hesitated before she said, "No, Buzzy. Steven doesn't need to do that. You've been generous enough."

Norman smashed a clove of garlic with the knife's blade and chopped it quickly and precisely. Norman added the chopped garlic, salt, pepper, and Worcestershire sauce to three pork chops. He set the chops aside to marinade and moved on to dress the potatoes before he put them into the oven.

"Steven will pay you and every performer he cheated every dime. It's what I want, what I must have him do. I've spoiled him all his life, and I'm not proud of the outcome. It will not do," Buzzy said. "In return, though, I need something from you, Maxine."

Chapter 40

MAXINE NO LONGER felt adrift.

With Norman and Buzzy's help and that of her therapist, Dr. Foyle, Maxine was working through her guilt, and Jesse was becoming a chapter of her past. Once Dr. Foyle dug deep into Maxine's psyche, she was able to work through the gnawing guilt and had her rethinking every past and present decision. With Dr. Foyle's help, Maxine could shake herself from the emotional constraints and understand that Jesse's actions were his.

Recognizing she was not to blame for Jesse's choices, Maxine opened up to Georgiana about what he did. Not many things got under Georgiana's skin, but hearing, for the first time, the reason for Jesse's departure did. Whether Georgiana felt partially responsible for Jesse's actions or guilty that his death broke her daughter, for the first time in her life, she reconciled her faith with her actions.

With Norman and Buzzy's support, Maxine wrote her book. Sir Barks-A-Lot, an illustrated hardcover, was selling better than Maxine anticipated. Sir Barks-A-Lot was inching up on the best-seller list, and Maxine's bank account quickly reached levels she did not imagine possible.

Maxine missed teaching and her children. She hoped to get back to it when memories faded. Everything had a shelf life.

After learning about Beth's scheming and learning she had sent Sister Fisk the Maxi Bass video, Maxine's heart broke before she filled with sadness. That her best friend could hurt her as she had was something Maxine could not come to terms with. Maxine made no effort to reach out to Beth, and Beth did not either. Trusting Beth again would take time, and Maxine was not there yet. Besides Maxine's broken trust, she imagined Beth would not react well when she discovered that Norman proposed to her and they were planning their wedding.

Steven paid the one million dollars he stole from the handful of performers over the years. Steven thought limiting his theft from new performers who would rather sacrifice money over stage time would not raise attention. His scheme may have worked had he not stolen the money from Maxine at Beth's prodding.

"You thought with the wrong organ, Steven," Buzzy said.

Disappointed by her son's actions, Buzzy took control of Steven's trust fund. Buzzy demanded Steven sell his downtown penthouse to use the money to compensate performers for the stolen funds. Steven refused, but under Buzzy's icy stare, he reluctantly agreed.

Faced with a second difficult choice, Steven grudgingly agreed to work at Ba-Dum-Bump under Jack Sievers's supervision. Not that Buzzy gave Steven much of a choice. Steven either complied or faced a permanent ban from the club and risked losing the master of ceremony job, the one thing Steven loved to do.

Maxine moved into Norman's home, and Buzzy and Carol Burnett moved in with Lester at his sprawling estate north of the city. Carol Burnett and Ginger, Lester's white and brown spaniel, spent their days roaming the grounds together and chasing squirrels.

The humble home Buzzy and Maxine owned became Steven's residence. Buzzy compelled Steven to pay Maxine to rent directly from his monthly allowance. It did not go over well with Steven, but Buzzy was unwavering. Buzzy held Steven accountable for his daily existence for the first time in her life. It might be too late for lessons, but Buzzy had to teach Steven to stand on his own two feet.

To say Georgiana was ecstatic to hear Maxine was engaged to a man from the teaching profession was an understatement.

"Norman will make a decent woman of you yet," Georgiana said, unaware of Maxine and Norman's living arrangements because what Georgiana did not know would not hurt her.

Maxine, Norman, and Buzzy would not have to keep the secret of Norman and Maxine's ungodly cohabitation from Georgiana for too long. Summer was only months away when Maxine and Norman planned to get married in a small, intimate wedding.

Ambivalence was no longer a factor in Maxine's life. She had become the resolute woman who strived to persevere after her worst life experience because of a wonderful friend and a good man who stood with her.

Sneak peek at M.L. Lexi's new novel

THE INVINCIBLE WOMAN

Prologue

REALITY STRUCK AND it all came out.

The betrayal, lying, and plotting that was a part of Antonia Trevi's life like a second skin caused her life to come crashing down like a Jenga tower when the one block that held it together was removed. In a matter of minutes, Antonia—known to her friends as Toni—found herself stripped of everything that had meaning in her life.

Toni had betrayed Bianca, her employer and the only person who believed in her. As a result, Toni lost the job she loved and excelled at. Toni lost the love of the only friends and family she knew. Worse than that, Toni deceived Christian, the only man who gave her unconditional love and expected nothing in return but her love.

Toni's response was to run away, far away from everyone she hurt.

Toni fled to Milan, the only home she knew to welcome her. Putting an ocean between her and the web of lies she concocted was the only plausible conclusion to the situation she created.

Toni couldn't face Christian. It was difficult for Toni to confess her betrayal to Christian's sister, Bianca, but more daunting was revealing to Christian who she truly was. Telling Christian the shameful things Toni did and revealing the humiliation that was her life was something

Toni couldn't bring herself to do. The pain of the revelation was all-encompassing, and Toni wouldn't hurt Christian. Toni wouldn't allow Christian to inherit her trauma.

Absence makes the heart grow fonder, and her absence weighs on him, and he sets off to find her.

When Christian finds Toni, the dam bursts, and she tells him the sordid truth of who she was, what she did, and the lies she had told. With reluctance, Toni revealed she was the type of woman who engaged in relationships with men—many, many men—to extort money from them. Toni told Christian she was a woman who engaged in sexual affairs with older men to satisfy her mother's need for money. Toni conceded she was the type of woman whose questionable past didn't blend with his impeccable upbringing.

Christian held up a silencing hand, but Toni pushed on. "No, Christian. I must tell you everything."

"I have no interest in your past. I'm only interested in the here and now," Christian said.

"You need to care, Christian. My sullied past is unsuited to meld with your unblemished life. A secret like mine is corrosive. It will come between us, your family, Bianca. I must tell you everything about me, and you must decide if you still feel the same about me afterward. I will understand if you do not."

Coming Soon

The Complete Woman
The Conflicted Woman
The Spiteful Woman
The Tortured Woman

The Relentless Woman Duology

The Relentless Woman
The Vindictive Women

The Unbreakable Woman Trilogy

The Unbreakable Woman
The Brave Woman
The Valiant Woman

Contact us

Email us at mllexiauthor@gmail.com to receive emails whenever M.L. Lexi publishes a new book. There is no charge or obligation and your information will remain confidential.

Visit us at www.mllexi.com to read excerpts of upcoming releases.

www.ingramcontent.com/pod-product-compliance
Lightning Source LLC
Chambersburg PA
CBHW050723180626
46814CB00002B/578